REIGN OF ERROR

The Worst Detective Ever
Mystery Series
Book 2

by Christy Barritt

Reign of Error

Christy Barritt

Reign of Error

Season 1, Episode 2:
The case of the inadequate investigator who
couldn't stop trying—
but not by her own volition.

Reign of Error

CHAPTER 1

"I don't want to do this." I rubbed my goosebump-freckled arms. I was freezing, and I hadn't even gone in the ocean yet. Still, the churning water in the distance taunted me, as if it knew the pain I was about to endure and delighted in my future suffering.

"This is going to be so much fun." Zane Oakley, my neighbor and one of my only friends since I'd moved to the area, made peace signs with his fingers and crossed his hands together. "Hashtag: awesome. Hashtag: bucketlist."

Of *course* he would say that. He lived for stuff like this. Things that stretched both the limits of the human body and all good sense. "Fun? Do I need to remind you that cold water is what killed Leonardo DiCaprio in *Titanic*?"

He shot me a lopsided glance. "Is that confirmed? Because I'm pretty sure he drowned."

"Either way, cold water and the human body are not a good combination." I shivered again as a gust of wind billowed over the area, sending with it a smattering of sand. "I've been practicing for this all week."

Zane narrowed his eyes, totally unaffected by

the jostling crowd all around. "Practicing how?"

"I've been jumping in and out of the cold shower." And it had been painful. More like a practice in futility than preparation for this. But still, I didn't want to look like an idiot. It was the same reason I'd had my toenails done in the winter. People would see them. Pictures could be taken. I had to be camera ready because . . . well, old habits died hard.

"Jumping in the shower is dangerous. You could fall and hit your head."

I slapped his chest when I saw his smile. "All the crazy things you do, and you're going to tell me that getting in and out of the shower is dangerous?"

He shrugged. "Just trying to look out for you!"

"Well, I'm glad someone has my back."

He lowered his gaze, all signs of teasing gone. "Always."

I swallowed hard when I saw the look in his eyes. Was I reading too much into this, or did Zane like me? Like, really like me? I wasn't sure. But I did know the possibility both thrilled me and filled me with dread. I loved love and being in love, but I so wasn't ready for a relationship.

"By the way, the mayor is trying to flag you down over there." Zane nodded toward an overzealous man on a makeshift stage in the distance.

I'd been trying to avoid eye contact with Mayor Roger Allen. Ever since I'd been accused of interfering with a police investigation, he had been using my dilemma to his advantage. Instead of pressing charges, Mayor Allen assigned me to whatever selective community service he saw fit.

That selective community service always somehow involved capitalizing on my star power and using it to help promote the Outer Banks, or the OBX, as most called it. Since I'd come here, my goal was to remain low key. However, that hadn't really been working out.

Take today, for example. Did I want to host and participate in the Polar Plunge Challenge? No way.

For starters, it was February on the Outer Banks of North Carolina. The temperature outside was thirty-something degrees, and I could only imagine how cold the ocean water was. Someone had told me, but I blocked out that information in an ignorance-is-bliss moment.

Secondly, all my vegan/raw-food/no-gluten—it depended on the day—diet goals had been an abysmal failure lately, yet I had to wear a bathing suit. In public. So much for being able to bulk up in the winter, the season of oversized sweaters and forgiving jeans.

Thirdly, crowds bothered me. They had ever since two men—one who remained faceless—had decided to stalk me. Even worse than stalking, they'd taunted and threatened me until I played their morbid little let's-resurrect-Raven-Remington game. I'd portrayed the invincible detective on the hit TV show *Relentless* for five seasons, and some fans had trouble handling the word "canceled."

But since I didn't want to add jailbird to my illustrious résumé, here I was.

As I walked across the lumpy sand toward the platform where Mayor Allen stood, I glanced toward the foot of the platform and saw Jackson Sullivan standing there. He wore a heavy black jacket with the police emblem on the pocket and his customary scowl. His arms were crossed, daring anyone to defy him.

My stomach turned at the sight.

We hadn't spoken in three weeks. We hadn't had a reason to. The last time we had seen each other was when a criminal was on the cusp of sharing information about my father, who had disappeared three months ago. Before Mr. Bad Guy could reveal anything, Detective Sullivan shot him. Granted, the man was about to shoot me. But still.

Then I'd found out that Jackson, whom I'd always assumed to be honorable, had stolen Zane's girlfriend way back when. No honorable man would steal another man's woman.

Jackson Sullivan was not who I thought he was. His intense green eyes, sexy stubble, and solid, stare-worthy build wouldn't persuade me otherwise.

I looked away from him as I greeted the mayor with a nod. "Yes, Mayor Allen?"

I was utilizing my acting skills in every way because I didn't feel pleasant or agreeable at the moment. I nearly clasped my hands beneath my chin and fluttered my eyelashes, but I figured that would be overkill.

The jolly man grinned at me. "You ready for this? Everyone is anxious to get their plunge on."

Get their plunge on? Oh my. It sounded even funnier because he looked and spoke like the Sicilian Vizzini from *The Princess Bride*.

Best. Movie. Ever.

"I'm ready." My voice was accented with fake enthusiasm. I did not want to do this. At all.

I hated being too cold. Or too hot.

I really just liked being comfortable. But didn't everyone? Except Zane maybe.

The mayor tapped the microphone and got the crowd's attention. There were probably three hundred people here. Three hundred people who wanted to raise money for the local police fraternity. Which was ironic, since this was the very police department I wasn't sure I trusted.

The mayor did an introduction before saying, "Everyone, here's the incredible Joey Darling, star of the hit series *Relentless*. Let's give her a warm Outer Banks welcome!"

I stepped up to the microphone, and everyone cheered. The attention-loving side of me ate it up. Every minute. Every handclap. Every moment of approval.

And that was what always got me in trouble. That, and my love affair with love itself.

I offered my most camera-worthy smile to the crowd. "It's my honor to be here today and to be able to call the Outer Banks home for the past month. The local police are a vital part of a healthy community. Even though I didn't play an official investigator on *Relentless*, I did learn to appreciate the work the police do. Our local department is in need of new equipment and new vehicles, and I'm excited to say we're freezing for a reason today. Thanks to all of you, we've met our fundraising goal, and it's all because of your outstanding efforts. Without further ado, let's . . ." I stared at the note cards that had been prepared for me by the city's PR department. "Let's . . . get our plunge on!"

It hurt me to say the words. But I did it anyway. Mostly because Mayor Allen was staring over my shoulder, waiting with childlike giddiness for me to read the prepared script.

Another super-fortunate (not!) thing I got to do for this was to be the leader of the pack. I, like a Viking going into battle, would be the first into the bitterly frigid waters of the Atlantic Ocean. And just like a skirmish, there would be pain involved for at least one of the parties. My bets were on me and not the ocean.

I removed my winter coat and revealed the one-piece bathing suit and swim shorts underneath. Immediately I regretted all the cheeseburgers I'd been indulging in recently. I'd probably put on ten pounds. Not good.

Especially when I saw the cameras appear. The *National Instigator* would have a ball with this! I could see the headlines now. "Joey Darling Lets Herself Go." "Joey Darling Dying of Mysterious Illness: Medication Makes Her Look Bloated." "Could Joey Darling Be Pregnant?" At the thought, my hand went to my stomach. As it did, a camera clicked.

Stupid camera.

Putting my personal feelings aside, I tapped into my inner showman. I ran toward the crowd, giving people high fives as I did so, just like that time I'd been on *Live with Kelly*! Zane waited for me at the front of the pack. He would be my moral support during this. He grabbed my hand, ensuring I couldn't escape this torture . . . er, humbling experience in fundraising.

I had to wait for everyone to disrobe. And by disrobe I meant take off their sweatshirts or coats. Some had written messages in body paint on their chests and arms. Others wore wigs and crazy hats and snorkels. Whatever floated their boats.

"Do we have to go under?" the man on the other side of me yelled over the noise of the crowd and the pulsating music that began in the background.

I glanced over, my teeth already chattering as another gust swept over the beach. Seagulls squawked overhead, warning us to go back before it was too late. It was true. I'd seen it once in a Disney movie.

"I'm not sure," I told the man.

I did a double take. I recognized this man . . . from somewhere. I tried to place him. Short— probably my height of five foot six or an inch taller— with a stocky build and a buzzed haircut. Probably in his forties, he reminded me a bit of a younger Mark Hamill.

I drew a blank as to where I'd seen him before though.

13

"You cut my hair two days ago," he reminded me.

"Oh, that's right! Fancy seeing you here!" I did remember him coming in. But business at the salon had boomed once word had spread that I was here researching a role.

Yes, researching a role. I supposed in some ways I *was* researching the role of a lifetime. It was a handy excuse that stopped people from asking too many questions about my true intentions for moving here and cutting hair. I didn't want people to know the truth.

He shivered. "I'm ready to get this over with."

"You and me both. May the force be with you."

He lowered his voice. "Be careful out there."

His words stunned me a moment. Be careful out there? Was that a warning? Or was he simply telling me that because I was about to immerse myself in ice-cold water?

I didn't have time to think about it now. It was time for me to get started.

"Is everyone ready?" I shouted with enough fake enthusiasm that my acting coach would be so proud. Hollywood might even give me an Oscar.

Everyone cheered back.

"Then let's do this," I yelled. "In three. Two. One!"

I charged forward. Toward the ocean. The cold, cold ocean.

As soon as my foot hit the Atlantic, the rest of my body rebelled. It was like stepping into ice water. Or purposefully falling into a frozen pond. Or having a death wish. In Antarctica.

Why had I ever agreed to this? My dad had taught me better. *If everyone else is jumping off a bridge, would you do it?* Apparently, the answer was yes.

But adrenaline pushed me onward. First, my foot. Then my calf. Then my entire leg, waist, and chest. I moved as quickly as possible, even though time felt frozen.

Zane didn't let go of my hand. It was almost as if he knew I might change my mind and run for my life . . . or at least run to Sunset Coffee Co., where anyone with good sense would be instead of here.

"This is awesome!" he yelled, like only an adrenaline junky might. Then he took a breath and dove into the water.

I could no longer feel my legs. People surrounded me. Totally surrounded me. Diving in. Screaming with elation. Shivering like mad.

The waves whipped over me, all the way to my shoulders, in cold fury. I could only think of one thing: pneumonia. I was done. I ran back to the shore, desperate for warmth.

Quickly I pulled my coat on and took the coffee a volunteer cocooned in ski gear thrust into my hand. I watched as everyone slowly trickled out of the water, looking as I felt: frozen. Medics stood by just in case anyone had health issues.

Event: done. One more thing I could mark off my list.

Until the mayor thought of something else I

should participate in to make amends. Stupid amends.

And, for real, I was deathly cold right now. I had to get inside. I needed some glorious heat. But at the same time, I was the host. I was supposed to change and then kick off a winter beach party. Stupid winter beach parties.

I looked back at the ocean. Zane came out, water dripping from his wild, curly hair. He looked like he could have stepped off the set of *Baywatch* with his lean beach body and carefree movements. He was a good six inches taller than I, perpetually tan, and had sun-kissed brown hair cut short on the sides but curly and long up top.

Just as he reached me, he shook his head like a wet dog as someone handed him a blanket. "That was awesome!"

"Not the word I was thinking of myself." But I smiled anyway, his enthusiasm never ceasing to amaze me. "I'm ready to get inside that tent."

He hooked his arm around my neck, and specks of water rained on me. "Let's go!"

I took one last look back, making sure everyone was out of the water so we could get our party started.

That was when I saw something tumble ashore.

Or should I say someone.

A body.

I sucked in a breath.

Mark Hamill.

CHAPTER 2

The mood inside the tent changed from celebratory to downright uptight as the police questioned all the Polar Plunge participants. At least there was coffee and hot chocolate freely flowing, although most people would have preferred alcohol at this point.

The heat had been cranked up, and everyone huddled in their coats. Too bad everyone's wet hair had been frozen, giving all of us a Jack Frost vibe. Some people even had snot icicles. Ew . . .

The event was now a disaster. The good news was that it wasn't my fault for once.

Zane put his arms around me in a friendly bear hug. "Body heat is the best way to stay warm."

"That's what they say," I muttered into his chest. And who exactly were *they*? The elusive group showed up in studies and statistics all the time, yet they remained nameless and faceless.

Which was what I would like to be right now.

Despite how affectionate Zane was, we were just friends. I thought he was adorable, but I wasn't in a place to date anyone. No, I was still recovering from a nasty divorce that had made me lose faith in relationships. Maybe for now. Maybe for always. I hadn't decided yet, though I was leaning toward always. It seemed like a better bet.

"Joey, I need to talk to you."

I turned as I recognized the deep voice behind me.

"Detective Sullivan." My voice sounded colder than the ocean. I stepped away from Zane's embrace—but not before I heard another camera and saw the flash. "Of course."

My goodness. Couldn't I ever catch a break?

Rag mags like the *National Instigator* loved to see the famous fall, and I'd given them plenty of fodder.

Jackson nodded toward the door flap. "Privately, please."

Okay, I wasn't expecting that. But I could handle privacy. Privacy was my friend.

"Can we stay inside? I'm freezing," I said.

"Sure thing." He led me to a corner instead.

I crossed my arms, ignoring the fact that my heart rate had kicked up a notch. "What's going on?"

Jackson narrowed his eyes, as he always did when he either looked at me or was thinking hard, which was apparently every time we were together. "Joey, how did you know Douglas Murray?"

"I'm assuming he's the Mark Hamill look-alike."

"The man who died. Yes."

I shook my head. "I did not know him."

He twisted his head, his studious gaze remaining on me. "Are you sure about that?"

"Of course. Why?" It didn't matter why. I already didn't like this. My gut instinct, which had let me down plenty of times before, indicated bad news was coming.

"Several people said you were the last person seen speaking with him before he went in the water."

I opened my mouth and shut it, considering my words and knowing that anything I said could and would be used against me either in a court of law or of public opinion.

Finally, I said, "Yes, that could be true. We were chatting right before he went in."

Jackson shifted, his laser-beam eyes shooting through me. "What were you chatting about?"

I did the whole open-and-shut-my-mouth thing again, as I realized how this could all look. "Well, he actually got his hair cut at Beach Combers two days ago."

He muttered an uninterpretable "Okay."

I already didn't like where this was going. "I hadn't ever seen him before. He was just another client on a growing list. I didn't think anything about it. Then he was beside me at the Polar Plunge, and I just figured it was an it's-a-small-world type of thing, minus the weird animatronic animals."

He let out an unreadable "hmm" as he stared at me.

Animatronic animals? Come on, Joey. Stop blathering around Jackson.

"What?" I finally asked, tired of his scrutiny.

"I'm going to have to take you down to the station."

Alarm rushed through me, and all thoughts of

robotic, singing animals left my mind. "Why in the world do you need to do that?"

He took my arm and started toward the cold, frigid world outside. "Let's not make a scene. We just need to ask you more questions."

"Jackson—Detective Sullivan, I mean—please tell me what's going on." My alarm turned to panic. Raven Remington 101 had taught me this wasn't normal. That was right: everything I ever needed to know in life, I'd learned by being an actress.

His jaw flexed, but he paused. "We found pictures of you in Mr. Murray's pocket, if you must know."

"Pictures? Of me?" My heart pounded in my ears. Why in the world would the man have pictures of me? It made no sense.

"That's right. Now, can we talk more down at the station before that nosy reporter over there catches wind of this?"

I glanced over at a man holding a camera and smiling. Paparazzi? I wasn't sure. But getting out of here sounded like a great idea. Because stories of my demise had *not* been greatly exaggerated.

***

"I'm telling you, I have no idea how that man ended up with my pictures," I repeated for the umpteenth time.

The detective didn't appear to believe me. That was nothing new. "I'm not saying you knew him. But I am saying he had pictures of you in his pocket."

"Are you sure that was his jacket? There were a lot of jackets on that beach." Even if that was true, the fact that *anyone* had my pictures and was carrying them around was disturbing.

Jackson held up a driver's license. "That's his name and picture, also found in the coat."

"How do you know he didn't just die of natural causes?"

"We won't know for sure until the autopsy comes back," he said. "But there's initial evidence that make it appear he put up a fight. Skin under his fingernails. Possible bruising on his shoulders. It's too early to tell exactly what happened."

"Wouldn't someone have seen someone holding someone else under water?"

"Not when you consider the sheer number of people in the water. Everyone was splashing, and it was mass chaos."

"I suppose you're right." It had been crazy out there. We'd been like a flock of seagulls swarming a shrimp trawler.

"Anyway, those facts mixed with your photos being found in his coat is why we brought you in for questioning."

I shivered, but I wasn't ready to drop my ability to rationalize this yet. "Maybe he's a fan who wanted an autograph."

Jackson held up the pictures. "Do these look like your normal pictures that you'd autograph?"

I cringed. No, they didn't. These were strange

pictures of me. One leaving Beach Combers. Another standing on the shore at dusk. Still another of me taking out the trash. Each taken when I was unaware.

I shivered at the thought. "Maybe he's the unknown part of my super-stalker duo."

"That's . . . quite a title."

"Isn't it though? But think about it, Jack—Detective Sullivan." Why did I keep reverting to calling him Jackson, as if we were friends? Because we weren't.

I had so many reasons not to be this man's friend. So. Many. Reasons. Yet another part of me remembered the moments Jackson and I had shared. They were few and far between, but they were there. I thought we'd connected—on a deep level, at that—but I'd been wrong. Again.

"I've had this feeling from the start that I somehow knew the stalker without knowing who he was," I said. "Maybe Douglas what's-his-name is our guy."

"Our guy?" He cocked an eyebrow. He did that a lot. And scowled. Mostly at me.

"Your guy. My guy. Whatever!" I threw my hands in the air. Hysterics at their best.

Jackson leaned back, a tiny smile playing at the corner of his lips, but only for a second. Then he snapped back to all business again. "I suppose that is a theory. But the problem we're looking at right now is you're our only suspect."

"Well, that's the craziest thing I've heard since Kanye stole the spotlight from Taylor Swift at the

VMAs. I had no reason to kill him."

Jackson did a half eye roll. "Unless he was your stalker."

My jaw went slack. "That's ridiculous."

"But is it? That was your theory, after all."

"I never had a theory that I killed him because he was my stalker."

"No, but you thought he could be your stalker, which would give you motive to kill him."

"What . . . I . . . What are you trying to do? Talk me into a corner? I know nothing, Jackson." My words came out faster and faster as my hackles went up. Yes, my hackles went up. I grew up in a small mountain town, and the colloquialisms I'd learned there reared their heads at the most cockeyed times.

Someone tapped on the glass window beside us. I'd seen it before on *Relentless*, and I knew what it meant: new information. New information to make me look guilty or innocent? That was the question.

"Excuse me a minute," Jackson said.

How had I gone from being the guest of honor to being the main act in an interrogation room? What would the mayor think?

On the bright side, maybe he wouldn't ask me to do any more polar plunges.

I pulled the sleeves of my sweater over my hands. Jackson had allowed me to drive here in my own car, provided he could follow me in his unmarked police sedan. I found an old gray sweater in the trunk, which I'd pulled on, as well as some high heels. It wasn't my best look, but the heels were slightly warmer than my flip-flops. I draped my coat over my bare legs, wondering why they kept this room so incredibly cold.

This stunk. Plain and simple.

Whoever had written this script needed to make some changes. Pronto. The problem was this wasn't a script, and there were no rewrites allowed. Double stunk.

Finally, Jackson came back into the room. Should I ask for a lawyer? Why hadn't I thought of that earlier?

Raven Remington, my fictional alter ego, would have. Or she'd be smart enough to watch what she said. Had I watched anything? Considered a single word I'd said? No, I hadn't. I might have even blathered more, but at least I hadn't mentioned any more animatronic animals. I might have brought up the movie *Alive* and people eating other people though. Why had I brought that up again? Maybe because those people had nearly frozen to death also. I wasn't sure.

Jackson definitely knew something new. And I didn't like it.

He strode over to the chair across from me, his steps heavy and measured. He pulled the seat out, the metallic sound of the legs scraping against the floor causing my skin to crawl. If he ever wanted to go into acting, I'd totally recommend him for *Law and Order*. He had the whole intimidation thing down pat. Plus, he was handsome to boot. The cameras would love him, as would all the single ladies longing for the perfect fantasy man.

"Douglas Murray doesn't appear to be his real name," Jackson stated.

"And you're blaming that on me also?" What would he blame me for next? The fact that *The Lone Ranger* movie lost nearly $190 million at the box office?

His lips twisted in a frown. "I didn't say I was blaming you for his death, Joey."

I crossed my arms. "That's how it sounds to me."

"We're just trying to find some answers."

"I've heard that one before."

He reached into his pocket and pulled out one more thing. "We found another picture. In a different pocket inside his coat. Do you recognize this?"

I picked up the photo, and my eyes widened. It was a picture of me from high school. I stood in front of the Roanoke River Gorge after my dad and I had hiked all day—one of our favorite pastimes together.

The edges of the photo were wrinkled, and it was already yellowing slightly. This wasn't a new copy of an old photo. My hands trembled as I turned it over. A cry caught in my throat.

There was my father's handwriting, crude but strong. He'd scribbled the date on the bottom right corner. Just as he always did.

Mark Hamill had one of my father's photos.

Everything spun around me. This just took this mystery to a whole new level.

***

Jackson released me but asked that I remain in town. I knew what that meant. It meant I was a suspect, despite the fact that Jackson said he wasn't *necessarily* blaming me.

Whoever Mark Hamill was, I could only come to two possible conclusions: the man was my stalker, or he was connected with my father. Either way, that picture proved he was somehow connected with me, and I didn't like that. Especially when considering he was now deader than my career.

How had he gotten that photo belonging to my dad? Had the man taken it from my dad? Or had my father given it to him?

The whole reason I'd come to this area was because my father had disappeared without a trace. And that was unlike my responsible, always-there-for-me dad. I had to figure out what happened to him because he was the only person I had left in this world . . . and I loved him more than anything.

Seeing that photo had stirred up something deep inside me. It had made me remember some of my long talks with Dad. Talks where he'd reminded me that family and faith were everything. Talks where neither of us had said a word, yet unbreakable bonds had been forged as we hiked or whittled wood or fished. When I looked back on the most important moments of my life, those were some of them. Family.

As I walked out of the police station, my head spun. More than ever, I wanted answers. I wanted to know what happened to my dad. Someone out there knew, and they weren't sharing that information.

My bad day felt ten times worse than it had earlier.

Until a woman stepped in my path, and ten times became one hundred times. She had a microphone, a camera crew, and wore a cheap business suit. I knew what this meant: an on-air ambush.

"Joey Darling, what do you know about the man who died at the Polar Plunge?" The thirtysomething blonde shoved a microphone in front of my face.

I froze, totally not expecting this. Nor had I expected the camera.

My gaze traveled behind her, and I spotted a news van with their call letters emblazoned across the side. The media had caught wind of this and come down from Norfolk, Virginia, where all the local stations for this area were based.

"He . . . um, he's dead." *Good one, Joey.*

"We're aware of that. Was he murdered?"

"The police are working on it." I tried to take a step, but she blocked me.

"Did you know the man?"

"Who? Douglas Murray?" As soon as the words left my lips, my stomach sank. Had I actually said his name out loud? I was toast, pure and simple. Not even with cinnamon and sugar on top. Just plain, dry, and tasteless bread.

"Is that his name?" The reporter's eyes lit like a hunter who'd just locked on her prey.

"I don't know what you're talking about."

"You said Douglas Murray."

"I think I said don't go smearing. As in smearing my name or what I said." *I am so lame. Just stop talking, Joey!*

"What else can you tell us?"

My thoughts stopped spinning for a minute. Was this my chance to send a message? To let whoever did this know that *I* knew about *their* connection with my father? Was this an opportunity to draw the bad guy out and end this once and for all?

I didn't know, but I had to make a quick decision.

I stared right into the camera, the thespian in me taking charge. "I'd like to say this: whoever is toying with me, I'm not playing these games any longer. I have a message for you. Come out of the shadows and act like a big boy. Only wimps hide and threaten and antagonize from the safety of anonymity. Man up or shut up."

The reporter followed behind me, still asking questions, but I ignored her and climbed into my car.

What had I just done? It didn't matter because it was too late to take my words back. I'd made my intentions clear and, in the course of it, challenged a faceless villain. I may have just sent an invitation to my demise.

What had I been thinking?

CHAPTER 3

I stared at the computer screen as I sat at the little corner desk in my oceanfront duplex. Adrenaline pumped through my blood as the implications of everything that had happened replayed in my mind like a broken movie reel. Or *Groundhog Day*, the movie. No, no . . . I was going to stick with the broken movie reel. It had a bit more style to it.

Those pictures that had been found in the man's pocket had stirred something deep inside me, something I was unable to let go of. Something I wouldn't be able to let go, even if I wanted to. Douglas Murray was linked with my father, and I had to know why.

Which was what had brought me to my computer and to the Internet in search of answers. It wasn't a crystal ball, but it was the closest thing I had to one.

As I studied the words on the screen, trying to let them sink in, I felt someone behind me.

Zane. He'd come over to my place to hang out after the police station fiasco. He'd brought my favorite drink, a sparkling flavored juice called Izze, as well as guacamole and baked blue corn chips.

When I'd come downstairs after my shower, he'd been watching Bob Ross on Netflix, so I'd snuck over to my computer, hoping for a moment alone.

Sneaky, I was not, I reminded myself in my best Yoda voice.

"Are you really looking up 'How to ID a John Doe'?" Zane leaned close, so close that I could feel his body heat behind me, and an involuntary shiver went up my spine.

I quickly shut my laptop, surprisingly embarrassed that he'd caught me doing such a rudimentary Internet search.

"Yes. Yes, I am. I have no shame." None that I'd admit to, at least. Hashtag: liarliarpantsonfire.

Zane nodded slowly at first and then more quickly as he seemed to get used to the idea. "Cool." He said the word with a surfer-like inflection that always made me smile.

I leaned back and sighed. My thoughts were more tangled than a fishing net in turbulent waters. "I don't want to get involved in this investigation. I don't. But, that said, my picture was found in the dead man's pocket. I want to know why."

Zane perched himself on the wide window frame beside me, forming a striking picture as the remnant colors of sunset smeared behind him over the ocean. Remnant because the sun actually set on the other side of the island, but its east coast gladly shared in the smear of pastels.

"I thought his name was Douglas or something," Zane said.

I pushed my chair back to a more comfortable angle to chat. "That wasn't his real name. If I'm going to figure out any answers here, I have to figure out who that man was. And since I'm not with the police, that's going to be difficult."

"Why?"

I let out a pent-up breath of frustration. "Well, for starters, I have no idea where this guy lives or even how to figure out where he lives. If someone reports him missing, they'll tell the police, not me. There's just so much that I don't have access to. I don't know where to start."

"What did Google tell you? Google is all knowing, right?"

"Google told me exactly what I just said. Check his personal belongings, his residence, his friends." I rested my hands on my forehead. "I'm so terrible at this detective thing. I have a case staring me right in the face, and I have no idea how to proceed. I'm a disgrace to imaginary detectives everywhere."

Zane pulled up a chair and sat beside me. "No, you're not. Look at the last case you solved."

"I almost died, and I almost got you killed," I reminded him. "I'm not cut out for this."

"You have a whole legion of fans who would disagree. They think you and Raven Remington are one and the same."

"Well, the public is wrong. What can I say? We're day and night, ebony and ivory, Laverne and Shirley."

"*Laverne and Shirley*? I loved that show!" His chuckles faded, and he sat up straighter. "I know how you can get answers."

"Pray tell." I wasn't holding on to the hope though.

"The mayor likes you, right?"

"That's how it appears."

"And he's looking for publicity for the area, right?"

"Yes, he is."

Zane's eyes lit. "See if he'll let you do a Castle/Beckett type of thing."

"What?" I had not expected him to say that.

"You know, the TV show."

"Yes, I know about *Castle*. I loved that show. Nathan Fillion is the one who taught me the 'Faces of the Soap Take.'"

"What?"

"You know, the *Did I leave the stove on?* expression?" I demonstrated with a concerned look. Then I realized Zane totally wasn't getting the acting tip and moved on. "Look it up on YouTube when you have the chance. It's spot on. Anyway . . . I still don't understand what you're getting at."

"Easy. See if the mayor will let you work with Jackson to solve the case. You could be a consultant and bring some good PR to the area. People would eat it up."

"There's only one problem with that: I don't *want* to work with Jackson."

"Sure you do. If it means getting answers, you do."

I mulled over his words a moment. He had valid

points, but I had more reservations about this than my aunt and uncle on their cross-country campground tour. "I don't know, Zane."

"I'm sure the mayor would be happy to oblige you. He's always wanted to put the Outer Banks on the map."

"But the Outer Banks *is* on the map. People come from all over to vacation here."

"Tourism has climbed under his reign—er, leadership here. Tourism is what keeps this area alive. Without it, no one would survive. We depend on that income from out-of-towners. It's just a way of life here."

I shook my head. "I don't know. I'm going to have to think about that one, Zane."

"I think it's got gold written all over it. In the meantime, there's only one way I can think to cheer you up."

"What's that? Let me guess: Bob Ross?"

"Not this time, although my man Bob is almost as awesome as the beach on a cloudless day—no, make that a *nearly* cloudless day. Let's add some happy little clouds in there for good measure." Zane reached behind him. "But I have a better idea: pillow fight!"

He hit me with one of the pillows from the window seat.

I sat stunned for a minute. Then I grabbed a pillow and swung it back at him.

And I remembered again why I was so glad Zane was my friend.

***

I woke up the next morning with more questions than answers.

I had a lot of want but so little know-how. I was like a novelist wanting to create the next great American novel but suffering a terrible case of writer's block. How did I figure out who the dead guy really was? Because that was the first step in figuring out his connection with my dad.

Did I drive aimlessly all over town? Question random people in stores and restaurants? Go the Castle and Beckett route? That last one was tempting. Very tempting. If it weren't for Jackson, that was. I supposed I could suggest working with other detectives in the department, but my gut instinct told me that I would still end up working with Jackson.

The thoughts continued to circle my mind all day on what was supposed to be a lazy Sunday morning. I had been attending my father's church, but today I had to help Dizzy with wedding party updos at Beach Combers.

"Do you realize that our murder rate here in town has gone up since you arrived?" Dizzy took a break from humming Christmas music, which blared from the overhead—in February—and stared at me, her oriental folding fan in hand. She always had that thing in hand. Hot flashes, she claimed.

Dizzy owned the salon where I was temporarily working until I could find my dad. It was a long story, but yes, I had to work and earn some cash because of some bad decisions and naïveté on my part. Long story short: the IRS was garnishing my wages.

Dizzy had been married to my uncle, but only for a few years. I'd been in California for most of those years, so I hardly knew her. She was in her late fifties, wore her hair piled high on her head, and loved her blue eye shadow that stretched all the way to her brows.

Unfortunately, she was also a suspect because, of the few items I'd found of my father's, an oriental fan was one of them. And it had blood on it. I hated to suspect the woman, because she truly did seem kind, but I couldn't look past the evidence.

"I do apologize for the fact that crime is skyrocketing since my arrival," I said, holding the curling iron on my client's hair. That should totally be the opening line in a movie. And it should be said with a British accent. And the lady who'd played the lead role on *Supernanny* should star in it.

"So are you going to track down the bad guy again?" Dizzy put her fan down and began rearranging our stock of shampoos and conditioners.

I remembered the foolish challenge I'd thrown out to the TV camera and frowned. I'd backed myself into a corner, hadn't I? "We'll see."

I continued to curl the hair of the woman in front of me. The mother of the groom remained quiet, but I could tell she was listening to every word. The rest of the party was gone, but she'd volunteered to go last, claiming the bridal party talked way too much.

"But you did so well with that last case!" Dizzy

said.

"I had no choice but to get involved in the last case since some psycho was threatening me." I frowned at the memories, holding the curling iron in place a little too long in the process. I only noticed because I smelled the stench of burnt hair.

I released it and held my breath. Whew. The woman's hair was still intact. Hopefully, when I touched it, the strands wouldn't disintegrate like ashes from a cigarette.

Just then my cell phone rang. I glanced down and saw the name of my manager. Interesting. He'd actually tried to call a few times before, but I'd always let it go to voicemail. I knew I had to answer it now, thanks to an upcoming movie release we had to discuss.

"Could you finish up for me, Dizzy? She just needs some hairspray." I held up my phone. "I really have to take this."

She nodded.

I thanked the mother of the groom, and then I scurried toward the back room.

"Hi, Rutherford." Rutherford James Seamore III, to be exact. And his name fit him to a T. He was slick. Literally. As in, his dark wavy hair was slicked back from his face like a wannabe GQ model. Pockmarks belied his nerdy past before he'd transformed into a hotshot manager to the stars, including Jennifer Lawrence, Emma Stone, and Betty White.

He'd been at my beck and call until the Great Implosion of 2016. And by implosion, I was referring to myself.

"Joey Darling. I thought you'd disappeared off the face of the earth. To hear Eric talk, you have."

I frowned. Rutherford had always liked Eric, which was one of the reasons I'd chosen to distance myself from my manager. That, and the fact that it just wasn't Rutherford's hair that was slick.

"No, I didn't disappear. I'm still alive and kicking." The kicking part was important. Kicking had kept me alive.

"Excellent news."

He didn't really think my blasé update was excellent news. He was just going through the formalities before getting to his point, because he always had a point, and that point usually had something to do with his paycheck. Me no worky meant him no payee.

"Listen, we really need to talk about your career." His voice changed from friendly to business in 2.5 seconds.

And there it was: the reason for this call. "I'm taking a break."

"You know what 'break' spells in Hollywood, don't you? It spells failure. Remember Miranda Meadows."

He *had* to bring Miranda Meadows up again, didn't he? He kept dangling her in front of my face as an example of how to have a great fan base via her *Fiona the Werewolf Hunter* show and then ruin everything.

"I'll have you know Miranda wrote a very

successful cookbook recently. And I understand your concerns, but . . . I can't go back right now." The mere thought of going back caused tension to grow in my chest, stomach, back, and everywhere else in between.

"I had a feeling you'd say that. That's why I'm not coming to you with any movie auditions. But *Dancing with the Stars* has expressed interest."

"Talk about kiss of death. The dancers are usually more famous than the stars." Was this really where I was at in my career?

"True, but it could be a good opportunity. There's also a new version of *Celebrity Survivor* coming up. Your name was tossed around."

"Over my dead body." Seriously. I'd probably die if I went on that show. For starters, there was no coffee. And you had to eat bugs. No, thank you. It would be like the Polar Plunge, only on a tropical island. In other words: torture.

"You haven't forgotten about the press junket coming up for *Family Secrets*, right? You and Jessica. It's part of your contract."

I frowned. "I haven't forgotten. But I still have a few weeks until that kicks off."

"I'll email you the details. I think the movie is going to be a hit. You and Jessica Alba? How can you go wrong? Viewers are going to eat it up. Your fading star power is going to become a thing of the past."

Wasn't that what I wanted? For my star power to fade so I could disappear into obscurity? Yet a part of me craved fame and everything that came with it.

Me being in Hollywood was like an alcoholic being in a bar.

In the movie, Jessica Alba and I starred as sisters who were secretly competing spies. I'd filmed it over a year ago, but the release had been delayed. My agent thought it would thrust me back into the spotlight and secure my position as a rising A-lister.

"Between this and the fact that you made one of *People* magazine's '50 Most Beautiful People' last year, you're going to make a comeback. You do need to work on bulking up your Facebook followers."

"I have four million."

"Jessica has five."

"Is that why you called?" I finally asked.

"No, it actually isn't. Maria Salvatore from ABC News contacted me. She heard something about you solving a crime a few weeks back in that little beach town where you're living now."

"Nags Head."

"That's the one. Anyway, they want to do a story on you."

I was going to politely decline this one. "That's okay. The whole murder-solving thing wasn't a big deal."

"Well, actually, Maria called me, and then she called the mayor, and then she called me back, trying to arrange this interview. She's a shark, I tell you. A fierce but beautiful shark. Apparently the mayor pretty much already said that you and the detective that helped you—"

The detective that *helped* me? Jackson was going

to have a fit if he heard that. Jackson had tried to *stop* me.

"... are available for the interview and the town would love to welcome ABC News. I wanted to give you a heads-up."

Suddenly my whole day just got a whole lot worse. I sagged against the wall, nearly knocking down several bottles of hair dye. "Are you serious? I do have a say in this."

"Of course you do. But talk to the mayor. He said something about you owing him one."

I sighed and rubbed my temple. I could totally see Mayor Allen pressing this. In fact, he probably already had a plan as to why I *had* to do this. I wasn't sure what was worse: having to bring attention to myself by doing the interview or working with Jackson to do so.

"I'll be in touch," Rutherford said.

I had no doubt he would be.

As soon as I stepped out into the salon area, someone else stepped inside.

I cringed when I saw Jackson there. Scowling. Of course.

I braced myself for our conversation, knowing, without a doubt, it wouldn't be a pleasant one.

CHAPTER 4

"Can I have a word with you?" Jackson asked.

Dizzy let out a soft but loaded "oh" in the background and continued to sweep up hair to the tune of "Rockin' around the Christmas Tree." She thought my life was a soap opera, and she loved soap operas. Especially Christmas-themed soap operas. In February.

It was too late to disappear, and with no clients in sight, I couldn't feign being busy. "Of course."

"In private."

"Ya'll go on back to the office. I'll stay out here and hold the fort down," Dizzy said, sounding suspiciously affable and almost like a blue-eye-shadowed Cupid. Her overzealous wink only added to the melodrama.

"Thanks." Without waiting for my approval, Jackson took my arm and pulled me toward the back. As soon as the door shut, the fire in his eyes grew to an inferno. "What were you thinking, Joey?"

I tried to figure out what exactly he referred to, because I had a rather long list of actions that question could apply to. "What do you mean?"

Jackson held up his phone. A video played on the

screen. It was the reporter from yesterday doing a story on the murder during the Polar Plunge. Unfortunately, my face popped onto the screen.

"You mean Douglas Murray?"

I'd looked rather confused as I'd stared at the camera. I quickly noted how my makeshift outfit from the Polar Plunge made me look like I was wearing nothing beneath my coat. Almost like a stripper. That was just . . . awesome.

"Is that his name?"

"I don't know what you're talking about."

"You said Douglas Murray. What else can you tell us?"

The blond reporter had conveniently left out my "don't go smearing" response. Which could be good because it halfway made me sound like an idiot.

I nibbled on my bottom lip. "Oh that," I muttered.

The Christmas music on the overhead did nothing to extinguish the chestnuts roasting in the open fire . . . of Jackson's eyes. *"Oh, that?* Do you realize what you've done, Joey? You shared the victim's name before we could even get in contact with his relatives."

"It wasn't his real name, I thought." My argument was weak, at best.

"It doesn't matter! What if he was living under an assumed identity with his family?"

"Then that would be bad," I whispered as guilt crashed inside me. "I didn't mean to say it, Jackson. That reporter cornered me."

"I'm not denying that. But how about this?" He

held up his phone again.

This time, my challenge to the killer scrolled across the screen. I'd looked fierce when I spoke into the camera. Like Raven Remington actually. It was totally a move she would have taken. A touch of satisfaction washed over me.

Until my words sank in.

"Whoever is toying with me, I'm not playing these games any longer. I have a message for you. Come out of the shadows and act like a big boy. Only wimps hide and threaten and antagonize from the safety of anonymity. Man up or shut up."

"Have you lost your mind?" Jackson stepped closer, totally in my face. "Why do you look happy right now? You should look terrified."

My satisfaction shriveled faster than a slug in a salt shower. "I'm not really sure what got into me. Except for the fact that this man is obviously connected with me and my father in some way. I need to know how. I'm tired of living under someone else's rules. I'm taking the bull by the horns." I fisted my hands and pretended to grab thus-said horns.

"When you take the bull by the horns, you end up either tossed across the arena or with a mortal wound in your gut! Whoever came up with that saying either had a wicked sense of humor or should be permanently silenced for giving that kind of advice!"

"Oh." I frowned.

He lowered his voice and shifted. Though there was ample space back here, Jackson seemed to fill the entirety of it. "Joey, there are several things concerning me right now. For one thing, you put yourself out there. A lot of people know you're in this area now, and that makes you a target. Secondly, whoever this person is who killed our victim has been given a challenge. And thirdly, you released our victim's alias, which could hinder our investigation."

I sat down hard on the rickety table behind me, which was meant for lunch breaks. A pile of magazines stacked there fell to the floor, but I didn't bother to retrieve them. Not now. "I screwed up. I'm sorry. I have no idea how to make things right."

"You can't make it right. You just have to deal with the consequences."

"Then I'll deal. I'll take the conses by their quences and show them who's the boss."

He swung his head back and forth before squeezing his eyes shut. "Did you really just say that?"

"I did. Look, I didn't get paid to write scripts. I just acted. I'm doing my best here, but I have very little to work with."

He ran a hand over his face and seemed to snap out of his Joey-induced stupor. "Okay, you just need to stay low key. That's all I can say. And please don't talk to any more reporters."

"I won't." I frowned and chewed on a fingernail. "Well, I won't except for Maria Salvatore."

Jackson's gaze darkened. "I heard."

"It wasn't my idea."

"I heard that also."

"You could decline and not take part in it," I said.

"Have you met Mayor Allen?"

"True. Then again, Maria Salvatore is well documented to be a cheater who doesn't respect commitment—in both marriage and TV network loyalty. Maybe you should get along just fine."

What was I saying? Why were these repressed feelings popping to the surface now? Did I want to make a bad situation worse?

Jackson paused, and his hands went to his hips. "What's that mean?"

"Nothing." *Another bad move on your part, Joey.*

"What's your problem, Joey? I thought we were . . ."

I waited, nearly holding my breath, which made no sense since I didn't even like Jackson. "We were . . ."

He shrugged, his expression hardening again. "Friends. I thought we were friends."

I resisted a harrumph and considered my words. I couldn't show my hand.

My dad wasn't the one who'd taught me that poker move. No, he hadn't ever played cards. My *ex-husband* had taught me that wisdom, yet I'd been clueless to the reality that he actually had a poker problem. Despite those facts, the words seemed relevant now. I couldn't let Jackson know that I knew he could be somehow involved in my dad's disappearance.

I wanted to tell Jackson that everything was fine and I'd misspoken. But that wasn't the truth. It wasn't fine.

All because Zane's words kept ringing in my ears. *Jackson stole my girlfriend from me.*

I raised my chin. *Bull by the horns, even if you get tossed or gorged.* "I know that you stole Claire from Zane."

His eyebrows skyrocketed. "I stole Claire from Zane?"

I nodded. "That's right. I didn't think you were that type of person."

"What type of person is that?"

"The type who's once a cheater, always a cheater."

"I'm not a cheater, but even if I was, what does that have to do with us?"

I cringed. "It . . . doesn't. Except it shows your character. Your very lousy character that's carefully concealed under a noble facade."

His gaze clouded, and he leaned closer. "I can only imagine who told you that information."

I shrugged this time, wanting to shrink like Ant-Man. "Someone."

"Zane." He released a long breath, and when he was done, fire reignited in his gaze. "Well, let me teach you something, Ms. Up-and-Coming Detective: You have to be careful what sources you trust. Trusting the wrong information from the wrong person can get you killed—or ruin your life."

His words caused me to blanch. For the blood to leave my face. For my lungs to tighten.

Before I could respond—not that I knew what to

say—he turned on his heel and left.

Take the conses by the quences, I told myself.

That had to be the dumbest expression I'd ever made up. But I was sticking to it.

***

After I finished at Beach Combers, I headed over to Oh Buoy, my favorite smoothie bar and a place that was quickly becoming a regular hangout. A mix of a tropical tiki bar and nautical diner, it hands down had the best smoothies in the area.

Right now, "Kokomo" by the Beach Boys played overhead, but even the warm-fuzzy-inducing song couldn't undo my crankiness. I didn't want to do an interview with ABC, nor did I want to do it with Jackson. I never wanted to see him again after our disastrous talk.

After Jackson left Beach Combers, I'd promptly called Mayor Allen, and he basically twisted my arm and told me saying no to the interview wasn't an option. He actually said, "Publicity. Good Publicity." And he said it with the same inflection as "Wuv, twue wuv" from *The Princess Bride*. Had he done that on purpose? I wasn't sure. But I was fascinated.

However, that was neither here nor there. I still didn't see how murder could be good publicity for the tourist town, but what did I know?

The whole conversation made me rethink Zane's Castle/Beckett idea though. If I could get an "in" at the police station, maybe I would stand a chance at solving not only this case but also my father's disappearance. I had to face the fact that I was getting nowhere on my own. I didn't have Raven's instincts or training. But if I planned carefully, maybe I could find some advantages that I *did* have. Like fame.

"You look like you have a lot on your mind." Phoebe Waters, an on-again, off-again employee at Oh Buoy, set my smoothie down on the bamboo-topped table and then slid in across the booth from me. "I'm on break, and I'm a good listener."

I stared at her a minute. She'd become a good friend since I'd been in town, and I looked forward to our talks. They were mostly here at Oh Buoy, but twice we'd gone out to dinner together, and I'd enjoyed getting to know her. She was down to earth and as loyal to this area as the crew of the Nebuchadnezzar was to Morpheus in *The Matrix*.

She oozed everything that was good about beach dwellers, all the way from her sand-colored hair to her easy smile to her laid-back attitude. She thrived on being with people she loved, doing jobs she enjoyed, and appreciating the natural beauty around her.

Still, despite her easygoing ways and great listening skills, what bothered me at this moment was that I was going to have to work with Jackson when I did this stupid ABC interview, and Jackson just happened to be Phoebe's brother-in-law. Or former brother-in-law, depending on how you looked at it. Claire had been her sister.

"It would be awkward if I told you what was on

my mind," I started, absently rubbing the side of my smoothie cup. Mirlo Sunrise, or, as I called it, Heaven on Earth. The fruity drink was named after a local beach.

Phoebe narrowed her eyes in thought and studied me a minute. "Is it about Jackson?"

"Why do you assume that?"

"Lucky guess."

I took a sip of my smoothie and contemplated my words. I hadn't ever opened up to Phoebe about . . . well, anything. Not my past. Not my real reasons for being here. Definitely not men problems. But I thought I could trust her. She wasn't the emotional type, and that could be a good thing because it would balance out my a-little-too-emotional side.

"Is it true that Jackson stole Claire from Zane?" My words came out confoundingly fast. If I hadn't said them quickly, I might not have said them at all because they revealed an ultra-personal side of myself that I tried to keep private.

Phoebe frowned and let her head fall back slightly. "Who on this green earth told you that?"

I swallowed hard, the acidity from the orange juice burning my throat—that had to be it, not regret—before blurting, "Zane."

She shook her head, something akin to anger in her gaze. She spread her hands, which were partially covered with an ocean-blue hybrid henley/sweatshirt, on the table. "You really don't know, do you?"

"Know what?" My words caught.

"About Zane."

I didn't like where this was going, but I couldn't stop now. "I know he's my neighbor. The life of the party. Thrill seeker."

She pressed her lips together, contemplation clear on her wholesome features. "Do you want the truth, Joey?"

"I think I do." I wished I didn't sound so uncertain. But the truth could be a lot to handle sometimes. I knew that firsthand. Living in la-la land was much more fun.

She let out a long breath, glanced out the window, and absently tapped her ultrashort, well-chewed fingernails against the table. She was fighting bad memories, I realized. I recognized it because I'd been there before.

"Yes, Zane and Claire were dating," she began, her laid-back vibes long gone. "They dated all throughout high school and into college. But they had problems. A lot of problems."

"Like what?" *Don't ask. Don't ask.* But I couldn't stop myself. I wanted a glimpse into the past. I needed more information, even if it wasn't my business.

Phoebe's jaw flexed, and her gaze flickered up to mine. "Like the fact that Zane was doing drugs."

My bottom lip separated from my top. "But I thought Zane went off to college and got the job of his dreams?"

"He did. Eventually. But before that, drugs nearly did him in. Claire tried to fix him. To change him. But she couldn't. No one could. And he made her life miserable."

My entire body felt tense enough to snap. My mind tried to transport me back in time to when my ex had made my life miserable. Actually, miserable was an understatement. Eric had been downright abusive.

"What do you mean 'made her life miserable'?" My voice squeaked out.

She locked gazes with me, her eyes as stormy as a hurricane. "Drugs change people, Joey."

I rubbed my arm. "He didn't . . . hurt her, did he? Physically?"

"No, not that I know of. But he yelled a lot, especially when he was coming off a high. He depleted her energy, her hope . . . When Jackson came along, he was the best thing that could have happened to Claire. She'd already broken up with Zane, but he just couldn't accept it. He was sure she would change her mind."

"So Jackson didn't steal her away." How could I have been so stupid? Yet I'd had no reason to think Zane would lie to me. He was . . . my friend. I'd thought.

"No. But I would have applauded Jackson if he did. He would have been rescuing her from a desperate situation."

I shook my head, guilt pressing in on me yet again. I couldn't do anything right. "I believed the worst about him."

"Well, Zane has hated Jackson ever since. I'm

sure Zane doesn't like the fact that Jackson is your friend. Especially since I see the way Zane looks at you."

Did Zane look at me a certain way? I'd wondered about that. "He's clean now."

Phoebe nodded, almost uncertainly, and glanced at her watch. "Yep. Okay, I've got to get back to work. You're still coming down to my house this weekend, right?"

"Am I still invited?" Or had I messed up this friendship also?

"Of course." She paused. "Oh, and I heard about the dead guy."

"Who hasn't?"

"He was in here, you know."

I froze with my smoothie in midair. "Who?"

"The dead guy. He came in every day last week and sat in that booth." She nodded toward one in the distance.

I glanced over at it. That booth had the perfect view of Beach Combers. Had Douglas Whatever-His-Real-Name-Was come here to watch me?

I didn't know, but I didn't like the idea of it. Not at all.

CHAPTER 5

"You guys are talking about that guy who died at the Polar Plunge?" a customer sitting at a nearby booth said. "Right?"

I glanced over at the woman, who was probably in her early twenties and proudly sported multiple piercings and a severe wedge haircut. Papers and some notebooks were spread out in front of her, and she held a red pen in her hands. I'd seen her in here before, meeting with a writing group or book club or something.

"Yes, he's the one." I stepped closer, and Phoebe was right behind me as I extended my hand. "I'm Joey."

"I'm Alexa. I saw that man in here too." She closed her leather-bound notebook and crossed her arms. "Had a couple of conversations with him, for that matter."

She now had my full attention. "Did he say anything interesting?"

"He asked about you. You're Raven Remington, right?" She raised a pierced eyebrow as she waited for my answer.

"Not really. But I did play her on TV." If I had a

penny for every time I said that, I wouldn't be in this financial pickle right now.

"Yeah, he asked if I'd ever talked to you. He acted all fanboy about it, which was weird since he was so old. Men in their forties shouldn't be fanboy about anything except *Star Wars* and Apple products."

My back muscles tightened so quickly that I barely registered her ageist insult. "Is that right?"

Maybe that man had been a fan, but that wouldn't explain why he had one of my father's photos.

"That's not entirely unusual," Phoebe piped up behind me. "People are fascinated that you're living here in town. You're the most exciting thing since Lowe's opened a store in the area."

As long as I was giving people something to talk about . . . me and a big-box home improvement store.

"Did he say anything else?" I asked.

Alexa tapped her pen against her lips. "Nothing interesting. He said he's from Pennsylvania. He was here doing some work. And that he loved your TV show and thought it was really cool you were in the Outer Banks. I was hoping he'd be in here this morning to give his opinion on your TV interview yesterday. Then I realized he was the one who died. Talk about bummer."

Phoebe shot me a questioning look, and I shrugged. Phoebe obviously hadn't watched the news today, or she would know about my throw down.

"Did this guy say where he was staying, by chance?"

Alexa absently rubbed the top of her leather notebook. "Not really. But when he pulled out his keys, there was a plastic black diamond keychain on it with the number 611."

My shoulders sagged. That was observant, but it didn't help me. "That could be for anywhere around here."

"Actually, it's not." Alexa grinned like there was a canary nearby, just waiting to be eaten. "I clean houses around here in the summer to pick up some extra money. That key chain is for the Seaside Condos down the road."

My heart leapt into my throat. "Are you sure?"

An imaginary yellow feather escaped from her lips. "Absolutely."

***

I headed over to the Seaside Condos after I left Oh Buoy. Maybe I should have called Jackson with the information, but I wanted to confirm that Douglas Whatever-His-Real-Name-Was—let's just stick with Mark Hamill—had actually been staying there.

That made sense, right? I couldn't be the girl who cried wolf. There was an entire episode of *Relentless* on that, and it hadn't ended well for the college girl in peril who had continually sounded false alarms.

However, when I pulled up to the condo complex, three police cars were already there, which made me want to turn around. Before I could, Jackson

Sullivan's laser-beam eyes bored into my car. He paused right there in the parking lot and scowled.

I sighed and put the car in park, knowing I'd need to explain my reasons for being here, lest I look even more guilty.

I climbed out, slammed the door, and slogged my way toward him. On the bright side, the day was cold but sunny. I pulled my coat closer, not so much because of the breeze but to guard myself against the onslaught of questions and accusations I was certain would come.

Jackson waited for me like a corrections officer with a grudge and a binge habit of watching *Prison Break*.

"What are you doing here?" Jackson asked.

Guilt—one of my closest companions lately—pounded in my chest. I'd pegged him all wrong, and now he hated me for it. Somehow I needed to make things right, but this wasn't the time or place. "I heard a rumor the mystery man may have been staying in 611."

"And how did you hear that?"

"Through talking to someone at Oh Buoy. You?"

He tilted his head. "You know I can't tell you that."

"Was he staying here?"

"I can't tell you that either."

"Well, what can you tell me?" I pressed.

"That you should stay out of this."

"I can't stay out of it. I look guilty." Plus, I'd put myself out there. On TV. And now it was a race to find

56

the killer before the killer found me.

"Being here doesn't help," Jackson said.

"Douglas Murray went into Oh Buoy frequently and watched Beach Combers from his little seat by the window. He asked people about me. What if he's my stalker, Jack—Detective Sullivan?"

He stepped closer. "Listen, if it makes you feel better—or worse, I'm not sure which—this *is* where he was staying. But he's only been here a week. Your super-stalker duo, as you call them, has been here in the area for at least six weeks."

"They could have switched locations. Or maybe they left the area and came back." Why was I talking like this topic was ordinary? Or like my stalkers were my friends? They terrified me. But at this very moment, I was separating myself from the reality of scary stalkerdom in order to get answers.

Jackson shrugged. "You never know. They could have."

"Why else would this guy have my picture?" Unless he was a stalker or connected with my dad . . .

Another shadow passed his gaze. "We're trying to figure that out."

"Did you get the autopsy back yet?"

His jaw flexed. "We did."

"And? Please don't say you can't tell me."

"He drowned."

"Accidental?"

"There were bruises on his shoulders."

My blood went cold. "Like he was held under the water," I muttered.

"I'm only sharing that information to remind you of how serious this situation is." He shifted. "I need to get back now. Stay away from this, Joey. Please."

I raised my chin. "I don't know that I can do that."

"Try."

Without waiting for my response, Jackson walked away.

And I remained right where I was.

CHAPTER 6

I stood at the perimeter of the crowd, hoping to spot a clue as to what the police were doing. I stared at the scene around me. Why were there so many police cars here? That was what didn't make sense. Sure, a murdered man had stayed here. But it wasn't like he was here now. All the police seemed like overkill.

At least, it would seem like that if we were filming *Relentless*. Though I knew Hollywood wasn't always accurate, I'd learned a lot in my limited PI work.

A small crowd had gathered, all waiting to see what the commotion was about. Even though no police line had been strung, we'd formed somewhat of an imaginary boundary. I watched as officers came and went from the condo.

While waiting there, I realized something very important: I couldn't stand back passively and wait. I was a showman, and I needed to do what I did best. I needed to act as an unconventional hostess of sorts.

Take the conses by the quences.

Note to self: stop saying that annoying phrase.

"Excuse me. May I have everyone's attention?" I turned to address onlookers. The small crowd looked at me, some surprised, others trying to avoid eye contact. "I'm desperate to find out information about the man who was staying in condo 611. I'm trying to identify who he is, where he was from, and why he was in this area. Did anyone here talk to him?"

Everyone remained quiet a moment, so I waited.

"Anyone?" I asked again.

Finally, a man cleared his throat. He was probably in his early thirties, lanky and tall with dark straight hair. Mostly what I noticed was that he had a leg brace and an arm crutch, causing his steps to be staggered as he moved toward me.

"I talked to him once," he said.

"And?"

He rubbed his jaw. "He seemed nice enough."

"What did he say? Anything that gave any hints about what might have happened?"

He remained quiet a moment. "I don't know. He was pretty friendly. But I saw some shady guys hanging around. I thought they might be going to the condo next door to him, but they went to his."

"What do you mean by shady?"

He shrugged. "You know, the kind who sag their pants and wear massive gold jewelry. They had shifty gazes. I don't know. I don't want to stereotype."

"I see. In other words, the guy staying in 611 didn't seem like the type to hang out with those kind of people. More like someone who liked *Star Wars*."

"Exactly."

"Anything else you can share to identify these shady characters?"

"They wore black jackets with something gold on the back." He glanced at me. "I'm Shawn, by the way."

"I'm Joey."

He shrugged, almost looking embarrassed. "Yeah, I know."

"Did you tell the police what you told me, Shawn?"

"Not yet. I didn't realize he was the guy who'd been killed until about an hour ago."

"Did this guy, by chance, say what kind of work he was doing while he was in the area?"

Shawn shrugged. "Survey work, I think."

A chill rushed through me. Survey work? It could be surveying land, I supposed, like for an upcoming building project. But I wondered if it meant surveying *me*. Who would have hired him for that? The paparazzi? I just didn't know.

"He was kind of weird," added a woman wearing a flowered, floppy beach hat.

"How so?"

"I don't know." She tugged on her floppy hat and frowned. "He seemed like he was creeping around, if you ask me. It was just the way he moved."

"And his shoes were always muddy," the man beside her said. "I can understand sandy around here, but muddy? That raised some red flags."

"I thought he smelled like fish," another person added. "Then again, who doesn't in this area?"

"Thank you all for your help. If you remember anything else, you can find me at Beach Combers on the main highway." I paused. "In the meantime, would anyone like an autograph?"

***

Finally, the crowd began to dwindle until there was just me standing at the imaginary police line. A shiver ran up my spine, and my throw down from yesterday replayed in my mind.

I glanced around, suddenly feeling paranoid. Was someone watching me now? Waiting for just the right moment to pounce? I knew one thing: I wouldn't feel safe until whoever killed Mark Hamill was behind bars.

I could only think of one way to find out why so many police were here. It wasn't my first choice, but I had no other ideas. I was desperate.

Zane had a friend with loose lips who worked for the police. Lips that would share things that weren't meant to be shared. Lips that would sink ships. He was a living and breathing piece of the Graveyard of the Atlantic.

After a moment of contemplation, I texted Zane and asked him to see what he could find out from his friend. Just as I expected, Zane seemed more than willing to help.

Sure thing. I'll let you know what he says. #thisisfun

Zane and his hashtags. Texting him now

reminded me that the two of us needed to have a serious talk about the whole drugs/Claire thing. Later.

"What are you doing?"

Jackson's voice made me jump out of my skin, and my phone nearly tottered from my hand. I quickly grabbed it and turned the screen away before he could see the text message.

"Nothing." I straightened my jacket. "Are you in the habit of scaring innocent bystanders?"

He narrowed his eyes. "I'm not so sure you're innocent."

"We've been over this. I didn't—"

"That's not what I meant, Joey." He glanced at my phone. "What are you being so secretive about?"

"What did you find inside his place? Tit for tat."

"You know I can't tell you."

At that moment, my phone buzzed. Did Zane already text me back? I looked up and saw his officer friend—I thought his name was Danny, but I wasn't 100 percent sure—at the door to Mark Hamill's condo. He winked at me.

My cheeks heated. I had such a hard time hiding my guilt. How had I ever made a living as an actress?

I shrugged those thoughts aside. "I guess there's nothing left to see here."

"Now that I'm leaving, you mean?"

Jackson thought I'd only come here to see him? Now *that* was embarrassing and needed to be immediately corrected. "That's not what I meant—"

He chuckled, obviously in a much jollier mood

now than earlier. "Goodbye, Joey."

"Very funny, Jack—I mean, Detective Sullivan." The man did have a sense of humor. What would happen next? Ricky Gervais would be asked to host the Golden Globes for a third time?

"Joey, just call me Jackson. Really."

"Okay . . . Jackson."

As soon as I was sure he was gone, I looked at Zane's text. I held my breath as I read what he wrote.

Note found at Douglas's place reading "we know who you are."

A chill washed over me. That sounded an awful lot like my stalkers. They'd always said "we."

Was Douglas one of my stalkers? Had he written the note with the intention of delivering it to me? Or had my stalkers—who tended to both threaten me and watch out for me—sent the note to the man after noticing he was watching me?

I didn't know, but I somehow needed to find out.

CHAPTER 7

I arrived back at my duplex in time to see a pretty honey-blonde with amazing platinum highlights leaving Zane's place.

A woman departing from my neighbor's wasn't an unusual sight. Zane wore many hats, including Realtor, surfboard restorer, and licensed massage therapist. He worked out of his home doing thus-said massages, which still sounded sketchy to me, but I supposed it could be legit. At least it explained why a different woman left his place each night.

In his defense, Zane definitely knew how to work kinks out of muscles. I'd been the recipient a few times, and his fingers felt amazing on my neck and shoulders. He tended to make me want to ignore my boundaries and jump into a relationship. But I had many issues with that, including the fact that I wasn't sure Zane was the committing type. Double plus, I wasn't sure I could trust him after the whole drugs and Claire fiasco.

I slipped inside my house, wanting to compose myself before talking to Zane. The two of us had developed a little routine. Every night we went out on our connecting balconies to look at the ocean. The joint space was only separated by a wood divider, so if we leaned over the railing, we could see each other and talk easily.

Zane would make up conversations that the people on the beach were having. From the leotard-wearing yoga guy, to the ultraserious photographer, to the chronic jogger man with the fluorescent jumpsuits, to numerous other regulars in the area, Zane purported to know what each of them was thinking and offered his free commentary. There was something comforting—and entertaining—about the routine.

But tonight I had a bone to pick with Zane. A big one.

I stepped out and pulled a warm fake-fur blanket around me. Tonight, the ocean smelled fishy and the waves were loud and constant. Stars fluttered overhead, and the sliver of a waning crescent moon teased like a hanging chad. This was one of my favorite places in the world.

A few minutes after I stepped out, I heard the adjoining sliding-glass door roll across its track. Zane's head popped around the divider. "I'm so sorry, Joey."

His pronouncement threw me off guard. I hadn't even scolded him yet. "Sorry for what?"

Could he possibly know I'd found out about his exaggeration? This wasn't going how I'd envisioned.

"I saw the article," he said.

My muscles were suddenly tight, and my blanket no longer felt warm at his ominous words. "What article?"

"You didn't see it?"

"I have no idea what you're talking about."

"Wait right there." He disappeared for a second before returning. His hands gripped the divider as his feet appeared on the railing, and he pulled himself up.

"Zane, you're going to kill yourself!" We were two stories high, and there was nothing to catch him except mounds of hard sand below.

"I've got this!" Like a skilled rock climber, he maneuvered his way over the railing and landed in one piece on my side of the balcony.

The whole exhibition both fascinated me and disturbed me. It made me realize how easy it would be for someone to get into my place, if they wanted to. I pulled the blanket closer, feeling more exposed than ever.

Zane bounced before straightening. I studied his outfit quickly: bright-orange lounge pants and a tank top. Somehow, the clean-cut hippie look worked for him.

He grabbed something on the other side of the divider and plopped it in my hands. "This."

I glanced down at a print copy of the *Instigator*, and my stomach sank. It was a picture. Of me. From yesterday.

I wore high heels and a coat with what appeared to be nothing beneath it. My hair had dried in a wet bun on top of my head, giving it a greasy effect. Between the water, cold, and accusations thrown at me, my face looked pale and gaunt. I was leaving after my interrogation, and a sign on the door behind me clearly stated *Police Station*.

The headline read, "Joey Darling arrested on prostitution charges."

My mouth dropped open. "You've got to be kidding me!"

"I know. These people are jerks, Joey."

"What's even worse is the fact that this picture totally looks legit." I squeezed the skin between my eyes. *Please don't let my dad see this. Please.* "What am I going to do?"

He flipped the magazine open and pointed. "And there's this."

I scanned the text. It was a quote. From Eric, my jerky ex. I read it aloud. "I've been worried about Joey's erratic behavior for a long time now. I just pray she can get the help she needs. Our marriage didn't survive, but I truly hope she can pull through this and get her life back together again."

Fire swept through my veins like lighted dynamite waiting to explode. "You have to be kidding me. Eric said that. The little two-faced, poppy-squatting jerk."

"We'll address your poor use of name-calling later, but for now, I'm really sorry."

I shook my head again, hoping this was a dream and I'd wake up soon. But I knew it wasn't. "How could he do this?"

"Some people will do anything for publicity."

Just then my cell rang. It was Rutherford. No doubt he'd just seen this article also and would be worried about how it might affect ratings of *Family Secrets*. I let it go to voicemail.

"Men can be jerks," Zane said.

As soon as the words left his lips, I remembered how mad I was at him also. All my man frustration was suddenly focused on every man who'd ever lied to me, starting with Zane.

"Speaking of which—Zane, you told me that Jackson stole Claire from you. That wasn't true. She'd already broken up with you when she met Jackson."

Zane glanced away from me, toward the ocean, and narrowed his eyes. "This wasn't exactly the subject change I'd been hoping for, but since you mentioned it, Claire and I were going to get back together. We'd broken up many times before. It was never permanent."

I raised my chin, ignoring the fact that my nose was an ice cube. I'd invite Zane inside for this conversation, but I didn't want him to be too comfortable, not until I knew the truth. It was another move I'd learned from Raven.

"Why?" I asked.

A hood came down over his gaze. "Why what?"

"Why'd you tell me that Jackson stole your girl, Zane?" I needed an answer, and he wasn't going to charm his way out of this one.

"Because it's true."

I paused, feeling like I'd been plopped into the middle of a Nicholas Sparks movie. All the elements were in place: the idyllic beach, the small North Carolina town, the melodramatic secrets. If one of us died by the end of this, that would seal the deal. Rutherford would rush to get the film rights and pad his bottom dollar.

"I get that you don't like Jackson, and I even get that you might feel that he stole her. But you know it's not the truth."

Zane's jaw flexed, and his hands tightened on the railing. "Jackson moved in on Claire during a weak moment. It was a cheap play."

I licked my lips before asking my next question. "Is it true that you were on drugs? That your relationship with Claire was volatile because of it?"

His spine straightened, and not even the stars sparkling overhead could soften this *Erin Brockovich* confrontation. "Look, I'm not the person I was. Neither are you. Right?"

His words hit me. Hard. It was true. I didn't want to be remembered for everything I'd done wrong. If the *Instigator* had anything to do with it, that was exactly what would happen. "No, I'm not."

"If I could go back, I would have done things differently. But I can't do that. I only have to live with my mistakes now."

I lowered my voice. "What happened?"

His face looked stony as he stared off into the distance again. Whatever was on his mind was heavy and painful. "I was in a car accident. You know those pictures you saw at my place? The ones where I helped disabled kids learn to surf?"

I nodded. They were in an album on his coffee table.

"Well, my little brother is one of those kids. He hasn't always been that way. We were in a car accident when he was only ten. I was driving. I walked away okay—long term, at least—and he's in a wheelchair for the rest of his life."

Everything went still inside me until all I heard was my heartbeat. "I'm so sorry."

"I was in a lot of pain because of my injuries for a while, and I became hooked on the painkillers I was taking. When I couldn't get more prescriptions, I discovered heroin. Anything to stop the pain. It wasn't my proudest moment, but it happened. I finally got myself clean. Went to college. Got a real job. Then I realized that I had everything I wanted right here in the Outer Banks. Life is too short to get caught up in the rat race."

"And Claire?"

His jaw flexed, and he looked away. "Claire was the love of my life. We met in high school. She was two years younger. She loved the beach almost more than I did. I'd be lying if I said things didn't change after that accident my senior year."

"Did you guys go to school with Jackson?" I couldn't remember if he was native to the area or not, though I seemed to remember he wasn't.

"No, he came here every summer on vacation with his family. That's where he and Claire met. She was surfing, and he was on the beach. And that was the end of my happy-ever-after story."

"But he didn't steal her. You had broken up. Right?"

He shrugged. "I guess. It was just a matter of time before we got back together though. I was about to go to rehab. I'd realized I was a train wreck waiting to happen."

"How long are you going to hold it against Jackson?"

He finally looked at me. "Why? You have a thing for him or something?"

"It's like I told you, Zane. I'm not looking for a relationship." I held up the *Instigator* and pointed to Eric's quote. "I've got a bad track record. Besides, Jackson hates me."

Zane let out a quick puff of air and an almost bitter chuckle. "Yeah, sure he does."

"Really. He does. I'm a thorn in his side."

He ran a hand through his hair, leaving curls standing on end. "More like a rose."

"What does that mean?"

Zane shook his head, the tension radiating from him practically transforming him into a different person. He snapped his head up and turned toward me. "Listen, I'm sorry. Do you forgive me?"

"I forgive you, Zane." How could I not? He'd been there for me since we met. "Of course I do. I just want us to shoot straight with each other."

"We will. *I* will."

"Excellent."

He turned toward me, his features softening. "This is all serious. This isn't us. We have fun together. We relieve stress. So can we talk about something else?"

Silence fell, and I tried to think of something to say. I tugged the blanket closer. "You had a client tonight?"

"A client?"

I mentally sighed. "I saw her leaving when I came home."

"Oh, April? No, she's not a client." He chuckled slowly, almost awkwardly, and his hands went to his hips. "She's . . . uh, she's . . . my girlfriend."

I blinked. "What? I didn't know you were dating someone."

He'd just kissed me a few weeks ago. Men were so confusing. Or maybe I was the type not worth waiting for or who could be gotten over quickly. That seemed most likely, given my track record.

"Well, we went out a week or so ago and hit it off, you know. She just started working at the realty office with me."

"I had no idea. That's . . . that's great, Zane."

"Yeah, she's a pretty cool girl. We're heading out of town for a wedding together this weekend, FYI."

"A wedding out of town together? You guys got serious fast. Aren't weddings usually level two of dating?"

He shrugged. "What can I say? Go big or go home, right? Anyway, listen. I have some fondue I was going to make. You want some?"

Fondue? The thought made my mouth water. Veggies and cheese. I could do that. No meat. No bread. I could stick to my diet . . . if I could remember which one I was on right now.

But . . . "What will April think about us hanging out?"

"She's knows about you. She's cool with the fact we're friends. Why wouldn't she be?"

Exactly. Why wouldn't she be? It wasn't like we'd kissed or anything.

Except we had.

It was my turn to shrug. "No reason. And fondue sounds good."

"Great. Then I'm going to tell you about that guy over there fishing." Zane pointed toward the beach. "He actually told his wife he had to go into the office . . ."

***

That evening after fondue, I went to a spare bedroom of my rental and to the little closet where I kept all the information on my dad's disappearance. Zane had bought me a dry-erase board—he'd said it was because every detective in those TV shows always had one to organize their clues.

On one side, I'd written all the facts I knew connected with my dad's disappearance. So far, I had:

- Bloody oriental fan
- A torn paper with random numbers
- A key to something unknown
- A picture taken of my dad with Jackson only days before Dad disappeared

- A witness who'd seen my dad eating at Fatty's with a man with a skull-and-crossbones tattoo
- Shoes left at my place with traces of salt water, polyurethane, and red diesel, signaling a connection to a marina
- Dad's personal items were missing, including his treasured grandfather clock and an old trunk

It seemed like a lot, but it really wasn't. Nothing was concrete enough to point me toward the next logical step in my search for Dad.

But the board had two sides, so I flipped it over to write down clues about this Douglas guy.

I started with the fact that I didn't know his real name.

- Alias: Douglas Murray
- In town approximately a week
- Traveling to do supposed survey work
- My pictures found in his pocket—including one that belonged to Dad
- I'd cut his hair—a ploy to talk to me?
- Done the Polar Plunge
- Seen meeting with some punks
- Mud on shoes
- Smelled like fish

- Note found at the rental. *We know who you are*
- He'd warned me to be careful right before he died

None of that made a bit of sense.

Not even a smidgen.

I stared at the list.

I had no idea where to go with this. And maybe I shouldn't go anywhere with it. Maybe I should just bow out and not get involved.

Except I *was* involved. Douglas had involved me, both when he came in to get his hair cut and when he'd carried my picture with him.

I sighed. I just wanted to find my dad. I wanted to be frustrated with this case for preventing me from doing so, but that wasn't even the truth. Reality was that I didn't have any good leads. Even if I hadn't become wrapped up in this new mystery, I would still have no answers about what happened to my dad.

And that was unacceptable. My alter ego would have never approached an investigation so lackadaisically. And I shouldn't either.

I began brainstorming ways to figure this mystery out. Nothing was off the table.

CHAPTER 8

The next morning, on a break at work, I called Mayor Allen.

I had a plan. It could be a lousy plan, but at least it was something.

Now I was going to be like Will Smith in *The Pursuit of Happyness*: determined and unstoppable. I would see success, even if I had to be laughed at and unconventional to do so.

"If it isn't my favorite celebrity," Mayor Allen said.

"And my favorite mayor." My throat hurt even saying the honey-dipped words. I absently began folding freshly washed towels that Dizzy had brought in.

"Oh stop." His voice warmed under my compliment. "What's going on, Joey?"

I paused from folding when I saw a copy of the *National Instigator* at the bottom of the pile. I scowled. Of course it was the newest one that featured my recent "scandal." Dizzy must have bought a copy. Nice.

I cleared my throat, putting those thoughts aside. "Mayor Allen, I was wondering if I could see the publicity shots from the Polar Plunge."

"Oh, Joey." His voice dropped, almost like he was talking to a child. "We won't be using those. Not after what happened."

"I realize that . . . but I still wondered if I might see them. To . . . uh, add the experience to my portfolio." I threw a towel over the magazine, tempted to take it home and burn it.

"Oh well, I suppose it couldn't hurt then." He perked up. "I'll put my assistant on it. Is email okay?"

"Email would be great." That way I could blow the photos up and really look at the faces there. The killer had been present at the event. It was just a matter of pinpointing whom.

"I'll do that then. Oh, and you heard from ABC News, I take it?"

I frowned at the mention. "I did."

"This is going to be fantastic!"

"I'm not sure a murder in Nags Head is fantastic." I had to get that thought out of my mind, because it kept circling and circling with nowhere to go.

"The murder isn't fantastic. But solving a crime and a bad guy getting justice? People love that. As long as it's not a serial killer." His laugh quickly faded. "Serial killers are bad."

At least we were both on the same page with that one.

I paused. Should I ask him about the whole Castle/Beckett thing Zane had suggested? I couldn't bring myself to do it. Not yet.

"Thanks for all your help, Mayor," I said instead. "I appreciate it."

It was probably a long shot, but the killer should be in one of those pictures. Would I recognize him? I couldn't say. But it was worth trying, especially since I'd put it out there that I was coming for him. Not my brightest move. Almost as bright as a burned-out light bulb, for that matter.

***

"You want pictures, huh?" Dizzy said when I emerged.

Eavesdropper. Even worse, an *Instigator*-loving, Christmas-music-obsessed eavesdropper.

"I do."

Her eyes danced with excitement as she sat at the counter, balancing the books. "You're investigating, aren't you?"

I shrugged. "Why would I do that?"

"It's in your blood."

"You're confusing me with Raven Remington."

She laughed so hard she slapped her knee. The force of wind from the action sent some receipts floating to the floor, and she scrambled to pick them up. "You're so funny! Of course I'm not. I can just see the fire in your eyes."

Self-preservation. That was really what it was. But I kept my mouth shut because I knew it wouldn't change her opinion.

"Besides, there are some things you can't fake," she continued, punching more numbers into the calculator. "Raven Remington has always been a part of you, deep down inside."

Her words gave me pause. I couldn't think about them too long. Because they were wrong. Raven and I were nothing alike.

Raven was a sharpshooter. Was I? No.

She was a genius. I wasn't.

A martial arts expert. No way.

Amazingly adept on the computer. Me? Nope, I couldn't even remember my passwords.

"How's the love life going?" Dizzy asked, changing the subject like Raven changed lanes on the freeway in rush-hour traffic—brashly and without apology.

I'd answered this very question before, and I really felt like I needed something more interesting to tell her today. "I'm going to move to Tuscany while battling career obstacles and in hopes of meeting a handsome Italian while recovering from a lousy ex-husband who took all of my money."

"What?"

"*Under the Tuscan Sun*? That movie is much more interesting than my life right now." I sighed, surprised at what my life had in common with that film, now that I thought about it. "I don't have a love life."

Seriously. We'd been over this before. Many times. Just because Raven always found love didn't mean I would. Especially not after Eric.

"Oh, come on. Admit it." She wiggled her eyebrows, her blue eye shadow reminding me of cartoon dolphins breaking the surface of the ocean on a clear day. "You're interested."

"In whom? A handsome Italian?"

"No, of course not. I can't decide. Either Zane or Jackson. I don't know which one is better for you."

"Neither are interested. Jackson, for obvious reasons. And Zane is dating someone." I really needed to change the subject. "We don't have any appointments scheduled, do we?"

"No, we don't. It's a slow day."

I rose from my twirly chair. "Do you care if I head out? I have some things I need to do."

"Are they Raven Remington type of things?"

"Actually, they are."

"Then I insist you take the time off today. Go get 'em, Tiger!"

***

Last night, Zane had mentioned that he had nothing scheduled for today, so I called him, hoping I wasn't interrupting his time with April. I sat in my car with the heat cranked as I waited for him to answer.

"Joey? What's going on?" He sounded like he'd just woken up.

I glanced at my watch. It was already 11:30. Sheesh. Talk about a sleepyhead. "Zane, where would people who are up to no good hang out in this area?"

"What?"

I wiped some dust from the dash with my fingers. I really needed to have this car detailed.

Except I had no money. Which meant I should do it myself. Which meant it probably wouldn't get done.

"I need to track down people who are troublemakers," I continued. "Where would they be in this area? Any hot spots? I'm guessing they probably can't afford one of these beach houses, but they're here somewhere."

"Okay . . . um, I need to think."

Thinking was good. Except when it led to thoughts like *Why hasn't the bad guy tried to kill me yet?*

Then it hit me: maybe he hadn't seen the video yet because he had more important things to do than watch TV. Things like kill people.

"Do I need to bring you coffee?" I finally asked when I realized Zane was still thinking.

"Do that. I'll get dressed. And I'll look at the map to figure out what places to hit and in what order."

"That sounds so organized."

"I *am* a Realtor. This is kind of my jam. I'll even go with you."

"But April . . ." I was seriously worried about this whole April thing. I didn't want to cross any boundaries.

"I told you—she's cool. We'll hit some vape shops. Maybe an old marina. Campgrounds are always good. We'll have a plan. Hashtag: adventure!"

***

Zane and I went to ten different places. Yes, ten. We

went to four pawnshops, three vape shops, and one store with drug paraphernalia everywhere. We also went to an arcade and the cheapest hotel on the beach.

I told Zane only one more place, and then I was giving up. I'd given it the good old college try.

Our final stop was at a secondhand store—a mix of a pawnshop and thrift store. I approached the front counter, where a man with flaky white hair stood picking stuff out of his ear with his keys.

Gross.

The only thing that redeemed this place was the big sign hanging over the register reading, *Our junk can be your junk*. Well, that and the eighties death-metal music on the overhead. It almost made me forget the ear picking, as well as the strange scent of garbage and body odor.

"How can I help you?" The man took his key from his ear and examined the end of it.

I leaned on the counter, trying to turn on my charm, and glanced at his name tag. "Hi, Terry. I'm looking for someone. A few someones, for that matter."

"Like who?"

"Unfortunately, I don't know much about them. Three guys in their late teens, early twenties. They look like troublemakers. You know the type, right? Not to stereotype, but—"

"Yeah, I know the type." He straightened, as if he was above doing business with that type of customer.

I highly doubted it.

"Anyway, there were three of them," I continued. "They were all wearing the same black jacket with a gold patch of some sort on the back."

He nodded slowly, flicking something off the glass counter in front of him. "Oh yeah, I know who you're talking about."

I straightened, hoping this might actually be something. And also hoping that whatever he flicked hadn't come from his ear, because it had been aimed right at my jeans. "What do you know about them? I'm looking for any information I can find."

He paused, a John Wayne expression on his face as he lowered his voice. "Are they up to no good?"

"Quite possibly."

He pursed his lips and nodded. "Okay, what do you need to know? I haven't actually seen them myself."

My hope sank.

He snapped his fingers. "I know who has. Go talk to Hal at Hal's World RV Park in Kitty Hawk. He was having some trouble with them. They were staying there in a camper, if I understand correctly. He was talking about them at breakfast the other morning."

I glanced at Zane. Answers. Could I finally get some? I had no idea, but a girl could hope.

CHAPTER 9

We pulled up to Hal's World, and I immediately recognized that this wasn't one of the nicer RV parks in the area. There would be no glamping (glamorous camping, in case you were not in the know) taking place here like that occurring at some of the other nicer campgrounds in the area. Some of them were located oceanside and contained recreational vehicles that cost more than many houses did. They had playgrounds and mini golf courses and other amenities people enjoyed.

Hal's World, on the other hand, featured campers that were on the back of truck beds. And not nice trucks. Run-down, rusted trucks. A few tents popped up in the midst of them. The RV park was located far from the ocean, back in a part of the area that I didn't even know existed, near another little Outer Banks town called Colington.

A resort, this was not.

I parked on the side of a gravel road and stepped out. The place smelled like a junkyard. Trash drifted with the wind. Empty bottles and old tires had been discarded in ditches, and a ratty couch sat at the curb.

A little shed had been erected in the center of it

all. A little window had been cut out in the middle of one side, and a piece of flimsy pressed wood hung down beneath it, water damage swelling the edges.

"Here goes nothing," I muttered to Zane.

A man was inside, and he looked like someone who'd hang out with Flaky White from the secondhand store. He had a toothpick in his mouth, stains on his white T-shirt, and hair that was a little too greasy.

"Hal?"

He nodded. "That's me."

"Terry from down the street said we could find you here," I started.

Hal counted some dollar bills and placed them in a money drawer, barely looking at us. "That right?"

"We're looking for three guys who might be staying here," I said.

"You're going to have to give me more information than that."

I pulled out my wallet and flashed my driver's license. "Josephine Schermerhorn. I'm with . . . a government agency."

The man went pale. He closed his money box and slid it under the counter, suddenly giving me his full attention. "Okay."

I leaned closer, knowing that I needed to both tap into my acting abilities and come up with a quick cover story. In other words, I needed to think of a movie where two agents went in search of bad guys. There was only one that came to mind, and I hoped it would work.

"We believe we've uncovered a deadly plot by them to assassinate two ambassadors from opposing . . . Middle East countries. We believe they're currently living in this area and that they're extremely dangerous."

Zane glanced and me, and I shrugged. *Men in Black*, Outer Banks version. What could I say? *If all else fails, tap into your overwhelming database of movie knowledge.*

Hal's eyes widened. "What do these assassins look like?"

"They wear black jackets with a gold logo on the back," Zane added.

"Oh, them troublemakers. Yeah, I know who you're talking about."

"Are the aliens here now?" I asked.

"Aliens?"

I snapped back to reality. "I meant illegal aliens. Not the intergalactic sort. Of course."

Hal shrugged, unfazed by my rambling. "Nope, they sure aren't. They were here for about a week, I guess."

"Can you tell us which camper was theirs?" I asked.

"Nope, it's gone now."

"They took it?" Zane asked.

"Nope, they didn't take it. Someone else did."

Irritation clawed at me. "Who took it?"

"The police," Hal said. "They beat you to it. Sounds like you need to work on interagency communication."

I did a Jackson and scowled. "Just tell us what happened. Please."

"Those three were apparently breaking into rentals around here. You know most of the places are abandoned and won't be opened up again until the spring. It's the perfect time for thieves to hit. And they do."

"Of course I know that. I do work for the government." *Don't forget your cover, Joey!*

"Anyway, that's what they were in town doing. They came here just long enough to break into a handful of homes and a couple of condos. Of course I didn't know any of that until the police arrested them the other day. They hadn't counted on one of the homes having security cameras. Not very smart for international assassins."

"I never said they were smart."

They'd been arrested. That meant that Jackson had known all of this. If that was the case, it made my blood even hotter than before. Not that I expected him to share information. But still.

"That's right," Hal continued. "Happened right here at the campground. The detective had a warrant and all."

"Do you know any more details?" Zane asked. "We'll talk to the police to confirm all of this. Of course."

"I know they hit some of those condos over in Nags Head. I overheard the police saying that when they arrested them."

Condos over in Nags Head? Did that mean those

guys weren't associated with Douglas Murray's death at all? Did they just happen to be ripping off the very condo where the man had been staying?

I took a mental tally.

Bad luck: two

Joey: zero

At the rate I was going, I was never going to get to the bottom of this.

***

I'd nearly forgotten I promised Dizzy I'd come for cake at her place this evening. I showed up with a bag of pretzel M&Ms—it was better than being empty handed, right?—and met three of her friends. Apparently, this was a weekly ritual.

It was my first time going to Dizzy's place, even though she'd invited me before. She lived in a little bungalow tucked away from the main highway that cut through the island. Even though the island was only three miles wide at its thickest point, this neighborhood almost seemed normal, absent of stilt-ridden beach houses, tourists, and souvenir shops. I would imagine that this was where the area's teachers and police officers and firemen lived.

The inside was decorated just as uniquely as I might suspect for Dizzy. Bright-blue walls. Purple accessories. Boas instead of curtains.

Boas?

Whatever floated her boat.

Her friends greeted me. Maxine, who owned

Utter Clutter, a store that sold fabulous repurposed furniture. There was also Geraldine, who'd been a homemaker, and MaryAnn, who'd retired from teaching. All four were widows and in their late fifties or early sixties. Apparently, they called themselves "The Hot Chicks."

"Anyone want some cake by the ocean?" Dizzy held up a glass platter full of luscious yellow slices of heaven. She snickered. "Get it? Cake by the ocean?"

I squirmed in horror as she began singing the song by the same title. "I don't think that song's actually about a beachfront birthday party."

She paused midlyric, with her hip jutted out in a frozen dance move. "Really? What's it about then?"

I cringed. "I'm . . . not really sure. But I think it's inappropriate."

"Good to know." She licked some icing from her finger, looking unaffected.

I took a piece she offered and quickly consumed a bite before she asked more questions about any Joe Jonas songs. "This is delicious. And it's so moist. What's your hack?"

Her eyes widened, and her free hand rushed to her hip. "I'm no hack."

I raised a hand, realizing I was digging a deeper and deeper hole for myself. "No, no. That's not what I meant. Hack just means tip or shortcut, not fake. Pretending is more of my jam than yours."

"You want a jam recipe?" Geraldine said. "I've got a good one for spiced pear."

I just smiled, realizing I needed to change my

mind-set from twentysomething to more appropriate for the Hot Chicks. Otherwise, these ladies really *would* have something to talk about in their social circles. *Did you hear that hack Joey Darling likes to eat cake and make jam by the ocean?* No, thank you.

As we ate some of the tastiest lemon pound cake I'd ever had and sipped on coffee that could have been instant—I'd try not to hold that against anyone—they asked questions about Hollywood, and I asked questions about life in this area.

They told stories about growing up here at the beach and talked about the lifeguards they'd dated back when they still looked cute in bikinis—their words, not mine. Of course, now they were all pleasantly plump and not the beach-going types. But I'd say getting old enough to be pleasantly plump and happy was quite an accomplishment. I hoped I lived to see it one day.

Then I told them about the last case I'd somehow solved. These ladies were better than any sound-effect machine or even cue cards. They clapped at the good parts, gasped at the scary parts, and got teary eyed at the happy ending.

As my story concluded, the TV in the background caught my ear. The reporter finished a report on some shipping trucks that had been heisted recently in the state. Then she launched into the next story.

"Four months after the death of Anastasia Chernova, an international student worker from the Ukraine, police still have no answers," the newscaster said.

I gravitated closer to the TV, frowning at the familiar face on the screen—the ambush reporter. I hardly cared. Four months ago was when my father had disappeared. Possibilities began to circle in my head.

A picture of a smiling young woman came on the screen. She had long dark hair with a touch of wave and auburn highlights, olive skin, and a fabulous smile. A simple gold cross necklace hung around her neck, and she made a peace sign with her fingers.

"Anastasia arrived in the area in May and was scheduled to head back home at the end of September. She hoped to study criminal justice, according to her friends in the area, and eventually come back to the States. Her body was found in the Roanoke Sound by some fishermen. Her death was initially ruled accidental, but upon analysis by the medical examiner, it was found she was strangled. The police have no suspects."

"Isn't that just terrible." Dizzy came up beside me and shook her head. "That murder was the talk of the town. Don't get me wrong—it was terrible when that man turned up dead at the hotel a few weeks ago. And now that guy drowned during the Polar Plunge. But this young woman was beautiful, and you know the beautiful ones always get more media attention. That's just the way it is, fair or not."

"The media probably wouldn't care a thing about old broads like us!" Geraldine cackled.

The rest of the women laughed with her.

I supposed it was good to have a sense of humor

about these things, even though I thought their revelation was a sad testament to society.

"Now you, Joey Darling, would get plenty of media coverage," Dizzy said.

"My death would be no more important than anyone else's," I said softly. "You said she came here from the Ukraine?"

"She was one of those international workers we have," Dizzy said. "You know, with the surge in business in the summer, we don't have enough locals to fill in the workforce. So business owners bring in college kids from overseas to work. Mostly in hotels, restaurants, and retail stores, but occasionally other businesses too. She was one of them. Where did she work? Do any of you ladies remember?"

"I think it was somewhere in Manteo," MaryAnn said. "Maybe that drugstore?"

"Even drugstores around here are essentially souvenir shops, at least in the summer, you know?" Dizzy said, fanning her face again. "I believe that was the one where I got my fan, wasn't it?"

Her fan? The oriental one Dizzy always used? The one just like the bloody one left in a bag with the rest of my father's things?

My breath caught. What if the mystery of my father's disappearance was all somehow connected with this Anastasia girl? Or was that a stretch?

"Funny that this is the first I've heard about her murder," I finally said, hungry for more information. "I would think it would be the talk of the town."

"It's because every lead went dry," Dizzy said.

"MaryAnn's son is a police officer. He told her all about it."

MaryAnn waved. She was the demure, sweet one of the group.

"Is your son Danny, by chance?" I asked.

She nodded, beaming as she did so. "My sweet Danny. He loves to talk to his mama, and I raised him to know he could tell me anything. So he does."

Perfect. "So what did he tell you about this case? Anything?"

She blinked, as if thinking about it, even though I could tell she was eager to share. "It was all very strange. She was a very quiet girl. Kept to herself, and not many friends. No one truly understands what could have happened to her, but I do know it's made some of the agencies who send the workers over very hesitant. That's not good news for the local businesses who depend on them."

I shifted on the purple couch, grabbing a fuzzy, lime-green pillow and putting it in my lap. "What do you all think about this guy who died at the Polar Plunge? Have you heard anything about him?"

"There are lots of rumors flying," Maxine said. "Maybe he was with the mob."

"Or he was a hit man," Geraldine added.

"I heard he was part of an assassination attempt," MaryAnn said.

My cheeks heated. Had that information really got around to them already? Oh my. I had to remember the perils of living in a small town.

"There's really no telling," Dizzy said. "This area

is known for having harbored pirates. Who knows who we're harboring now?"

Her words left an ice cube in my chest.

The subject quickly moved to a new hotel that was being built in the Outer Banks. *No one wanted it. This area couldn't become another Myrtle Beach. Part of the Outer Banks' charm was that it was undeveloped.* And more and more and more.

I only halfway listened. Because my mind rehashed everything I knew and tried to figure out where to go next.

CHAPTER 10

Zane stopped by when I got home, to see if anything new had happened. Just as we were sitting down on my couch with some Izzes to chat, my phone buzzed. I looked at the screen and saw that Mayor Allen had emailed me.

I clicked on the email. Bingo! Pictures from the Polar Plunge.

"What is it?" Zane peered over my shoulder.

"I need to see this on my computer." I rushed to my feet. "You'll want to see it also."

"Now you've got me curious." He took a long sip of his drink.

I grabbed my laptop and sat back down beside Zane—not too close though. I opened the email and clicked on the first picture, anxious to see if I'd discover anything.

"Polar Plunge photos," I told Zane. "If someone killed Douglas Whatever-His-Real-Name-Is, then his or her picture should be in here somewhere. It's a start at least."

"You are brilliant."

"Not always. But this was one of my more decent ideas." I scrolled through the photos. I saw pictures of

Mayor Allen. I saw pictures of me on the stage. I saw Zane holding my hand up. Jackson watching quietly in the background. There were participants wearing costumes and crazy hats and ones with their chests painted.

I scanned the faces. Surprisingly, I recognized more than one person. I saw Billy, who owned Willie Wahoo's, a local bar and grill. The man had been a possible suspect in my last investigation when his father's car—that Billy was borrowing—was seen at a house belonging to a nearly dead woman. Plus, his dad, Winston Corbina, was one of the wealthiest men in the area, and there was something about him I didn't trust.

I also saw the girl from Oh Buoy, the writer chick who'd told me where Douglas was staying. I saw Yoga Man, who religiously worked out on the oceanfront no matter the weather. I recognized other people who were regulars in the area or who'd come into Beach Combers before.

"Look in the background there." Zane pointed at one picture. "Can you blow it up?"

"I can try." I made the picture as large as I could without pixelating it. There in the background, near the walkover atop a sand dune, was Hal from Hal's World. Also interesting. He didn't seem like the type to enjoy charity work or police fundraisers.

I flipped through a couple more photos. I wasn't sure if these were sent in chronological order or not, but in the next frames, Hal was gone. Or had he mixed in with the crowd somehow?

"There's one more person there." I pointed to a man standing in the background. It was none other than Winston Corbina himself.

"He doesn't seem like the Polar Plunge type either," Zane said. "He's above events like these. Plus, I heard he can't stand the police chief, so why head out to support the department?"

"Good question. But he does seem like the type who has enough money to hire someone to do his dirty work. Maybe he was just there to oversee things."

Just then I heard something in the distance. Zane and I froze.

When I looked over at the balcony, I noticed the table had overturned. I was about to blame the wind, when movement caught my eye.

It was a man. In black. Jumping over the balcony railing.

Zane ran toward him, and I was on his heels. He threw the door open and lunged outside. I reached the railing just in time to see a figure in black running down the beach. Zane started to launch himself over the balcony, when I grabbed his arm.

"No, don't." All I could think about was when Zane had been harmed in my last investigation. I didn't want that to happen again. I couldn't live with myself if he got hurt because of me.

He stopped, but I could feel the adrenaline pulsing off him. He gripped the railing and stared at the man's fleeing figure. The intruder was all the way across the beach and soon faded into the night.

"Why would someone have been on the balcony?" I muttered, running through everything in my mind.

"Spying on you? Maybe he was waiting until I left so he could try to get inside. Maybe it was the paparazzi. I have no idea." He rubbed his jaw. "But I don't like it."

"I don't like it either." I glanced around to see if he left any clues. A piece of paper lay on the floor.

My hands trembled as I picked it up. They trembled worse when I read the words there.

> *Did you miss us? Because we missed you. Stay tuned for more instructions. Your biggest fans*

CHAPTER 11

My throat tightened as Jackson Sullivan strode into Beach Combers the next morning for a haircut. I figured he'd never trust me with his hair again since I'd royally messed it up last time. But apparently, I was wrong.

"Fancy seeing you here." I flapped open a cape and fastened it around his neck.

"I've got to look good since I have a big interview on Thursday." He didn't appear entirely thrilled about it. Or thrilled at all. Kind of disgusted about it, for that matter.

But that wasn't my fault. It was Mayor Allen's. "Same cut as before?"

"Please."

I pulled out the clippers and slipped on the guard. As I stepped toward Jackson, I got a whiff of his spicy cologne. I imagined running my fingers through his hair. Touching his stubble.

I snapped out of it. I shouldn't be thinking about romance. I should be channeling my energy on the note I got last night from my "biggest fans." My stalkers had finally given themselves names, but it didn't make me feel any better. Nor did "Christmas

Island" blaring on the overhead. I was so over
Christmas music right now.

My back muscles constricted as I turned my
attention fully on Jackson. I needed to apologize to
him. I'd thrown an accusation at him, and it hadn't
been correct. When he left today, I'd walk him out
and apologize. I should have done it earlier, but I'd
gotten distracted.

I worked as I talked. "So what do you know
about this Anastasia girl who died four months ago?"

It was supposed to sound casual. It didn't.

"Anastasia? Don't you have enough on your plate
without adding her death to your list of things to
stick your nose into?"

I frowned. "Asking questions doesn't mean I'm
adding it to my plate."

"Doesn't mean you're not."

"So . . ." I refused to drop the subject.

"It wasn't my case. Dare County Sheriff's Office is
handling it."

"So you know nothing?"

"Nothing I'm willing to share."

I accidentally let out a "harrumph." It had been
worth a shot.

Jackson's eyes met mine in the mirror—deep,
mysterious eyes that always made me wonder. "You
wouldn't, by chance, know anything about some
fugitives who are hiding out in the area before
assassinating some ambassadors from the Middle
East?"

My hand slipped, and I nearly nicked his neck.

"Why would you say that?"

"Oh, I don't know. Maybe because you fit the description of the government agent someone said was looking for them."

I frowned. "Someone? You mean Hal?"

"Yes, Hal."

"Funny, he doesn't seem like the type to be overly social and share information like that."

"Only when he's drunk. And you should really stay away from Hal's World RV Park. Some shady stuff has gone down there."

I paused. "Speaking of shady . . . Have you ever looked into this Hal guy? Because his gaze was kind of shifty, and he hid some money when he heard I was a . . ." I almost said a government worker. Instead I said, "A TV detective."

"A TV detective? Is that all you told him?" He carefully watched me in the reflection of the mirror.

I cringed, hating the weight of his studious gaze. "I may have used the plot from *Men in Black*, minus the funny little aliens and intergalactic war. It was all I could think of."

"I've told you before that you need to be careful what you stick your nose into."

I shrugged and continued working. "I have little choice. My picture was in that man's pocket. And I got another threat."

He stiffened. "Another threat?"

"Yes, and you can't straighten like that, or I'm going to ruin your haircut." I whacked his shoulder in reprimand and then waited for him to say, "Ruin my haircut like last time?" But he didn't. Maybe he was a gentleman deep down inside.

"What did the note say?"

I told him.

"I don't like the sound of that, Joey."

"Believe me—I don't either."

"You should bring it by the station so we can file it as evidence."

"Of course."

"And if you get any more, you should report it right away."

"Right." I shifted. "So, I guess you, uh, arrested the three guys staying there. The ones who were at Douglas Murray's rental."

"Maybe."

Before I could ask any more questions, the door jangled and pulled my attention away from the conversation. To my surprise, Shawn from Seaside Condos walked in.

"Hey, Joey," he said, lingering by the front desk and leaning on his crutch.

"Fancy seeing you here. You need a cut?" I glanced at his coiffed dark hair, which appeared neat and trimmed.

"No."

"A manicure? Wait, an eyebrow wax?" I leaned closer and waggled my own eyebrows in exaggeration as I studied his rather bushy ones.

He chuckled and leaned against the counter, like he had all the time in the world. Island time. That was what it was called around here.

"No, I actually stopped by to see you."

"Oh?" Dizzy said, suddenly popping up from behind the desk.

"You said to come by if anything else came up," Shawn said.

Aha! Now that made more sense. "Something came up?"

Jackson grunted in front of me. All of this was against the no-snooping clause he'd tried to unofficially impose. Thankfully, I'd never agreed to it.

"I was hoping you might like to get coffee," he continued. "Maybe at Sunrise Coffee Co."

Hearing those words was music to my ears. I loved Sunrise almost as much as I loved Oh Buoy. "I am supposed to be working for the next two hour—"

"Oh, no. You go right ahead," Dizzy said, waving her hand in the air flippantly. "I can handle things here."

"Are you sure?"

"Oh, I'm more than sure. It's the winter lull." She smiled a little too brightly. She really wanted to see me with someone.

The next thing I knew she'd be happy to set me up with my stalker. As long as I was with *someone*.

Sheesh.

I nodded at Shawn. "How about if I meet you there in ten? I just need to finish up here."

He smiled. "Great. I'll see you then."

As he left, I finished edging Jackson's hair and brushed some powder on his neck.

Jackson gave me a look, and I smiled as if I hadn't

noticed.

"It's been a pleasure," I told him, resting a hand on his shoulder like I might any customer. Except, I became entirely too aware that I was touching him and quickly pulled my hand away. Instead, I took off his cape, ready to wrap this up and go talk to Shawn.

"Joey . . ." he warned.

"I'm just having coffee."

"Sure." He sounded unconvinced.

I expected nothing less.

After he paid, I grabbed my purse and walked with Jackson outside. Now was the time. The moment I'd apologize to him for assuming the worst. I was nervous, which was ridiculous, really. I'd apologized for stupid things a million times before, and I'd do it a million times again in the future. I just had to say *I'm sorry* and get it over with.

I slowed my steps in the gravel parking lot as we approached his unmarked sedan. "Jackson—"

Before I could finish, his phone rang.

"Hold that thought." He answered and grunted into the mouthpiece before turning toward me. "Sorry, Joey, but I've got to run."

"Of course. Duty calls. I'll see you later."

***

I smiled at Shawn when I walked inside Sunrise and tried to quell my curiosity as to why he wanted to meet and what he'd learned. I had to act like I had some manners, so I couldn't just jump into my questions . . . right?

I paused beside him at the counter and looked up at the menu board, as if I didn't know what I wanted.

"I think you're a latte kind of girl, but I can't decide between mocha or caramel."

"Good guess. I'm actually both."

He narrowed his eyes thoughtfully. "Soy?"

"You know it."

"I figured it was a Hollywood thing." He shrugged nonchalantly. "Anything to make a drink sound fancy."

"Well, you know . . . it makes all of us famous people feel special when we make all these demands." I raised my nose in exaggerated snootiness. "We thrive off that."

"I was going to say it makes you seem complicated." He flashed a grin.

Before I could order, the barista thrust my drink into my hand. Yes, coffee and eating out were my vices. I was on a budget now, and I really needed to stop this indulgence.

"Here you go, Joey," the barista said. "I started it as soon as I saw you pull in."

"Thanks, Shannon." I raised my cup and nodded at her.

"You must come here often," Shawn said.

"Guilty as charged. Coffee Lovers Anonymous knows me on a first-name basis." I was on a roll.

He chuckled again. "Let me order real quick. You get a table?"

I paid and found a seat in the corner, anxious to hear what he'd discovered.

As I waited, I scanned the quaint interior of the place. It wasn't polished like most of the coffeehouses I'd enjoyed in Beverly Hills. No, Sunset Coffee Co. had mismatched chairs and tables and an old ratty couch. Goods by local craftsmen sat on shelves wherever there was room, mostly mugs and coasters. Even the menu board wasn't nice or fancy. No, it was just a chalkboard that changed daily. I loved it here.

As I waited for Shawn, I pulled out my phone and scanned my emails. No angry messages from Rutherford or scary threats from stalkers. I could officially label this a good day.

"Anything good on there?" Shawn asked.

I slid my phone back into my pocket. "No, nothing. But checking it is addicting, unfortunately."

"I'm surprised you don't just hire a social media manager or something." He sat down across from me and stretched out his bad leg on an extra chair.

"Oh, I've had those. Everything was going fine until I told her to post that Steven Spielberg was a public treasure."

"What's wrong with that?"

"Well, let's just say she left a letter out of 'public' and changed the whole meaning of the sentence."

He nearly spit out his coffee. "Are you serious?'

"All too serious." I shifted.

"That's awful. Hilarious, but awful."

As the strands of "You Say Nothing at All" crooned overhead, Alfred the tabby cat tiptoed over and rubbed against my legs. I reached down and ran a hand behind his ears before clearing my throat. "If you don't mind me asking, what happened to your leg?"

"Iraq."

I raised my eyebrows. "You're a veteran."

"That's right. Army. On the ground. Stationed out of Fort Bragg."

"Thank you for your service."

"I'm glad I could fight for what I believe in. Life is too short not to."

"I wholeheartedly agree. What do you do now?"

"I work in management. It's not ideal, but it pays the bills."

I waited a moment for him to take charge of the conversation. When he didn't, I said, "So why did you want to have coffee with me, Shawn?"

"Isn't it obvious?" he asked.

"Of course. What was I thinking. You're fascinated with women who cut hair."

"You're funny. I thought you'd be more intense. Kind of like—"

"Raven?"

He shrugged. "Yeah, I guess so. Sorry. I know you probably hate that."

"Yeah, a little. But it is what it is." And what was with that saying? I really hated it. Like we had no control.

"I guess you want to know what I found out."

I leaned closer, curious now. "What's that?"

"I've been playing armchair detective, and I

found out something about that Douglas guy. Someone came by at his condo yesterday."

My blood spiked. "Did you recognize this someone?"

He shook his head. "No, I've never seen her before. But she looked . . . I don't know. Professional, for lack of a better word."

"What do you mean?" My mind went to so many places with that.

"Military-ish. You know, she wore utility pants, combat boots, a plain shirt. Her hair was pulled into a bun, and she carried herself like someone disciplined and tough."

"What did she do?"

"She knocked at his door. When he didn't answer, she tried to look into his windows. Then she left."

I chewed on that for a minute. Interesting. Very interesting.

"One other thing. Last night a few of us were playing horseshoes. I talked to one of the guys who happened to be staying next to Douglas. He said that Douglas told him he ran into someone he'd worked with before. It's probably nothing, but the man was from Pennsylvania also. What are the chances?"

"Slim."

"The interesting part was this guy seemed to have a grudge of some sort against Douglas."

"Why would you say that?"

"Apparently Douglas was upset after seeing him. He went on and on about what a jerk the guy was."

"Really? Where did Douglas see him?"

"He was playing pool over at Willie Wahoo's."

I nodded slowly, letting that sink in. "Did he give any indication what the man looked like?"

"He had hair so blond it was almost white."

I stored that information away. Because it could prove to be very, very helpful.

CHAPTER 12

I pulled into my driveway just as Zane walked from the shore in a wet suit, carrying his surfboard. He blogged for a local surf company, and because of that, he'd had a special wet suit made with a blue fin on the back. The suit fit him to a T, figuratively and literally.

"Isn't it cold to be in the ocean?" I yelled as I stepped from my car. Flashbacks from the Polar Plunge hit me, and I shuddered.

"There's no bad time to catch a wave." He bounded over the sand dune like a boss, set his board near the outdoor shower, and met me. Water dripped off his hair, yet he looked invigorated. "What are you up to?"

"That's what I'm trying to figure out. To say I'm stressed would be an understatement." I had no answers, I half expected Mark Hamill's killer to show up and silence me for good after my on-air threat, and I wouldn't be surprised if my stalkers suddenly appeared and let me know they'd been watching, critiquing, and plotting their own episode of *Relentless*. Yet, so far, all had been quiet. Eerily quiet.

"Stressed?" Zane said. "Being stressed is no fun.

You've been pushing yourself too hard. I have an idea that might be the perfect solution. It's something I've wanted to do for a long time. Want to come? Think: *Days of Thunder*."

I was intrigued. "Can I be Nicole Kidman?"

"Only if I can be Tom Cruise."

I tapped my foot in thought. Something not involving the mysteries plaguing me? Could I even consider it? I was enthralled. Maybe clearing my head would be good. "Tom and Nicole. You got it!"

He grinned. "Meet me out here in ten? You won't regret it. Hashtag: bucketlistsarefun!"

I shrugged, figuring I didn't have anything to lose. "Sounds good."

I drove, but Zane took me to a little go-carting place owned by one of his friends. It seemed like such a waste of time to have fun when so many things were pressing at me, but Zane's friend offered to let us take a spin around the track.

So we did. And there was something exhilarating about zooming around the little circle in the go-carts in fifty-degree weather.

Maybe it was just the stress reliever I needed.

Maybe *Zane* was just the stress reliever I needed. He was always so laid back and happy, like he didn't have a care in the world. He lived for the moment and made the most of each day. There was a lot to be said for that, and April was apparently very understanding.

When we finished go-carting, we went to Willie Wahoo's for an early dinner. It wasn't my favorite place, and I didn't trust Billy, the owner. But Zane was a regular around here, and he was a karaoke king. Besides, the white-blond man had been seen in here. What were the odds he'd be here again?

They had a decent vegan menu, and it was one of the few restaurants still open in the area at this time of the year. But I also knew a lot of trouble came out of this place. Fights. Back-alley drug deals. Inappropriate groping on the dance floor.

Jackson had gone through the list with me a few weeks ago.

"Racing builds up an appetite," Zane said. "I'm starving!"

"Then by all means, let's eat."

Inside the dimly lit windowless restaurant, Zane and I grabbed a high-top table and ordered a few appetizers. I let out a contented sigh and surveyed the place as I waited for our food. I'd eat a little and then get back home to prep for my big interview on Thursday. Rutherford had sent me some questions to review, and he wanted me to squeeze in a mention of *Family Secrets* if at all possible.

Zane called out hello to several friends. There was a steady flow of regulars, and the hum of chattering patrons intermingled with someone crooning "Blue Moon" on a stage in the corner. If you liked watching people, this was the place to be.

"So where's April tonight?" I asked, twirling my cucumber-and-mint seltzer water. I didn't drink. Not anymore. I'd made too many mistakes with alcohol in my system.

"Working." Zane didn't seem to think too much of it.

"Bummer."

"Yep."

Zane and I had a lot of fun together today, but suddenly guilt hit me. How would I feel if my boyfriend took his "friend" go-carting and went out to eat? *My Best Friend's Wedding* came to mind. I did not want to be Julia Roberts in that flick. I'd told myself that Zane and I could still hang out because we were pals, but maybe I needed to think a little more deeply about the subject.

Zane stood and held out his hand as "Blue Moon" ended. "Want to sing? We were a hit last time."

I stared as a basket of french fries was placed in the center of our table, along with some steamed shrimp, and veggies with hummus. What I really wanted was to eat. And watch people. And think deep thoughts. None of which was really like me.

"Maybe next time. I need to take a breather right now."

"Your loss."

I grabbed a fry and watched as Zane took the stage. A moment later he started singing "Little Red Riding Hood." The lyrics had never bothered me before, but right now they made me think of a stalker hunting his prey. I shivered, suddenly anxious for Zane to be done.

As I sat there, the hair on my neck prickled. I glanced around, and my breath caught. A man with white-blond hair sat at the bar, chatting away with

Billy. The boisterous man didn't seem to have a shortage of words.

I stood and edged closer, ordering more cucumber-and-mint seltzer. As I waited for it, I listened carefully to his conversation.

"Yeah, I was injured on the job and got an insurance payout," White Blond said. "I won't be working again for a while. In fact, my work is paying for me to be here right now. Got a great deal on one of the nicest houses on the beach."

"Which one is that?" Billy asked, drying a glass.

"The Sandblaster. It's the yellow one with the huge anchor in the front yard and an elevator on the side. If I'd known life could be so good after an injury, I would have injured myself a lot sooner." He laughed a little too loudly.

Interesting. This man didn't sound like a killer. And what kind of business had surveyor Mark Hamill had with him in the past?

The conversation veered to sports, and my water was delivered, so I went back to the table. Zane had finished singing. Everyone applauded, and he strode back toward me. I kept an eye on White Blond, ready to follow him when he left.

"Sounded good," I told Zane.

He shrugged. "What can I say? I try."

We ate for a few minutes in silence. Across the restaurant, I saw Hal from Hal's World. He was eating with Flakey White from the pawnshop. Interesting. I had no reason to suspect either of them, yet I couldn't help but feel neither was a star citizen.

Just then, White Blond stood and headed toward the door.

I dropped some cash on the table and turned to Zane. "I'm ready to go."

"But we just got here." His breath smelled like alcohol. How much had he drunk?

I glanced back at the door. This man was quickly disappearing. "I know, but I have to get ready for my interview. I have some prep work to do."

He didn't move.

"Do you want to get another ride home?" I asked.

He sighed. "Nah, I'm good. Let's go."

But as he stood, I could already tell he'd been drinking too much. I didn't love alcohol for this very reason. It made people act stupid.

The skin on my neck stood again. I glanced around. It wasn't White Blond who'd caused the reaction. He was gone. So far gone that I'd lost any hope of catching up. Hal and Flaky White were immersed in a game of cards.

I didn't see anyone else. Strange. Because my gut told me someone was watching me.

I slipped my arm around Zane's waist as we walked to my car. Before I closed the door, I gave one last glance back. No one suspicious caught my eye.

But I was certain someone in the crowd had been watching me.

My stalker? A fan? The killer? I had no idea.

And I'd lost White Blond. Double fail.

I stayed quiet for the short drive home, but Zane yammered beside me. At the house, I helped him to do the door.

"Are you sure you don't want to come in?" Zane asked.

"I'm sure." Alcohol always seemed to be liquid courage for people. Zane had definitely dropped some inhibitions, and I didn't want to see where that would lead. Nowhere good.

He looked down at me, that dopey smile on his face. "I like you, Joey Darling."

I squirmed. "Thanks, Zane. I like you too."

His gaze looked steamy as he leaned toward me. Leaned toward me? Oh no.

He was about to do something he'd regret, I realized.

I scooted back, my conscience whamming to the forefront of my awareness. Zane was dating someone. I couldn't do the very thing to Zane that I'd accused Jackson of doing with Claire. I couldn't be that woman. I needed to put some distance between the two of us, no matter how much that pained me, especially when considering he was one of my only friends in this area.

"You should call April," I told him, my voice hoarse.

Zane stepped back, his eyes still glazed but not nearly as warm now. "Yeah. Yeah, she's probably home by now."

"Have fun at the wedding with her this weekend."

He ran a hand through his hair and closed his eyes. When he opened them, a new emotion had taken residence inside. Anger? Disappointment? Resignation? I didn't know.

"I'm sure I will." His voice sounded flat and unconvincing.

Before anything else awkward could develop, I slipped inside my duplex, wondering why everything always had to change. Especially my relationships.

CHAPTER 13

The next morning, I knew exactly what I needed to do. I needed to figure out what White Blond was up to. I needed to know if he was involved in Mark Hamill's murder or not. I might have to take drastic measures for that to happen.

Just as I climbed into my car, a Jeep pulled in beside me, and Phoebe rolled down her window. I did the same.

"I guess I'm catching you at a bad time?" she said.

"I was just going . . . to see someone," I said. "What brings you by?"

"I stopped by Beach Combers to see if you wanted to hang out after work. Dizzy said you'd taken the day off. She practically volunteered me to stop by and make sure you were okay . . . which was a little weird."

Dizzy suspected me of investigating. Had she sent even-keeled Phoebe to be my watchdog?

I blinked, unsure how to respond. "I'd love to have some company, but—"

"Okay, great." She climbed from her Jeep, scurried over, and opened my passenger-side door.

"I'm having a bad day, and I really don't want to stay at the house all day by myself."

I still felt a touch of hesitancy. It was one thing if I got myself in trouble, but an entirely different story if I got Phoebe in trouble. Plus, where I was spontaneous, emotional, and far from levelheaded, Phoebe was an all-around good person who was well thought out and logical.

I swallowed hard as I pulled out of my driveway. I hadn't wanted to reject a new friendship. I needed people in my life. But I wasn't sure potentially getting Phoebe into trouble was the best way to win any points.

"Bad day?" I started down the road.

"Bad week. No offense, but I really don't want to talk about it. I just want to do something."

"So where are we going?" Phoebe asked.

I tapped my fingers on the steering wheel and contemplated lying. But I couldn't do it. I couldn't tap into my vast ability to pretend to be someone else in a scenario outside of reality. Our budding friendship would dissolve faster than that snobby clique in *Mean Girls*.

"Well . . ." I cleared my throat.

"You're investigating, aren't you?"

I shrugged, heat creeping up my neck. "Maybe. Honestly, I have an opportunity in front of me that I can't let slip through my fingers. It's concerning my father's disappearance. I feel like the answers are close. So close. And I'll never forgive myself if I don't do everything in my power to figure this out."

"Okay, where are you going to investigate?"

I pointed to a house in the distance. "Right there."

Sandblaster, the big yellow house with the gigantic anchor in the front yard, waited at the end of the imaginary line extending from my finger. I'd seen the place before and had known exactly where White Blond was talking about.

An SUV was parked in the driveway. Just as I drove past, White Blond stepped outside and strode toward the vehicle. I kept driving, hoping he hadn't seen me. But I kept an eye on him in my rearview mirror.

"Whose house?" Phoebe asked.

"I don't know his name. But he was one of the last people seen with the dead guy, and he's my only real lead at this point."

"So you're going to talk to him?" Phoebe played with the end of her braid.

"I . . . I don't know what I'm going to do. I like to play it by ear."

She nodded slowly, thoughtfully. "You're one of those kind of people."

"Is that bad?" I couldn't read her tone.

"No, I enjoy playing it by ear . . . in situations that aren't life or death, at least."

"Good point."

I watched as White Blond climbed into his car, backed out, and took off down the road. When he was out of sight, I turned around and parked in his neighbor's driveway. By all appearances, no one was staying at this house.

"What now?" Phoebe asked, surprisingly even keeled, considering what I was about to suggest.

I tried to choose my words very carefully.

"Well . . . I, uh . . ." How did I even say this? She was going to run for the hills faster than the von Trapps escaping the Nazis.

"You want to go into his house, don't you?" Phoebe stared at me with a smirk on her face.

And here I'd thought she'd been all small-town wholesome and incapable of smirking.

"How'd you know?" I asked.

She shrugged, appearing unaffected. "Lucky guess."

"I know this is weird, but you could wait in the car—"

"Oh, no, girl. I'm going with you."

"But—" I didn't know if that was a good idea.

"I know it's risky. But I'm not missing this. If anyone asks what we're doing there, we tell them I was supposed to come for a pet-sitting job, and we must have gotten the wrong house."

I raised my eyebrows, seriously impressed. "I have to admit—I didn't think you were the type to go along with something like this."

"I've learned to live without so much fear. In some areas of my life, at least. You never know what life will hand you, so you might as well go after what you want. And I know you need answers. There's more at stake here than simply your curiosity."

I hesitated one more minute before nodding and

opening my door. "Let's do this then."

I knew sneaking inside his house was a risky move, but White Blond probably wouldn't talk to me if I tried to ask him questions. Or he'd lie. Especially if he was the killer.

I also knew I probably shouldn't do this. But someone was shooting at my feet and yelling for me to dance. So I was putting on a show.

Had this man followed Douglas to the OBX, determined to get revenge for some prior wrongdoing? Was he the one who'd killed the man at the Polar Plunge?

Phoebe and I darted across the sandy ground between the houses, not stopping until we reached a door beneath the house. I knew it was a long shot that the door would be unlocked, but I rattled it anyway.

Locked. Go figure.

"We have to try the ones upstairs," Phoebe said. "You'd be surprised at how irresponsible people are with rentals."

"Okay, let's do it." I darted up the stairway at the back of the house, praying that no one saw me. At the top, a deck stretched around half the house. I felt exposed up here, so we had to move quickly.

I tried the first door.

Locked.

I moved to a sliding-glass door. Also locked.

I went to the next sliding-glass door.

And bingo.

It slid open.

I drew in a deep breath. Last time I'd sneaked into a house, US marshals had surrounded me—along with Jackson. It hadn't been my most flattering moment. But I'd had a lot of those. What was one more?

"The longer we wait, the more likely it is that we'll get caught," Phoebe said.

Had this woman been a cat burglar in a past life? Talk about wrong assumptions. I'd never in a million years seen this coming.

"Let's go then," I said.

Phoebe and I slipped inside, and I quickly scanned the place.

"Typical rental," Phoebe said.

And it was. Neutral furniture. Pastel paintings. An abundance of seashell accessories. Nothing appeared out of place.

"Let's check out the bedrooms," I said.

The first one appeared unused. As did the second. And third.

"How many bedrooms does this house have?" I muttered.

"The more bedrooms, the higher the dollar people pay."

"How do you know this? Did you work in real estate also?"

"We take classes on this in high school in this area."

I paused. "Really?"

She nodded. "Really. Tourism is our livelihood, in case you haven't noticed."

We headed up another set of stairs to the top floor. Another four doorways waited for us here. We went through the same routine, but it wasn't until we reached the last bedroom that we hit the proverbial jackpot. The master suite. Of course.

"Check this out," I whispered as I glanced around the place.

It was a Hollywood-worthy beauty. Large, with expansive views of the ocean, a high ceiling, and plenty of natural sunlight.

"I could get used to a place like this," Phoebe said, gravitating toward the window.

"Who couldn't?"

I wasn't here to admire the property, so I hurried to the closet and opened the door. A suitcase rested in the corner. I knelt beside it and read the tag attached to the handle. *Richard Williams.* His address was listed as *McKeesport, PA.* I used my cell phone to take a picture of it. I'd research him later.

"I have a name, at least," I muttered.

"It's a start."

I stepped back and glanced around the room. I didn't know exactly what I was looking for. I just needed to learn more about this man. I needed to think like Raven.

Pamphlets for parasailing and hang gliding and nighttime kayaking were sprawled on the dresser. If I had to guess, the owner had left them here for his guests. There was also some spare change, a ticket stub from the movies, and a business card from one of the local olive oil and wine shops.

Nothing suspicious. And nothing that gave me any clues.

I opened a drawer and paused. There was money in here. A lot of money. Cash, freshly wrapped in bundles from the bank.

"Check this out," I muttered.

Phoebe joined me. "That's a lot of mullah."

"Tell me about it. Maybe this guy was paid off to kill Mark Hamill?"

"It's a theory."

"Let's check the bathroom," Phoebe said. "It can say a lot about a person."

"I'm not sure what I'll find there." I walked into the oversized room anyway. The first thing I saw were the bottles huddled together in the corner. Aftershave, lotion, mouthwash. Boring.

I moved a couple and spotted some medicine bottles at the back. Acid-reflux medicine and pain reliever. Another one I didn't recognize, so I took a picture on my phone to look up later.

"You recognize this?" I asked Phoebe.

She shook her head. "I can't say I do."

"I risked a breaking-and-entering charge, and the payoff was not worth it," I said.

Phoebe shrugged. "Win some; lose some. At least you know now."

Just then something slammed downstairs. Then whistling cut the air. Keys rattled.

White Blond Richard was back, I realized.

Already?

Phoebe and I exchanged a glance, panic in each

of our gazes.

"What do we do?" Phoebe whispered.

My gaze darted around the room. We wouldn't make it to the balcony. Plus, we'd risk being locked out there in the cold. No, thank you.

Footsteps echoed. Coming up the stairs. Toward us. We didn't have much time.

So I did the only thing I could think of. I hid. In the shower. With Phoebe.

And I really hoped Richard wouldn't go a little mad and decide to re-create any shower scenes from *Psycho*.

CHAPTER 14

The whistle got louder and louder, closer and closer.

"Maybe this wasn't such a great idea," Phoebe whispered.

"Maybe not. I'm so sorry if I get you in trouble. I just want to tell you that in advance."

"You didn't make me do this. I practically forced it on you."

I glanced around. A seashell bath curtain offered our only protection from whoever was in the house. A dirty white washcloth hung on a silver bar below me. A soothing tan tile enclosure reminded me, at the moment, of walls at a mental ward.

The whistle was in the bedroom now. *Please stay there, and don't come in the bathroom!*

But what if White Blond Richard was home for good? What would we do then?

I ran a hand through my hair. What a predicament. And again, all for nothing. I'd discovered virtually no new information except his name. A lot of risk and no payoff.

When I didn't show up either at home or at work, Zane or Dizzy would eventually get worried. One of them might call the police. Which meant that

Jackson would probably get the memo.

He'd go looking for me. He'd eventually see my car parked at the house next door. He might come over here and eventually find me and Phoebe.

Or worse—he'd try to call me!

My phone, I realized with another surge of panic.

My hands trembled as I slipped the device from my back pocket. *Don't drop it, Joey. Don't drop it.* That would be my luck. Or that it would ring.

Is your phone on silent? I mouthed to Phoebe.

She nodded.

Well, at least one of us was on the ball.

I stared at my device, which I'd only had for a month or so. I didn't see any Off buttons. Wasn't there a way to disable this? I couldn't figure out how.

Daggonit!

Carefully, I flipped the sound to vibrate. And as a means to confirm what I'd done, my phone buzzed.

Stupid phone.

The whistling stopped.

I froze and exchanged a look with Phoebe.

Had the man heard the buzz?

If this man had killed Mark Hamill's doppelganger, he could kill me and Phoebe, and no one would be the wiser. He could even claim it was our fault, that we'd broken in.

Worst-case scenarios rushed through my mind, and my pulse spiked.

The whistle started again. *Mary Poppins,* I thought. Whatever floated his boat.

My skin crawled as the sound got louder and

louder.

I shrank closer to the wall.

Oh my goodness. He was in the bathroom. In. The. Bathroom!

Phoebe and I exchanged another look.

Sweat sprinkled across my forehead, and I pressed myself farther into the tile.

I heard water hitting water, and my cheeks heated.

He was not only using the bathroom, but he was literally *using the bathroom*.

I closed my eyes. I should not be in here. It was such an invasion of privacy, not to mention gross and inappropriate.

Yet I couldn't move. I couldn't do anything except stand here and try to disappear.

Please, phone, don't ring. Don't ring! Or vibrate!

I glanced up. Bottles of shampoo and conditioner and body wash were perched in a wire container hanging from the showerhead. If I moved just the wrong way, the whole thing could fall. And my shoulder was dangerously close to it.

Come on! Finish up! And whatever you do, don't take a shower!

I glanced at the shampoo again, then at the shower curtain. What if he could see my shadow beyond those happy-looking little starfish and conches? Was it translucent?

There were so many things that could go wrong here. So many things.

I was terrible at this detective thing. Had I

mentioned that yet? Good detectives didn't make this many errors.

I shifted ever so slightly as my leg began to tingle. When I did, the shampoo shifted. The whole rack hanging on the showerhead crept down by a fourth of an inch.

Phoebe squeezed my arm. Too many more shifts and the whole thing would fall down. Which would cause the man to check the shower to see what was going on. Which would then lead him to finding us.

And it would be the end of my reign of error. Yep, then I would go to jail. Or the mayor would let me off, but I'd have to promise the life of my firstborn—as well as my People's Choice Award— along with the commitment to remain in the Outer Banks and do whatever he said for the rest of my existence.

Finish up already! How long did it take to relieve yourself? A long time apparently. The man should win some kind of Guinness award. What an accomplishment.

Finally, the water-on-water noise stopped. Something zipped.

I squeezed the skin between my eyes. I should not be hearing this. It was against everything I'd been raised to . . . to hear, I supposed.

Scenes from *Psycho* flashed back again. I half expected Richard to pull back the curtain and stand there wielding a knife.

Or . . . maybe he would leave now. After he washed his hands, of course. Because not washing your hands after going potty was gross.

But before I heard the sink running, a phone rang.

My heart almost stopped.

Until I realized it wasn't my phone or Phoebe's. It was his. Richard's.

I held my breath.

"Yo, yo, Timmy!" Richard said. "What's up, my man?"

I waited. I still didn't hear the water running in the sink, but Richard remained in the bathroom, so maybe there was still hope he would practice good hygiene.

And that if he found me, he wouldn't kill me.

"Yeah, I know, man. I heard about it on the news," Richard continued. "It was totally the guy who was spying on me. Who would have thought he'd be here?"

He was talking about Mark Hamill!

Richard let out a laugh. I pictured him preening in the mirror.

It was risky, but I moved my head ever so slightly and was able to see out of a slit between the shower curtain and wall. Sure enough, the man stared at himself in the mirror, playing with his hair.

"No, man. I didn't go to the Polar Plunge. Are you crazy? It's way too cold for that. You do remember that I have a heart condition, right?"

Heart condition? That was interesting.

"But one other interesting thing happened. Guess who else I saw here? Joey Darling, the Raven

Remington girl. Yeah, she looks even hotter in person than she does on TV." Pause. "Yeah, I was going to give her my number, but she was with a guy. I figured it probably wasn't going to happen . . ."

Really? Guys were so weird.

"Okay, I've got to get back to my golf game here in a minute. I realized I needed to put some more layers on first. The wind is wicked . . ."

He wandered from the bathroom.

No washed hands? Shame on you. Shame. On. You.

His voice faded as he left the room.

The good news, I supposed, was that Richard didn't appear to be guilty. Either that or he was a really good actor. The conversation had sounded authentic. Plus, I didn't remember seeing him in any of the pictures from the Polar Plunge, and having a heart condition seemed like a good reason not to dive into ice-cold water.

To my relief, I finally heard the door slam. Then a car started.

I was pretty sure he was gone. Which meant Phoebe and I had to get out of here. Now.

CHAPTER 15

I went home and dropped Phoebe back at her Jeep.

Before she got out, she turned to me. "Well, that was fun. Thanks for the distraction."

I frowned, remembering what she'd said earlier. "Are you sure you don't want to talk?"

She nodded. "I'm sure. But thank you. I got a text from someone about dog sitting, so I should probably go follow up."

"Of course."

After saying goodbye, I slipped inside my duplex and changed. Then I went back out.

I didn't want to take any more guesses. Not when answers about my father could be so close. This situation called for a conversation, and I planned to have one.

That was why I went back to Richard's house. But I didn't park in the neighbor's driveway this time. No, this time I pulled right under his house. I got out and sat on the steps leading to the door I'd seen him leave from earlier.

And then I waited.

Two hours later, Richard came back. He paused midstep when he saw me, blinked several times, and then grinned. "Joey Darling?"

"The one and only."

He blinked again and shook his head, as if in disbelief. "I . . . I don't know what to say. I wasn't expecting to see you here."

I stood, careful to remain cool and aloof. "I need to ask you some questions."

His face lost a bit of its glow. He wasn't going to have quite the story to tell his friends that he'd hoped. "Okay . . . You want to go inside to talk?"

"No, I think it would be better if we stayed here."

He crossed his arms, suddenly appearing nervous. "What can I do for you, Joey?"

I pulled off my aviator sunglasses. They were the kind Raven always wore. I'd also donned all black, just for good measure, as well as high heels. Yes, I'd taken a moment to both change and look up what kind of medication Richard was taking. Sure enough, it was for a heart issue.

"What was Douglas Murray's real name?" I asked.

His face paled, and he shoved his hand in his pocket.

Classic body language that showed nervousness. It was Basic Acting 101.

"Who's Douglas Murray?" he asked.

"Don't play stupid, Richard Williams."

"You . . . you know my name?" He almost sounded flattered.

"You'd be surprised what I know." I shifted. "You were both visiting from out of town, but you have a connection from the past."

His head bobbed back and forth with excitement, like a kid on Christmas morning. "I thought you only played Raven Remington. I didn't know you actually *were* Raven Remington."

Illogical satisfaction surged through me. "I'll take that as a compliment. Now . . . tell me what you know."

He let out a breath and lowered his gaze in defeat. "His real name is Max Anderson."

That had been easier than I thought. "How do you know him?"

Richard's eyes widened. Was he actually scared? I couldn't believe my tough-girl act had worked!

"Are you going to do your baloney move on me?" His voice trembled.

"Not unless you give me a reason to. I'd suggest staying on my good side by answering my questions."

He raised a hand to placate me. "Okay, okay. Max was a private detective based out of Pittsburgh. He investigated me for worker's compensation fraud."

"Is that right?" A PI . . . I needed to let that sink in. I hadn't expected that little tidbit.

"He was watching me, trying to prove that I was committing fraud and hadn't really been injured on the job. Except I caught him and confronted him. It wasn't pretty. I did nothing wrong. But because of him, my civil suit was thrown out." He frowned.

"What happened?" I needed more details here.

His gaze darkened. "I work in a factory, okay? Or I used to, at least. Nothing exciting. Blue collar. I hurt my back while loading some boxes on a truck, and I've been out of work for the past four months. I'll probably have surgery."

"I suppose that made you have some hard feelings toward Max." I planted my feet. Another pose I'd learned from Raven. Who knew pretending to be a fictional character would pay off one day?

He raised his hands in the internationally known sign for innocence and backed up. "Look, maybe I didn't like the guy, but that doesn't mean I killed him. It was all just one big coincidence."

"I'm sure." I crossed my arms and kept my voice hard.

"It's true! I'm not a killer. Maybe an exaggerator, which is what's gotten me into this whole mess. But I really did hurt my back. There's no way I could have killed him." He paused. "Why are you looking into this anyway?"

"Personal reasons." I didn't owe him any explanations.

"Sounds . . . awesome."

"Crime in real life isn't as fun as it is on TV. Believe me." I narrowed my eyes, not finished yet. "Where'd you get all that cash?"

He tugged at his collar. "Cash? You know about my cash also? I . . . that's my insurance payout. That's where I got it. Once it's gone, it's gone."

I suppose that made sense.

He released his collar and drew in a deep breath. "So why are you here? Did you see me at Willie's last night?"

"I've been keeping an eye on you."

His face lit up again, like I'd handed him the biggest compliment in the world. "Have you? Why were you following me? How'd you know my name?"

I ignored his questions and slid my sunglasses on. "And I really hope you're telling the truth. Because I'd hate to have to come back and find you again."

"I am. I am!"

"Good. Now I've got to run."

***

Back at home, I collapsed onto my couch. I pulled my fake-fur blanket around me—after making a cup of coffee. The TV was off, and silence permeated the atmosphere.

Until Zane knocked on the door.

"What's going on?" he asked, coming inside and making himself at home.

I pulled the blanket up around me again. Earlier I'd vowed to keep my distance. But that didn't mean we couldn't talk, right? Because I really needed someone to talk with right now.

"I finally have some answers," I started.

"Please share."

"Let's see. Douglas Murray, also known as Max Anderson, the Mark Hamill look-alike, was a PI. He'd worked an insurance case involving Richard Williams—"

"Who's Richard Williams?"

"Richard Williams is a man with white-blond hair whom Max Anderson investigated. He also happened to be in this area."

"Good job finding that out."

"People don't mistake me for a detective for no reason." I flashed a halfhearted smile. "Anyway, if I was a betting woman, I'd say my father hired this guy Max."

"What?" He blinked. "Why would he do that?"

"I'm not sure. Maybe to keep an eye on me. But why was he killed? And by whom? Did he see something? Say something? Make someone mad, or make them feel threatened?

"All good questions."

I could safely rule out White Blond, a.k.a. Richard Williams, as the killer.

I could also rule out the punks I'd tracked down. They might be bad guys, but they weren't connected with this case.

"Who else are potential suspects?" Zane asked.

"Great question." Who else did I have to look at when it came to potential killers? Not many people. Actually, none that I could think of. That all meant that my already small suspect pool had shrunk to nothing. In fact, maybe I needed to look outside of my initial list of names I'd put together if I wanted to figure out what happened.

For all I knew, someone had breezed into town, killed Max, and left. All my searching could be in vain. My viral threat may have gone unseen by the guilty party, who'd remained suspiciously quiet.

I yawned.

"You getting tired?" Zane asked.

"But I'm going to check my email real quick." I grabbed my laptop and sat back on the couch. Immediately, one caught my eye. The subject read: *Doll Face*.

"Doll Face?" Zane asked.

"That was my dad's nickname for me."

My hand trembled as it hovered over the mousepad. But finally I clicked on it. As soon as I did, a video filled the screen.

I sucked in a breath as images captured my full attention.

The footage was of me. Voicing my challenge to the reporter. It looped over and over.

Whoever is toying with me, I'm not playing these games any longer. I have a message for you. Come out of the shadows and act like a big boy. Only wimps hide and threaten and antagonize from the safety of anonymity. Man up or shut up.

My blood went cold.

Maybe my message *hadn't* gone unseen.

Just when I thought this was all there was to it, a crackly voice sounded on the screen.

"Challenge accepted. Be careful what you wish for, Joey Darling. And be careful, whatever you do. Look over your shoulder. Behind your back. Not even your shadows will be able to save you this time."

Okay, that was a threat. A direct threat. My hands trembled, so I sat on them. This was like a bad movie. *Ghost in the Machine*. Okay, not really. But my mind was drawing a blank.

I was getting closer. Close enough that the killer was getting nervous.

That reality made me exceedingly nervous and a little too excited for my own good.

Despite my overwhelming fear, there was something I was missing, and I needed to figure out what.

No more Ms. Nice Girl.

I picked up the phone and called Mayor Allen. It was time to see if I could get an inside track at the police station. Doing the Castle/Beckett thing was the only solution I could think of.

Now I had to keep my fingers crossed that it would work.

CHAPTER 16

The next morning, I showed up at a million-dollar rental house oceanside. The place was deluxe with huge windows, freshly painted dark-blue siding, and every amenity possible. All of that equaled one thing: the perfect place to do an interview for ABC News.

I'd taken special care to dress presentably this morning in a black business suit. I'd smoothed my hair into gentle waves around my shoulders and painted my nails a lovely shade of pink.

I knew that Eric, my ex, would probably either see this interview or hear about it, and I didn't want to give him any more ammunition against me by appearing ragged or like the type who'd been arrested for solicitation, as the *Instigator* had proclaimed. Rumor had it he was already writing an unauthorized book about our marriage. I had to play this cool. No more missteps.

"Joey Darling!" the producer said when he answered the door. "You're looking even more fabulous than always. The beach must be good for you!"

I smiled, wondering if we'd met before. I couldn't remember, so I decided to avoid the subject. "The beach is good for everyone, isn't it?"

He led me inside, gave me a brief tour, and then took me to makeup.

Afterward, I met Maria Salvatore, and we chatted for several minutes as camera crews worked on lighting and angles. She was a petite, perky woman who did entertainment stories for the network. I'd met her once before, and she seemed nice enough.

"You remember that interview we did with you and Ryan Reynolds?" Maria said. "That was a hoot."

"It was fun," I told her.

Ryan and I had been voice actors for a cartoon about birds and airplanes called *Into the Sky*. For the interview, the network had set it up to take place on an actual biplane flying over the Caribbean. Memories.

Someone walked into the room, and the air around me changed.

Jackson Sullivan.

I sucked in a quick breath. He looked incredibly handsome. Really incredibly handsome. Knock-your-socks-off really incredibly handsome.

He wore a dark suit with a crisp white shirt and a green tie that matched his eyes. His beard looked neatly trimmed, and whoever had cut his hair had done a bang-up job. Ha!

"Detective." I nodded at him, hating how formal I sounded.

He nodded back, just as stiffly. "Joey."

We awkwardly sat beside each other in two little

armchairs.

Maria Salvatore clapped her hands together. "Okay, we're all here. I just want to reiterate that I think this is going to be a wonderful story. Thank you both so much for agreeing to this."

As if I'd had a choice. I hadn't.

"Okay, you two," Maria said. "Let's get this interview rolling. Joey Darling, is it true that you solved a murder, just like a real-life Raven Remington?"

I cringed. My publicist would have told me to say yes. But that felt like such a lie, even though, by most standards, I supposed it was the truth. The truth was that I'd accidentally solved it more than anyone else.

"That's . . . that's one version," I finally said.

"Well, that's what we heard. You set a trap for the bad guy—"

"A trap that went desperately wrong," I pointed out. Why was I belittling myself? Sheesh.

"But in the end, you did your baloney move and managed to escape, just as the police got there." She shook her head in amazement.

Who had told her all of this? It was a Hollywood-ized version, for sure. "I'm not sure I'd put it that way."

"Maybe we should start at the beginning," Maria said.

So we did. I told her about the woman who thought I was actually Raven Remington and who had hired me to track down her wayward boyfriend. How I'd found him dead in a hotel room and how the entire thing had been staged to look like an episode of my show. How a psycho had sent me notes, taunting me at first and threatening me later.

When I was done, she turned to Jackson. "What did you think of all of this?"

Jackson glanced at me, and I prepared myself to be reamed out. He didn't approve of my involvement, and I didn't think he ever truly would. I couldn't blame him.

"I think Joey did a fantastic job," he said.

Everything around me seemed to shrink, and all I heard were his words. Had he really said that? My heart pounded in my ears in shock and amazement.

"However, I would never encourage civilians to get involved in police investigations," he continued. "It's just not safe, no matter how much fun it may look on TV."

"Did you ever watch the show?" Maria continued. "*Relentless*?"

"I hadn't before all this happened. I'm not much of a TV guy—no offense."

Maria laughed. "No offense taken."

"But I've since watched the series, and I find it fascinating. I've become a fan."

A fan? Everything shrunk even smaller. I couldn't be hearing this right. It was like an episode of *The Twilight Zone*.

"Well, there's a lot to admire about Joey." She turned toward me. "Joey, are you planning on coming back to Hollywood soon?"

My throat tightened. I'd known this question

would probably come. I just hadn't decided on what was the best answer. Everyone thought I was here to research a role. Only a couple of people knew the truth.

"I'm just taking it easy right now," I said. "The past several years of filming have been grueling, and I need to take some time to take care of myself."

"I understand. You're not worried that will hurt your career?"

I shrugged. "I guess there's always that worry. But life is full of risks, right? Raven wouldn't have solved any of her cases without any risk."

"Maybe the two of you are more alike than you'd like to admit," Maria said.

I shrugged again, unsure what to say to that. "Raven's a lot braver than I am."

"I wouldn't be so sure of that," Jackson said.

"Oh, you two! I can tell you make a great team." Maria lost her smile. "What do you say we go to the crime scene where everything came to a head? The mayor said it was okay."

The mayor. He was the one who'd given her all of this information. Of course. It wouldn't surprise me if she interviewed him later.

I nodded and pulled out my keys. "That sounds good."

"Do you want to ride with me?" Jackson asked. "No need of everyone driving."

Would wonders ever cease? I nodded. "Okay. That sounds good."

Then I wondered: Was this just an excuse to

lecture me?

***

Awkward silence fell as Jackson and I sat side by side in his truck. I was sure he had things to say to me. Not nice things. But instead, silence sat like a rock between us as he started down the road.

All day I'd sensed that something else was wrong, something besides the fact that Jackson had been forced to do this interview with me. Jackson seemed to have a certain heaviness about him today. That realization made me desperately curious and concerned. Mostly concerned.

"I'm sorry, Jackson," I finally started.

He continued to stare straight ahead. "Sorry for what?"

"For assuming the worst about you." I didn't mention that there were some things I still reserved the right to believe the worst about, like his involvement or knowledge in my father's disappearance.

"You were led to believe the worst. There's a difference." His words were said without emotion, but his jaw flexed. The motion was a tell that Jackson wasn't happy. I'd studied tells in acting—those unconscious actions that betrayed an attempted deception. I figured I knew about as much as a trained psychologist at this point. Too bad I often forgot to watch for them.

I glanced down at my hands, which mangled

together in my lap. "I should have thought the best, and instead I accepted the worst."

He finally glanced at me. "It's okay, Joey."

"But is it? I want to make things right."

"You don't owe me anything."

For some reason, his words felt like a rejection. Like he didn't care. Like it didn't matter. Like *I* didn't matter. Which was stupid. Of course I didn't matter to him. We barely knew each other, and he owed me nothing.

"Listen, we all make mistakes," Jackson said. "We make assumptions. We don't do things right the first time. I'm just glad you know the truth now."

Relief slumped through me.

"Thank you." My voice cracked as I said the words.

"Now that we've talked about that, what's this I hear about you needing to do some research on police work?"

My cheeks heated. "The mayor told you?"

"He called me last night when I was already in bed. He was that excited."

"Did he? Oh, well, yes, I need to research how detectives operate." The words hurt my throat. Another lie. Or was it? I did need to research it, just not for a movie. Still, I was justifying my poor decisions, and that wasn't something to feel good about.

"For a movie?"

"Well . . ." I drew the word out until it was three syllables. *No more lies, Joey. No more lies.*

"You just want an inside scoop on the case," Jackson said.

"I didn't say that."

"You didn't have to."

I just needed to keep my mouth shut. That was all there was to it. Lie of omission? The lines all felt blurry right now.

More silence hung in the air like a dead man on a noose. I let it fall, something I generally wasn't good at. I liked to fill the awkwardness, usually with blathering about inconsequential things. But not with Jackson. He wasn't the inconsequential type, and I kind of liked that about him.

"My wife died three years ago today." Jackson's voice sounded deep and husky and full of emotion.

His words caused my heart to leap into my throat and stay there, pounding hard and heavy and oozing with compassion. The fact that Jackson was admitting this to me meant so much more than I could ever express.

My hand flew to his arm, and I squeezed, all my reservations disappearing—at least temporarily. "I'm so sorry, Jackson."

"I usually take the day off and stay home by myself to grieve. I decided to do something different this year."

"Because the mayor forced you to?"

He shrugged. "I could have said no. I thought maybe staying busy was a better option than mourning what could have—should have—been."

"I'm so sorry. I can't imagine what you're going

through."

"I just wanted you to know because I'm feeling a little off, you know?"

"I know." It suddenly made sense why Phoebe had been having a bad day yesterday. She'd probably been dreading the anniversary of losing her sister.

Jackson pulled to a stop and put his truck in park at our next location. "Let's get this over with."

***

When I saw the inside of the warehouse, nausea bubbled in my gut. I hadn't expected the reaction, but being here brought up so many bad memories of what had happened last time I'd been in this open, exposed, rusty place.

It was on the water, and windows at the top were permanently open. A couple birds darted onto the beams overhead. I remembered hearing the bad guy's voice. I remembered wondering if I was going to die. But mostly I remembered the man almost revealing what he knew about my dad, his gun pointed toward me. Then Jackson took a shot.

Yes, he'd saved my life, but not my sanity. Because I'd replayed that conversation over and over again. I'd been so close.

Jackson and I, along with Maria and her crew, walked through what had happened in the final showdown of my last investigation, ending with my famous baloney move that Raven had made popular. In reality, the move was something my father had taught me. When I'd told the producer about it, he'd insisted on making it one of Raven's signature moves also. Basically, it meant "below knee," and that was where I kicked someone when I needed to get away.

A lone chair had been placed in the center of the warehouse, just like when I'd been tied up here, which also was just like what had happened in an episode of *Relentless*. It was a long story, but one of the bad guys had insisted on reenacting that episode.

"It sounds like you guys make an amazing team," Maria said.

I winked, trying to keep the mood light. "An amazing one."

"The mayor tells me you're going to be working together to solve more cases," she continued.

My curiosity spiked. He'd told her that? Already? And here I'd thought I would just do a ride-along.

"The Nags Head Police Department is committed to keeping the community safe," Jackson said. "We also like to raise awareness about what we're doing in the area to help fight crime and make our streets safer. If Joey and I working together will help create and foster that environment, then it's something we're committed to doing."

My eyebrows shot up. He sounded so believable. Maybe Jackson should go into acting.

At that moment, something crashed in the corner. I looked over in time to see someone flee from behind some old pallets.

Someone had been watching us? Was it my stalker? The killer?

Jackson took off after the man.

I had to do something. I ran out a door on the opposite side of the building. The not-so-smart creeper ran right toward me.

I glanced around, knowing I couldn't stop him on my own.

A huge rope was on the ground, anchored to a pier in the distance.

My heart rammed into my rib cage over and over, faster and faster.

Just when the man was about to pass me, I pulled the rope. It caught his foot, and he sprawled to the ground.

I'd done it. I'd stopped the bad guy.

Jackson hauled him to his feet and jerked his hood down.

I held my breath as I waited to see if I recognized him.

CHAPTER 17

"Who are you?" Jackson demanded.

I stared at the man—or should I say boy's?—face, not even remotely recognizing him. He was probably a teenager, college if I had to guess. He had acne marks and messy brown hair, and his body hadn't caught up with his frame yet, if that made sense.

"My name is Adam." He raised his hands, his features slack and his limbs trembling.

"Why were you watching us?" Jackson asked.

"I saw Joey Darling. I just wanted another look."

"Did you follow us here?" Jackson's voice was just above a growl, but his grip had loosened on the teenager.

"No, I was on a break from work. I'm part time over at Shipwreck Bay Seafood. Anyway, I wondered what all of the commotion was about. No one ever comes here. When I peeked inside, I saw the cameras and . . . Joey Darling." He glanced at me, his cheeks turning red. "I'm a huge fan."

"I'll give you my autograph later," I offered.

When Jackson scowled at me, I looked into the air and did an imaginary whistle. Exaggerated innocence at its finest.

"I promise you I didn't mean any harm. I just . . ." His face reddened again when he looked at me. "I think you're great, Joey. I was so bummed when *Relentless* was canceled. I even have your poster in my bedroom, the one of you wearing that tight leather outfit and holding a gun—"

"Yeah, I know the one." The poster hadn't seemed like a bad idea at the time, but hearing him talk about it made me feel dirty somehow.

Jackson released him but still didn't look happy. At least Maria and her crew weren't on top of us right now. They stood in the background, as if too afraid to come closer.

"By the way, there's something you should know," Adam told me.

"What's that?" I braced myself for whatever he was about to say.

He shifted his weight from one foot to another and then back again. "It's like I said—I'm one of your biggest fans. I'm a part of your Facebook Fan Club. My goal was even to go to a fan convention one day and meet you face to face. You and Fiona the Werewolf Hunter."

"Okay," I said, waiting for the big reveal. If there really was one.

"As I was surfing around online, I came across this fan club that took fandom to a whole new level."

Jackson bristled beside me. "What do you mean?"

Adam shrugged, his face squeezing with concern

and thought. "Like, these people weren't normal. They were obsessed with you. They posted your schedule, your favorite foods, your hangouts. They even said you were in this area and that you worked at some hair place."

My spine went straight. "Okay . . . that's a little extreme."

"How many people were on this site?" Jackson asked.

Adam shrugged. "At least six, I'd say. But here's the weird thing: right after I discovered the site, it disappeared. I don't think I was supposed to find it, but I do web stuff. I'm studying cybersecurity in college. I just work here to help pay my tuition. Anyway, I guess you could say I've always been good with computers, and I know how to get into some dark channels of the underweb."

My blood grew colder and colder by the minute. Did this network include my stalkers? I'd always known I had more than one, but I assumed that the main guy—Leonard Shepherd, whom I'd had a restraining order against back in California—was the leader and he worked with a partner. But what if I was just skimming the surface in that assumption?

Ice filled my chest. I didn't like this. I didn't like this at all.

Just then Maria clapped her hands behind me. I turned and saw her standing there, her camera crew recording this whole thing.

"This is going to make for some great TV!" she squealed.

My stomach sank. Certainly my life was more important than ratings . . . wasn't it?

***

Jackson and I both let out a collective sigh when we closed the doors of his truck an hour later.

Adam had been released to go back to work after Jackson got his name and contact information in case the police had any more questions. Thankfully, Maria and her crew had been too far away to hear anything he said. I didn't want word of this secret fan club to be leaked, nor did I want Adam to be a target, since these people were obviously unbalanced.

"That was an experience," Jackson said, not making an effort to go anywhere yet. Maybe we both needed a moment to decompress.

"Or something like it." I rubbed my arms. I was still chilled to the core after Adam's confession. A whole group of potential psychopaths had banded together to talk about me? To stalk me? Not comforting.

"We'll figure out who these guys are, Joey," Jackson said.

"I hope so." But they were good. Really good. And from what I'd seen so far, they knew how to cover their tracks.

"We still have officers patrolling past your place."

I glanced over at Jackson in surprise. It was the first I'd heard of that. "You do?"

"We do. Just as a precaution. It's really not a bad idea to get some bodyguards, Joey. We don't know who we're up against at this point."

"We?"

"I'm in this with you."

"Whether you want to be or not, huh?" I shifted before he could respond. "Bodyguards aren't a possibility right now. It's not in my budget. Long story." And embarrassing. On more than one level.

"I know it's none of my business, Joey, but what happened to all of your money?" He shook his head and looked out the window. "You know what, never mind. It's like I said—none of my business. I just can't seem to figure you out."

"It's okay. I'm a bit of a mystery to people." I drew in a deep breath. Part of me wanted to tell him. Which was weird because the whole story didn't reflect well on me. Usually I thrived on presenting a good image and trying to bury the ugly side of me. It was one of the reasons I'd swept what Eric had done under the rug. It would show the world how weak I really was.

Despite that, I cleared my throat. "My ex told me he was really good with money, and so I put him in charge of our finances. But it was like the more money I made, the more we spent. On stupid things. Things I'm not proud of. Things I desperately wish I could have a take two on."

Jackson stretched his arm across the back of the bench seat and lightly touched my shoulder. "You don't have to tell me if you don't want to, Joey. I shouldn't have asked."

"No, I need to own my mistakes." I rubbed my fingers together. "I made some doozies. Anyway, Eric and I got into financial trouble—partly because of spending, partly because of his gambling problem. Eric talked to a lawyer who told him to put all our assets in one spouse's name and all the debt in the other. Really, it was all fishy and underhanded. But I had no reason to doubt Eric, so I put all the debts in my name and all the assets in his. It was supposed to be a temporary solution. When we divorced, he walked away with what we had left, and I walked away with the debt."

Jackson blinked and let out a quick puff of air. "Your ex was okay with that?"

"He was more than okay with it. He delighted in it, I think." Eric hadn't been the prince charming he'd presented himself to be when we met. At first he'd seemed like the stereotypical gentleman who'd treated me like a princess—until we got married and his career tanked soon after. Then everything became my fault, and his controlling side kicked in.

"What a jerk," Jackson said.

He only knew part of it. Eric had done a lot of other things that were even more reprehensible, but it all came to a head when he pushed me down the stairs and broke my ribs. He took my phone so I couldn't call 911. And then he'd left the house while I was still writhing on the floor in pain.

That had been my wake-up call.

"Listen, it's just past lunch time," Jackson said.

"Do you want to grab a bite to eat?"

I paused before nodding. "Yeah, that actually sounds nice. Let's do it. Just don't let me order any gluten. Or meat. Or veggies cooked at more than one hundred fifteen degrees. And definitely no fries."

CHAPTER 18

Jackson and I went to Fatty's. It was actually called the Fatty Shack, but locals just called it Fatty's. It was one of the first restaurants I'd eaten at here, and the waitress Erma was a fan. My autographed picture was now on the wall, right alongside Tiger Woods and Sandra Bullock.

The restaurant was located on the causeway between Nags Head and Roanoke Island. The dated inside was decorated with old crab pots and buoys. It smelled like fish and dirty cleaning solution. The floors were sticky and the tables boasted chipped Formica. But it felt authentic, and the food was good.

I ordered seafood nachos, which almost fit my guidelines. Jackson, meanwhile, got a crab-cake sandwich and fries. We made small talk—mostly about fishing and church and how Maria Salvatore could be a wolf in sheep's clothing.

A few people stopped by to talk to Jackson, and I enjoyed seeing him in a different environment other than work. He was much more relaxed here, and all of this had proven that he wasn't an antisocial monster who hated people.

"You're Lew's daughter, aren't you?" A man

paused by the table. "Joey?"

My heart leapt into my throat as I looked up at the man. I didn't recognize him. He was in his forties with thinning blond hair, a square face, and wire-framed glasses. He wore a golf shirt and khakis.

"I am."

"I thought I recognized you. I'm Bert. Bert Philpot."

"Nice to meet you, Bert."

He frowned and shook his head. "Sure do miss your dad. Do you know when he'll be back?"

I shook my head. "No, I wish I did. But I have no idea. How do you know him?"

"Through my nonprofit."

"What kind of nonprofit is that?"

"I call it Safe Harbor, and it's designed as an outreach to the international workers in the area. In the summertime, we have anywhere between twelve hundred to sixteen hundred seasonal student workers in the area. I started Safe Harbor after I discovered several of these workers were using a storage unit as their home. That's when I knew I had to do something."

"What do you do, exactly?" I asked, curious now.

"Many things. But I began by setting up people to provide transportation to work for these students. We evolved into connecting students to locals who'd serve as their mentors. Many of them can fall victim to scammers. They speak broken English, and they have no one to turn to when they need help."

"And my father helped you?"

He nodded. "That's right. He approached me about volunteering."

"Really?" This was the first I'd heard of that. My dad had been a good man. A really good man. He'd give someone the shirt off his back if needed. But I'd never known him to be the type to get involved with nonprofits. They were too organized and impersonal for my dad.

"He started helping me probably two months before he left. He was very faithful. He mostly helped with transportation."

"I'd love to talk to you more about that sometime."

"Of course." He paused and shook his head. "You know, your dad looked almost apologetic last time I saw him."

I put down the tortilla chip in my hand. "What do you mean?"

His eyes wrinkled at the corners. "I don't know. You could tell he was distracted. Not acting like himself. He wasn't the type to just up and leave, you know."

His words gripped my heart. He understood also. "Yes, I know. Did you ever ask him where he was going?"

Jackson remained surprisingly quiet in the background, but I could tell he was listening to every single word.

"He just said he had business to attend to. That was what was weird though, because your dad seemed like such a simple man. He enjoyed living a quiet life."

Exactly. That was my dad. That was another reason why none of this made sense. I had the deep feeling that he was in trouble. A lot of trouble. And I hated feeling powerless to do anything about it.

"I'm hoping to hear from him soon," I said, playing with my straw wrapper. "Is there anything he said that seemed strange or off, Bert? Or did he seem normal in the days before he disappeared?"

A strange shadow fell over his face, but he quickly snapped out of it. "No, I can't say there was. He mostly worked and fished."

My heart sank, and I nodded. "Thank you."

"It was good to meet you, Joey," Bert said. "Your food is getting cold, so I'll let you eat."

He turned to leave, when the emblem on Bert's shirt caught my eye. Bert's Storage.

"Bert?" I called. "Did my dad ever rent storage space from you?"

He froze and didn't say anything.

And I finally had my answer.

***

"So, you can just drop me back at my car," I told Jackson when we'd finished eating and went out to his truck. I kept my voice even so I wouldn't raise his suspicions.

Jackson stared at me and made no effort to start the truck. In fact, he crossed his arms. "How about if I go with you?"

I feigned a ladylike blush. "To my house? That's a little forward, isn't it?"

His head dropped slightly to the side in an *I know your game* expression. "You know that's not where you're going, Joey."

I dropped my act, realizing it wasn't worth the energy. The situation was so complicated. I wanted to find out what Jackson knew. Yet I feared he was involved somehow with Dad's disappearance. I could simply ask him, but then I might be putting myself at risk. I had trouble believing it, but my instincts weren't honed. In fact, I doubted them. A lot. It was safer to keep what I knew to myself.

I let out my breath, deciding to fess up to what he already knew. Denial would only end in an argument. "Yes, I'm going to the storage unit."

"Why don't you let me help you?"

Why won't you tell me how you're involved? I swallowed the question.

"It . . . it just feels private." It was a cop-out, but I couldn't formulate a comeback quickly enough. Not knowing whom to trust made everything so complicated.

"Joey, you don't know what you're getting into."

"Why would you say that?" *What do you know? Why won't you tell me? These questions are tearing me up inside, and you know that and remain silent.*

"I'm just basing that on everything that's happened . . . and everything that keeps happening. I don't want to see you in a situation that puts you in danger."

"I can't seem to stop that." Just like the fictional detective Monk couldn't resist trying to have absolute order in his world, I couldn't seem to resist danger—lately, at least. Tabloids, unflattering pictures, and bad reviews were no longer at the top of my worry list.

He stretched his arm across the back of the seat, and I yearned for him to touch my shoulder again. He didn't. Which was good. I just had to convince my heart of that. "I won't get in your way—unless you try and do something illegal or that will harm you."

Did he truly want to help me? Or did he secretly want to see what was in that storage unit for ulterior motives?

My emotions warred inside me. On one hand, it would be nice to have Jackson there. But that was only if I could trust him, and I wasn't sure if I could or not. I wanted to do a face palm.

Despite all my misgivings, I finally nodded. "Okay. But only since you said you wouldn't get in my way. Break our deal, and you're out faster than gluten from my diet."

***

Thirty minutes later we pulled up to Bert's Storage. I'd had to stop by my place and get the key that I'd found in a bag my dad had left at the marina. My hands trembled the entire time—from the moment I'd told Jackson he could come until we pulled up at the storage unit.

"What's the number on the key?" Jackson asked.

"Five thirty-four." *Please don't let this be a mistake. Please don't let this be a mistake.*

In between those anxieties, I feared what I might find. I anticipated it. I hoped for the best. I feared for the worst.

My emotions were more confusing than *2001: A Space Odyssey*.

Jackson pulled to a stop at the unit and turned to look at me. "You ready for this?"

"I don't know."

He reached over and squeezed my hand, something he'd done a total of two times now. Each time made me want to squeal like a fangirl.

A Jackson Sullivan fangirl? Ha! If he could read my thoughts, he would totally scowl.

"It's up to you, Joey," Jackson said.

"My hunch could be all wrong."

"Or it could be all right."

I did a double take. "You almost sound like you're starting to believe in me as a detective. As Raven Remington."

"I never said anything about Raven."

Did that mean he *could* see me as a detective though? I didn't ask. I would just believe what I wanted, and I chose to believe that was exactly what he was saying. It was more fun that way.

I sucked in a deep breath and nodded. "Okay, let's do this."

Before I could change my mind, I climbed from the truck and strutted toward the door. My hands continued to tremble as I held the key. Would it fit this unit? What if all this angst was for nothing?

I slipped the key into the lock. It fit.

I twisted.

Turned the handle.

Opened the door.

And braced myself.

CHAPTER 19

The first thing I saw was my father's grandfather clock. He'd made it with his own father, my grandfather. And it was a beautiful piece of mahogany and brass. I reached forward and touched it, running my hand across the ledge below the clock face. I had so many memories of this clock.

I remembered lying in bed, counting the dongs on sleepless nights when I couldn't wait until morning. I remembered waiting until it sounded six times, because I knew my dad would be home from work and my babysitter could leave. I remember getting in late from a date once and hearing twelve chimes, knowing I'd be in trouble.

So many memories in one little sound.

Beside it was the wooden trunk with rope handles that my grandfather had carried with him after the war. My dad had refurbished it, staining it a bright oak color and sealing it with varnish.

My throat tightened as I flipped the tiny metal latch and opened it. Inside, there was an American flag, which had also belonged to my granddad. There was my dad's well used Bible, my grandmother's handmade quilt, and an old statue of a bull that my father, for some reason, had loved. Memories hit me like a tidal wave.

Jackson's hand covered my shoulder. "Are you okay?"

I rocked back on my heels right there on the concrete floor. "I think so."

Before taking anything out of the trunk, I glanced around. The space was otherwise empty. Just these two items. My father had wanted to ensure they were safe. If I had to guess, he'd probably paid in advance to guarantee that. How far in advance? A year? Longer? Just how long did he plan on being gone?

I supposed the good news was that he had planned on it. I guessed this meant he hadn't been taken against his will. He also hadn't intended on me finding this, or he would have left some kind of clue.

My thoughts all crashed together, and I tried to make sense of them.

The thing was, if my father had left of his own free will and not told me, what did that say about our relationship? I'd said things I regretted during our last conversation, but my dad wasn't the kind to just leave without telling me. Without saying a brief goodbye, at least.

"Does everything look as you remember it?" Jackson asked.

I stared down at the trunk again. Just at first glance, nothing looked unusual. But to be sure, I pulled some items out. One by one. Carefully, as if these could be the last memories I had of my father.

At the very bottom was the metal container

where my father had always kept important papers. I wasn't even sure about the story behind it, if there was a history to it or not. I just knew he'd always used it, for as long as I could remember.

I sat down on the floor, and Jackson sat beside me. Carefully, I opened the container and began flipping through the papers inside. Just as I'd expected, there were birth certificates and social security cards and insurance information. Anything that would need to be safe in case of a fire.

But at the bottom, one thing caught my eye. One thing I'd never seen before.

A photo.

"Who's that?" Jackson knelt beside me.

I stared at the woman there, and my chest tightened. "It's my mom."

The words didn't sound right as they left my mouth.

"Your mom? You haven't seen her since you were a baby, right?"

I nodded. "Yes, but I'd recognize her anywhere. I used to stare at her picture for hours and wonder what it would be like if she'd stuck around."

Jackson's hand came down gently on my back, as if he knew how hard this was for me emotionally. Because this photo wasn't one of the ones I'd stared at as a child.

No, this picture was new. It was a photo of my mom in her fifties. And based on the background of the photos, it had been taken here in the Outer Banks.

***

When Jackson pulled up at the house where we'd been interviewed so I could pick up my car, I somehow felt reluctant to say goodbye. Which was weird. And unexplainable.

Maybe I didn't feel safe alone. Maybe when he'd admitted that his wife died three years ago today, it did something to my heart. Maybe it was because, if I was alone, I would dwell on my mother too much. I would think about how she'd left my father and me so she could pursue a career in modeling. How she'd never shown up again. Ever.

How my dad had kept the hope alive that she might return someday. No, he'd never told me that. But I'd caught him looking at pictures of her. I'd heard him talking to my grandma. I'd seen the way he never dated again.

And as much as I'd tried to prove that growing up without a mom hadn't affected me, it had. While other girls had nice braids in their hair and pretty dresses, I had mismatched outfits and messy hair until I was old enough to learn to fix myself up. While other girls had gone to their maternal units for advice, I'd gone to teachers or my grandma until she died of a heart attack at the young age of fifty-eight. When I became a woman, I had to ask my father to buy tampons for me.

My dad had done a great job. He'd been a father and a mother as much as he could. I'd relished our time together. But there had always been a small hole in my heart that my mom left behind. There would always be an underlying feeling of rejection.

"Listen, I know that was a lot to comprehend," Jackson said. "Do you want to talk?"

I considered his words a minute before shaking my head. "No, I actually want to decompress. Do you, by chance, have any desire to look at the stars?"

Jackson's eyebrows shot upward. "The stars?"

Fear of rejection stabbed at me, and I instantly regretted the invitation. But it was too late to take it back now. "There's supposed to be a meteor shower tonight. And it's not too cold. And the sky is cloudless."

I waited for him to say no. When he did, I'd quickly return to my car and pretend like this had never happened. This had all been a terrible idea.

"Why not?" he said. "I could use some time to decompress also."

Surprise rippled through me. He'd said yes.

I smiled, hating how satisfied I felt that he was coming. "Okay, great. Meet me at my house. I'll make us some coffee—"

"How about if I pick some up on the way?"

A laugh escaped before I could stop it. Then again, why would I want to stop it? "You know me better than I thought."

"Well, I have tasted your coffee before."

"Ouch. You know how to hit where it hurts." But it was true. "If you want to pick some up, that would be great."

"It might have to be from 7-Eleven. I think

Sunrise is already closed."

"Even 7-Eleven coffee is better than mine." Yes, I could ruin coffee. It was one of my many talents. "I'll see you back at the house."

He chuckled. I loved it when he chuckled. It was like a gift. It didn't happen that often, so when it did . . . it was amazing. A reward.

Back at the house, I gathered a couple of blankets so we could sit on the sand.

I couldn't remember the last time I felt this excited. Maybe it was when I was offered the role as Raven Remington? No, that was ridiculous. If I was a smart girl, I'd never put my faith in a man again.

Just as I stepped outside, Jackson arrived with our coffee. My heart stopped for a moment when I saw the look in his eyes. Something looked different, and I wasn't sure if it was different good or different bad.

"You have to go to work, don't you?"

He shook his head. "I don't."

"Oh, you looked all serious, and I figured something bad had happened."

That same shadow crossed his gaze. "Nothing happened."

He didn't offer any more information. So I didn't ask, because I figured it wasn't my business. That had never really stopped me before, but I needed a break from the drama that had been my life for too long now. Tonight I just wanted to enjoy the stars. Was that too much to ask for?

"You ready?" I asked.

"Let's go." He put his hand on my lower back as we walked down the stairs. It was such a simple, gentlemanly gesture. Yet it thrilled me beyond belief. Way more than it should.

He turned a flashlight on as we reached the dune and helped me over the hard-to-manage sand. I didn't know how everyone on TV managed to look so graceful while traversing over the sand, because I looked like a dunce.

We found a spot near the dune and laid out one blanket. I saved the other one to wrap around me when it got cold. Because it was going to get cold. Then we sat there in the darkness.

I was glad Jackson was with me out here. It was so isolated at this time of the year. Even though the town of Nags Head was full of life during the summer, right now this beach was abandoned and the perfect place for a crime to occur.

I'd had enough of that happening lately to put me on edge.

I stared out at the water in front of us. The waves crashed—the sound louder than I always expected—time and time again. Thankfully, there was no breeze, which made the night chilly but temperate.

"Shooting stars, you said?" Jackson started.

"That's what they said." I forgot about my coffee and lay back on the blanket. Diamonds sparkled overhead, decorating the blackish-blue canvas. It was extraordinary. "Do you ever get tired of it out here?"

Jackson leaned back on his elbows and looked

Christy Barritt

up. "It is beautiful, isn't it? Thanks for reminding me of that."

"You forgot?"

"I got preoccupied."

I glanced at him, saw him staring up at the heavens, and drank in just how handsome he was.

I wondered if Claire had liked doing this. I didn't ask. Why bring up the memories? I supposed they could be good, but they could also be really bad. He didn't talk about Claire, so I didn't either.

"You like being a cop, Jackson?"

"It's what I've always wanted to do, since I was a little boy. I never thought I'd be a cop in a place like this, I've got to say."

"You wanted to work in the big city?"

"That's right. I did for a while. Up in DC."

"Why DC?"

"I grew up near Baltimore. Being a capitol police officer was my dream."

"Was it as good as you thought it would be?"

He smiled softly, still looking upward. "It was good. But family is the most important thing."

"I understand." Guilt panged inside me though. Family should have been the most important thing to me also.

"My family took vacations down here on the Outer Banks," Jackson continued.

My pulse spiked. He was opening up! It shouldn't excite me so much, but it did.

"Is that how you met Claire?" I wanted to slap my hand over my mouth. I wasn't supposed to bring that up! Stupid, stupid, stupid.

"It is. She was from down here. We met on the beach. And that was that."

Their happy ever after hadn't turned out the way they'd wanted. Things often didn't in life. I knew that all too well.

"Look!" I pointed to the sky. "Did you see that?"

"I missed it."

"It was a shooting star!"

He lay back, settling down beside me. "I'm cold. I'm going to have to steal part of your blanket."

"Of course."

But something inside me was entirely too alert and too aware of the fact that we were sharing the blanket. I liked it too much.

"Did you know that in Greek mythology, if you had a star named after you, it was called catasterization?

"Castration?" Jackson asked.

I laughed. "No, but it could be a form of honor or punishment. Cassiopeia claimed to be more beautiful than the sea nymphs, so Poseidon made her go live in the sky as a result." I pointed upward. "You can see her right there."

"How do you know all of this?" Jackson asked.

"My dad taught me. He was quite the outdoorsman. There was no place else he'd rather be."

"Your dad sounds like a good man."

"He was. He is." I cleared my throat before Jackson could hear the emotion there, then pointed to the sky again. "Look, it's another shooting star!"

Thank goodness. Because I didn't want to ruin this moment by talking about my dad and how much I missed him.

"There's another one," Jackson said. "That really is amazing."

"They are, aren't they?"

"No, I was talking about you."

I looked over and saw that Jackson was now leaning on his elbow, facing me. "You're really beautiful, Joey Schermerhorn."

My heart skittered into my throat. Or ears. Or took over my entire body. I wasn't sure which.

Because Jackson was gazing at me. His eyes mesmerized me, and that familiar pull consumed my body. The pull toward Jackson.

Was it my imagination, or was he being pulled toward me also?

Before I could find out, I felt something on my leg. Something spindly and prickly and moving.

I gasped, shot up, and jerked the blanket away in record time. It was just as I feared. There was a . . .

"Crab!"

. . . walking up my pants leg!

I shook my leg and shook it some more until the little crustacean flew off and skittered away. I scrambled backward, also desperate to put distance between myself and the future all-you-can-eat-buffet participant.

When my heart slowed, I swallowed hard and dared to look at Jackson. "Overreaction?"

He smiled and shook his head. Then he stood, brushed the sand from his jeans, and offered me his hand. "How about we get inside before anymore crabs come?"

"Maybe that's a good idea."

But another part of me—a big part of me—was seriously . . . crabby.

CHAPTER 20

My pulse throbbed in my ears as Jackson and I walked inside my house. What a day. I had so much to think about. But mostly what I'd be thinking about tonight was that look I'd seen in Jackson's eyes on the beach. A moment of attraction. Of desire.

"It's been a fun day, Joey," Jackson said. His voice sounded hoarse. "I wasn't sure I should do this. Not today. But it's been good. Thank you."

Warmth filled me. My voice came out a little too fast and high pitched when I asked, "Would you like to sit down?"

He pressed his lips together. Stayed quiet a second. Released his breath and shook his head. "I would. But I can't. I need to run home and get Ripley."

Ripley was his Australian shepherd. "Of course," I said quickly.

What had I been thinking? The invitation had just slipped out, and now he probably thought I was hitting on him.

"Phoebe let him out for me earlier," Jackson explained. "She does that a lot."

"She's a good person."

"Speaking of which, I hear you're going to her

house Saturday."

That was right! I'd nearly forgotten about her invitation. And I was exceedingly grateful for the change in conversation. "Yes, I finally get to see where she lives. Hatteras Island. I can't wait."

He shifted, and his gaze became hooded by his incredible eyelashes. "She did tell you that I'm going to be there also, didn't she?"

A shock wave raced through my heart—the good kind, the kind that activated all my warm fuzzies. But I had to play it cool. "Actually, she didn't."

He shoved his hands into his pockets. "I can reschedule if you'd rather have time with her alone."

I stepped closer and lowered my voice, making sure I sounded ultraserious. "Just answer one question for me first."

"What's that?" His eyes widened as he waited for my response.

I paused dramatically and did the "soap take" face. "Are you bringing Ripley?"

A smile cracked his face, followed by a deep laugh. He rubbed his chin as he wagged his head back and forth. "Joey, Joey, Joey. Yes, I plan on bringing Ripley."

I kept my dramatically serious expression intact. "Then you can come too."

He shook his head slowly again, as if either in disbelief or totally flabbergasted. "You really do like that dog, don't you?"

"What's not to like about him? He's furry and sweet and cuddly."

"And out of control, rambunctious, hairy." His gaze caught on mine another moment, until he finally stepped back. "It's been fun, Joey."

I nodded, wishing he would stay longer. But I had no excuse to keep him here, unless I wanted to feign being scared or needing a light bulb changed. "It has been fun."

We walked slowly toward the front door and paused. Jackson turned toward me. "You want to ride together Saturday?"

"That would be nice." Nicer than it should be. Why did I enjoy spending time with someone who was so . . . so . . . impossible?

"I'll pick you up at 10:30."

"I'll see you then."

***

As soon as I paced into my living room, part of me instantly felt lonely. Which was weird. Because Jackson and I were just friends. I had the feeling he wasn't looking for a relationship any more than I was.

I knew I should try to focus all my energy on trying to solve at least one of the mysteries going on in my life. That picture of my mom only added more unanswered questions to my already long list.

But I couldn't resist hanging out with Phoebe, Jackson, and Ripley. The people-loving, extroverted part of me craved interacting with people.

My cell phone rang, and I saw the mayor's number on my screen. If he was calling at nine at night, he must have something to say, so I answered.

"I just finished my interview with Maria Salvatore," he started, excitement tingling his lispy voice. "She said everything went great with your interview earlier. People will eat up this story like chilled potato salad on a hot day."

"I'm glad to hear that." It was certainly better than people eating up other things . . . like processed foods.

His voice shifted to a business tone. "Listen, I've given my initial approval for you and Jackson to work together. You know, for your research. I think it's a great angle, and it will do wonderful things for the area."

"Awesome."

"It might take a couple of weeks to get the paperwork processed though. We have some forms for you to fill out and some insurance stuff to go through. It's more complicated than your average ride-along. That's what the city attorney tells me, at least."

A couple of weeks? I couldn't wait that long. I was so tired of waiting. I had to find information on both my dad and Douglas Murray/Max Anderson/Mark Hamill before that.

I couldn't sound ungrateful. "Thank you," I told the mayor.

"It's been my pleasure," he said. "You're going to be the best thing to happen to this area. We've got plans for you, Joey Darling. Big plans."

I didn't know if I liked the sound of that.

I hung up and paced into the kitchen, suddenly craving some hummus. Something on the table caught my eye. A slip of paper. One that hadn't been there before. I was certain.

With a touch of trepidation, I picked it up and carefully unfolded the square. My throat tightened, as if my body knew what I'd find even though my mind was in denial.

Familiar scrawl filled the white space.

Maybe you should kick this investigation up a notch. Don't make us spell everything out for you. Watch Episode 210. Signed, Your biggest fans.

My blood went cold.

They'd been in my house. Again.

How were they coming and going? Were they still here?

I swirled around as fear gripped me. These men hadn't hurt me.

Yet.

But that didn't mean they wouldn't. Anyone who'd break in someone's home like this should be feared.

I backed up until I hit the kitchen counter. My gaze was still fixated on my house, still watching for any sign of movement. I saw nothing.

Should I call Jackson?

No, he would just think I was being irrational. Or not. But I wasn't going to do it. I was going to be Raven Remington tough, which seemed like a silly resolution since my hands trembled like crazy.

I attempted to push my fear aside, and I grabbed a butcher knife. In my gut, I knew these guys weren't here. They'd only wanted to leave that note and send a message. But I was holding on to this knife, just in case.

I fumbled with my phone and called my landlord. I had to change the code to get into this place. Too bad I couldn't get one of those retinal scanners like they had on TV. But I wasn't sure one of those would even make me feel better. Whatever was happening here, I didn't like it.

And I forgot about the hummus. Instead, I sat on the couch and found Episode 210.

It was about . . . a bank heist? How in the world was that supposed to help me with this mystery involving Max Anderson? I hadn't heard about any robberies in the area since I'd arrived. That would have definitely been front-page news around here. Maybe my biggest fans were trying to lead me astray? It just didn't make any sense.

Then again, a lot of things didn't.

I opened my desk drawer and pulled out a picture of my father. My kind, kind father, whose gaze exuded compassion and grace. My father who'd begged me not to go to Hollywood. Who'd warned me about the pitfalls of chasing fame. Whose heart had been broken when he'd realized the person I'd become. A person in a violent marriage. Who'd started to drink. Who said and did things she deeply regretted.

First my mom had run off, choosing her career over her family. Then I'd essentially done the same thing.

How did my mom play into this? Why did he have a photo of her?

I ran my finger down the side of his face and felt tears pop to my eyes.

What kind of trouble had he gotten himself in?

He'd always been there for me. Now I had to be there for him.

CHAPTER 21

The next day, I pulled up to the marina where my father used to work. The business was based out of the fishing community of Wanchese, a small town located on Roanoke Island. The place was a true working man's marina, full of fishermen and home to a thriving seafood industry. Nothing about the place was pretty, though the rugged authenticity of the docks and piers had a certain intrigue about them. The overcast, almost dreary day only added to the effect.

My gut told me the answers could be found here. I'd even tucked my father's photo into my pocket so I could remember exactly why I was doing this. Nothing was more important than my dad—not my career, not my love life, not my financial situation. I was going to find answers if it was the last thing I did.

But seeing that picture of my mom had brought a certain somberness to me today. That somberness was somewhat of a buzzkill for me, dampening my ADHD-like thoughts. Where my life normally felt like a twisted rom com of sorts, today it felt like an aching complex saga that could end in tragedy.

I meandered up to the little building, a shack

really, that served as a base of operations for the dolphin-watching tours my father had conducted. Charlie McGowan owned the business, and he'd been a friend to my dad. During warm months, there was a little window that could be opened for ticket sales. Laminated signs indicating prices still hung there.

I knocked before stepping inside. Charlie sat behind a rickety desk, looking over charts of some sort. He stood when he saw me, and a wide grin stretched across his wrinkled face.

"If it isn't Joey Darling. I wasn't expecting to see you here."

I smiled. I'd only met Charlie three times, but I liked the man. He was down to earth, pleasantly wrinkled, and treated me like a family member. Something about him reminded me of Andy Griffith, which was kind of weird considering he lived his final days on this very island.

"Sorry to stop by unannounced." I closed the door to ward away the cold and leaned in the frame.

"Anytime." He placed his elbows on the desk. "What brings you this way?"

I rubbed my lips together, determined to dive into this completely. Being passive would get me nowhere. "I know it's probably a long shot, but I was actually hoping to do a dolphin tour."

For research. My normal excuse. But I couldn't bring myself to say it.

He frowned. "We don't do them in the winter. Not enough interest, plus the cold drives people away."

My heart sank. I wasn't sure what I'd hoped to achieve while on a tour except to possibly get a better feel for where my father went and where he might have seen my mom. If I could match the background from the photo to an area here on the water . . . It was a long shot, but it was worth considering.

Charlie tapped his pen on the table and studied me. "I should say, I'm not doing any dolphin tours, but I was going to head out for a joy ride. You interested?"

My heart lifted. "Yes."

"Did I mention it's going to be cold?"

"I'm okay with cold." I mean, I hated it. But a girl had to do what a girl had to do. It was what it was, and so on and so forth.

"Excellent. You're going to want some coffee. Go ahead and get yourself a cup."

I went to the little pot in the corner and did as I was told. I'd been often called a coffee snob, and as I took my first sip, I nearly spit the hot liquid out. This was military-grade coffee, the kind where the grounds and filter went unchanged for weeks at a time. In other words, it was awful. But I didn't insult Charlie by telling him that. Instead, I gripped my Styrofoam cup and smiled. Acting 101.

Charlie pulled on a knit hat before grabbing his keys and a thermos. "Let's go. Any excuse to get on the water. So what brought this about?"

I shrugged and followed behind him. We stepped outside and started toward a narrow pier lined with boat slips. "I miss my dad. I want to see what he used to do for a living. I'd always said the next time I came out to visit him, I would do this tour. Unfortunately, I never got the chance."

Even more unfortunately, we'd been in a huge fight and my last words to my father weren't something I was proud of. I would take them back if I could. I would yell "Take two!" and start over again. Start over with all of it. Even my acting career. Especially my marriage to Eric.

But I couldn't do that, so I had to make the best of my past. I had to learn from my mistakes and correct whatever I could.

"Your dad was great at this job." Charlie took my hand to help me aboard a giant catamaran named *Oh Charlie.*

I assumed in the summer the cabin of the vessel was open and exposed, but now a plastic liner had been pulled down over the edges to keep out the wind. Rows of benches stretched down the middle and lined the edges.

"Holds forty-eight," Charlie told me, pausing to look at the boat with a glint of pride in his eyes. "It's quite the operation. Especially when you consider that I started with a little pontoon that held ten."

"Impressive. What kind of operations are run out of this marina?"

"Well, there's fishing, of course. Over there is Shipwreck Bay, one of the largest fishing companies on the East Coast. They process the catches in that building before they're sent to restaurants from here to the Mississippi."

I glanced at the rusty building he pointed to, one lined with crates and wire pods and other equipment I didn't recognize. Considering the business was so successful, it didn't look all that impressive.

"Over there is where they build world-class yachts." He pointed to another aluminum-sided building on the other side of the harbor. "And that's where Tony Simmons is based out of. He has his own show on Animal Planet. It's our little slice of Hollywood."

"That's right. My dad told me about that." That fact had always delighted my dad. Maybe if I'd been a hostess on one of those shows, he would have actually been proud of me. Instead I'd compromised all the beliefs I'd grown up with in order to pursue my career goals.

In my defense, I had instigated a morals clause, and I'd turned down offers by some naughty magazines. I'd still maintained some standards— standards as far as Hollywood was concerned. My dad on the other hand . . . he didn't approve of my career, my marriage, or the fact that alcohol had become such a huge part of my lifestyle.

My father didn't know that I'd started to drink to numb the pain and emptiness inside me. To help me contend with the fact that my all-star husband was an abuser who liked to put me in my place as often as possible. To help me forget just how much I'd come to hate my life, despite the fact that people naively thought they wanted to be me.

I grabbed a metal support to hold myself steady

as Charlie guided the boat from the slip. I stared out over the water, trying to forget all those things. It almost felt like my life was three different acts at times. The first was my childhood, growing up with a single father in a small Virginia mountain town. The second was my life in Hollywood, living large and learning both the ins and outs of fame. The third was right now, trying to find myself again in this little beach community that seemed so far removed from either of my other lives.

I supposed within a person's lifetime, he or she lived many different lives and played many different roles. I was no exception. But what I wasn't sure about was how this portion of my timeline—this little beach movie—would end. Would it be a Shakespearean tragedy? A Hallmark-movie happy ending? Did happy endings actually exist in real life?

My thoughts overwhelmed me, but at the moment I felt still. For most of my life, I felt restless. But being out here on this boat, gliding across the water, made me feel somehow at peace. Water seemed to have that effect on people, and that was why so many longed to have homes on lakes and oceans and rivers.

"You said my father was good at this job, huh?" I asked Charlie over the roar of the motor.

He nodded and pulled his hat down lower. Even with the windshield, it was still cold out here. "That's right. People always requested him for their guide and came back year after year. He was good with people, kind of like you."

"I always thought of him as being quiet."

"He was. But he still loved people. And he was passionate about the water. He loved telling the tales of this area."

"That's funny because growing up, I thought he was a mountain man who worked on the railroad. Never saw him as the coastal-living type."

"There's a lot kids don't realize about their parents until they're adults."

I nodded. I wished I'd had the chance to find out. To really find out. But instead I'd been wrapped up in myself. "I'm glad he had the chance to do what he wanted."

Growing up, my dad's world had revolved around me. He hadn't dated or really had any life outside of working and being a father. As far as I knew, at least. I'd assumed he'd been happy like that. But apparently he'd harbored a secret dream of coming to this area and settling down.

So what had happened to cause him to leave here? That was what didn't make sense. My father wasn't the type to do that. He was responsible to a fault. He'd once gone back to a grocery store because they'd given him fifty-two cents in change more than they were supposed to. I'd asked him if it was worth it to drive six miles to return fifty-two cents, and he'd told me that integrity started with the small things. I'd never forgotten that.

I stared over the horizon as the boat picked up speed. It was rugged out here with open expanses of water. Beaches—some with sand, others packed with marsh grass—beckoned exploration. On occasion, I spotted rocky jetties and old pilings with seagulls on top and trawlers surrounded by swarms of birds.

"Can you tell me what my father's life was like here?" I was ashamed for the words to leave my lips. I should know this information, but I didn't. I'd been too wrapped up in myself.

Charlie took a long sip from his thermos. "It was simple, and that was the way he liked it. He worked five days a week for me. We did three tours a day. In the morning, afternoon, and at sunset. Sunsets were always the most popular. When he wasn't working, I know he enjoyed attending the community church in Nags Head."

"What about friends? Did he spend time with anyone in particular?"

Charlie let out a slow breath, maneuvering the boat around some crab pods. "That's a good question. I do believe there was a man he'd recently befriended. They met at Sea Oats and Berries for breakfast some."

"Do you remember anything about him?"

"He ran a nonprofit of some sort. They wanted to reach out to some of the international workers around here."

"Bert, you mean?"

Charlie snapped his fingers. "That's right. He's the one. Oh, and he met with a writer once."

"A writer? Why?" This was the first I'd heard of that.

"I'm not sure. She was a younger lady. She had a

funny haircut. Short in the back and long up front. It was funny colors also."

Realization rang in my ears. The writer from Oh Buoy. Alexa was her name, if I remembered correctly. Funny that she'd never mentioned meeting my dad. I needed to track her down.

I reached into my pocket and pulled out the photo of my mother. "How about her? Have you ever seen her?"

He studied the picture a moment before shaking his head. "No, I don't reckon I have. Pretty lady. Joey, you don't think there's anything criminal going on here, do you?"

"I'm not sure. I'd like to believe there's not. And I know my father was a good man, so I don't believe he got involved in anything illegal on his end. I just wonder if he was in the wrong place at the wrong time."

Charlie remained quiet.

"Do you know something?" I asked.

"It's probably nothing."

"Please share. I need to help my dad if he needs help."

He pressed his lips together and finally nodded. "Okay, but take it for what it's worth."

CHAPTER 22

"I can tell you this: your father insisted on working here late. On closing up the shop. I didn't think much of it. My wife was recovering from hip-replacement surgery at the time, and I thought he just wanted to help me out. And he probably did." He tugged on his hat again. "But I came back late one night. I'd forgotten some paperwork about my wife's surgery."

I gripped the metal support, even though my hand was freezing. "What did you see, Charlie?"

"It was probably nothing. But he was down at the docks, talking to some men who seemed less than approachable, if you catch my drift."

My stomach tightened. "They looked like trouble?"

He nodded. "I'd never seen them around here before, and I can't imagine what kind of business they might have had here so late. Anyway, he seemed upset."

"Did he see you?"

Charlie shook his head. "No, he didn't."

"Did you ever ask him about it?"

"Maybe I should have, but I figured it wasn't any of my business. He'd been a bit obsessed over some activity that had been taking place lately on the water at night."

"What do you mean?"

"Most people fish in the daylight, though there are exceptions. Lately, there's just been a lot of activity out there in the evenings. Boaters aren't using lights even. It's unusual, and it bothered your father. He asked about it several times."

"And you told him?"

Charlie shrugged. "I told him with the popularity of all those fishing shows, maybe people were just trying to emulate what they're seeing on TV. It doesn't take much to make people act foolish. I didn't think a lot of it."

"Is that activity still going on?" I asked.

"Some. I'm not here late very often."

I shifted, trying to phrase my next question very carefully. "Is there any reason you didn't mention this earlier when we spoke? You only said he didn't seem like himself in the days before he disappeared."

"I try to stick to the facts, and I didn't want to worry you for nothing. Those men . . . they seemed like they were up to no good. They're not the type I think should be messed with. I saw them again the other day, and it jogged my memory."

Maybe I was finally on to something. "How about the girl who died in this area four months ago— Anastasia? Did my dad ever say anything about her?"

"Everyone did. Her murder was the talk of the town for a while. Her body was found not far from here, you know." He pointed in the distance. "In that cove right over there. At first it looked like she'd been wrapped up in a fishing net, but the medical examiner discovered she was actually strangled."

I shivered at the thought. "That's terrible. Do you think we could get closer to that cove?"

Charlie pressed his lips together before shrugging. "I'll get as close as I can."

He slowed and puttered up close to the shoreline. However, there was still a good three feet of water between the boat and the shore.

"If I go any closer, I'll run ashore."

"I'd like to take a walk. Would that be okay?"

"Have at it."

Despite my good sense, I took off my shoes, rolled up my jeans, and stepped into the icy water. I closed my eyes as my feet instantly began to ache. Was this really worth it? I had to believe it was, even if it was just so I could satisfy my curiosity.

I finally reached the shore. The ache in my feet didn't subside. Despite that, I walked across the sand. Thick marsh grass bordered it, and I'd guess during high tide the whole area was covered in water.

I stared across the vast, mostly barren expanse. There, in the midst of the windswept landscape, stood a gnarled, weather-bare tree. I'd seen that tree before.

In the picture I'd found of my mother.

This very spot was where my dad had seen my mom.

I glanced around the isolated panorama surrounding me. Why had my mom been here? Had my dad stumbled across her, or had they arranged a meeting at this remote location?

I studied the picture more closely. It almost looked like it had been taken from the distance. From the boat? Nothing made sense.

I paced the shoreline, looking for any type of clue I might find. From the distance, this beach had looked untouched. But up close, the sand had obviously been disturbed. There were marks in it that weren't natural. What was this beach being used for?

I stopped as the sand ended and marsh grass took over. I couldn't traverse past this area. Plus, I needed to get warm.

I waded back to the boat, dried off with a towel Charlie handed me, and quickly pulled my Converse back on.

"Did you find what you were looking for?" Charlie asked.

I bit down. "I'm not sure."

"Joey, I'm not sure what you're thinking, but you should tread carefully."

"What do you mean?"

Charlie tugged his hat again. "Joey, these waters are the perfect place for someone to disappear. There are miles and miles of nothing. And I've always had this nagging feeling that your father was in trouble."

***

I tried to put Charlie's words out of my mind for the rest of the boat ride, but it was hard. I didn't want to think about my dad's body being found at the bottom of the ocean. I wanted to think he'd forgotten all of his good sense and simply left to live in the Caribbean with the woman of his dreams. I'd be mad at him for not telling me, but at least I could rest assured knowing he was happy . . . and alive.

Maybe there was something deep inside me that knew that wasn't the most likely case. I knew my dad well enough to know he wouldn't do that. If he left without telling anyone, he had a good reason. I just hoped he'd had a choice in the matter. I prayed that it wasn't because he was . . .

I could barely even complete the thought. I wouldn't think it. I wouldn't believe it.

My dad was alive, and I was going to find him.

Charlie seemed to sense that I needed to change the subject, so he started giving me a tour of the area. He told me how five different sounds came together here in the area where the boat was. He pointed out a house that had been built on a little island in the middle of the sound, one that was only accessible by boat. He told me interesting facts about the Bodie Island lighthouse in the distance, starting with the fact it was pronounced "body." Who would've thunk it?

We even saw two dolphins swimming behind us, in the wake of the boat. He told me how the fin of each dolphin was as unique as our fingerprints. How scientists in the area were able to identify more than three hundred distinctive bottlenose dolphins in the Roanoke Sound and had even named them, including the famous "Onion," whose fin had been mangled by a boat propeller. It was all fascinating.

I could totally picture my father doing this. Telling these tales. Listening to new ones shared by tourists or locals who wanted to look at the area from a different perspective. I imagined how the delighted squeals of kids on the boats would make my father smile. I pictured him talking about fishing and telling about their latest catches.

All of this seemed just like my dad.

I wiped away a tear.

Finally, it was time to go back to the dock. My hands were frozen. I'd long since poured my coffee out and thrown away the cup—without Charlie seeing, of course. And those nose icicles I'd seen on other people at the Polar Plunge? I hoped I didn't have any now.

Once we docked, I climbed off the boat and stepped into the chilly gray outdoors. Charlie and I walked silently back to his business shack, and I thanked him for his time today.

"You're welcome, Joey. Your father thought the world of you, and I can see why."

Tears rushed to my eyes again. Could that be true? After everything I'd put him through? "Thank you."

My voice cracked as I said the words. Inside, I just felt so broken and unlovable. That was the root of my problem, wasn't it? Eric's lies had gone deeper inside me than I thought. Had he caused irreparable harm? Until I fixed the messy parts of me, I would never truly be ready to love again, no matter how great the person was.

I started back to my car, mulling over everything I'd learned today. Before I climbed in, I paused and glanced around the marina one more time. Fishermen came in with their catches of the day. Another man pulled crab pods from a boat. Two others walked past talking something about barracudas.

It was all fascinating, an entirely different side of life than what I was used to. But what did it have to do with my dad? What had he discovered? Why had he felt the need to hire a PI to watch me?

I was certain that all those questions would lead to no good.

As I unlocked my car, a woman in the distance caught my eye. She strode from one of the larger buildings on the waterfront, one with huge fishing boats docked out front. Like a woman on a mission, she headed toward a sedan in the gravel lot.

I probably wouldn't have noticed her if it wasn't for the utility-style pants she wore and the way her hair was pulled into a tight bun.

Was this the woman Shawn had seen at Max Anderson's rental? Maybe it was a long shot. Maybe I was seeing things I wanted to see and making something out of nothing. But I needed to know.

My somberness suddenly lifted.

Military Woman paused as a man stepped from the sedan.

I blinked, certain I wasn't seeing this correctly.

Hal. Was that Hal?

They talked a couple of minutes before he handed her something. Was that a . . . a camera?

Military Woman examined it a moment before reaching into her pocket and shoving something into his hand. Money?

I froze. The last time I'd seen something like this take place here at this very spot, it had ended up being an eBay transaction. I had to be careful not to read too much into this.

Whom was I kidding? I was totally going to read as much into this as I pleased.

As quickly as the exchange happened, Military Woman and Hal both hopped back into their respective cars and pulled away.

I hopped into my car as well. I had to follow . . . someone.

CHAPTER 23

As Military Woman climbed into her sedan, I climbed into my Miata. I counted to ten before following after her. After my last fiasco in following someone, I'd decided to look up some tips so I wouldn't be so obvious. My red sports car didn't help.

To my surprise, the woman took the first right turn after the marina area. I held my breath, realizing I could be putting myself in a precarious position. After all, this road most likely ended at water, which would mean I'd be exposed. My covert tailing would become obvious tailing, which pretty much would render it invalid.

I gripped the wheel. Fear might keep me alive, but it wouldn't help me find any answers. Either I was all in, or I was out. Right now, I was as immersed in this investigation as Zane had been in the ocean during the Polar Plunge.

I stayed a safe distance behind Military Woman, far enough back that her car disappeared around a bend in the road. I hoped I didn't lose her. I passed a couple of houses before spotting a restaurant ahead.

A restaurant? Out here? Surprising.

Then I saw the sign up top. Shipwreck Bay Café.

The seafood company had its own restaurant. Cozy.

Military Woman's sedan was both parked outside and empty, which led me to believe she must have already gone in.

I had to go after her. She shouldn't recognize me. And the parking lot was full, which meant it was probably a tasty restaurant and it would be easier to blend in among the patrons inside.

With that decided, I parked. I pushed up my aviator sunglasses and pulled my black knit hat down lower on my head. Maybe it wasn't the best idea to wear this outfit, because I was more recognizable as Raven this way.

Regardless, I stepped into the restaurant and paused. A few people looked up from their tables and gave me a double take. Several people whispered. But no one rushed me. That was good.

I scanned the place again. Where had the woman gone? The bathroom?

She definitely wasn't in the dining area.

I observed the restaurant a moment while I waited to see if she emerged.

Simple would be an understatement to describe the inside. Patrons ordered at a counter, picked it up at a window, and utilized disposable silverware. Plastic tables normally used outside constituted the dining area inside. It smelled like a fish market—because it was—but despite what some people might consider flaws, the place was packed.

My Hollywood friends would have turned up their noses if they saw me eating in here now. Even though I could get fish and fries for only six dollars, they thought it was better to pay twenty dollars for two ounces of raw fish with some uncooked vegetables.

I waited near the door for several minutes, pretending to be interested in some local hot sauce. When the woman still didn't appear, I realized I had to change course.

I scanned the restaurant one more time before stepping outside. What if she hadn't gone in? It was a possibility.

On the other side of the building was Shipwreck Bay Seafood. I could only assume that the fresh catches of the day came in here, where they were sorted and cleaned and whatever else happened to them.

Out of curiosity, I climbed from the covered porch and walked around the corner. A cluttered view of the harbor came into sight. I said cluttered because there were crab pots and buoys and mounds of oyster shells and a pier that appeared to be half fallen into the water. Fishermen yelled at each other while carrying bushels of something up to the shore.

Fascinating. Really fascinating. It reminded me of scenes from the movie *The Perfect Storm*.

Before I could dwell on it any more, someone suddenly slammed into me, throwing me back against the building. I hadn't caught my breath, when someone flung me behind an outdoor shed, well out of sight.

When the stars finally left my eyes, I realized

who was attacking me.

"Why are you following me?" Military Woman pinned me against the back of the building. Her nostrils flared, her eyes looked buggy, and she was entirely stronger than I'd imagined her to be. She was thin but ripped, and I'd guess her to be a few years older than I. She was like Sigourney Weaver in *Aliens*.

Wood shards pricked into my back. "Who said I was following you?"

"Don't play stupid with me," she seethed. "You followed me here."

"I was going to get something to eat." I refused to let myself quiver under her glare. I'd had a lot of practice with that with Jackson, so at least I could thank him for the skill.

"So why'd you come back here?"

I glanced beyond her, trying to pull an answer out of thin air. "To get a glimpse of the water. It's beautiful."

She raised an eyebrow, obviously not buying it. "It looks like a dump from here."

I swallowed hard. "It has character, in a shabby chic kind of way."

She glared at me another moment before dropping her arm from my chest, where she had me pinned. I stepped away from the building behind me and rolled my shoulders.

"Now that we've cleared that up, I should go—" I started.

"Not so fast." She shoved me back.

Instead of letting fear flash in my eyes, I gave an

aloof, cold nod. Hopefully she didn't see my knees knocking together uncontrollably. "What do you want? I answered your questions."

"You're not fooling me." She narrowed her eyes. "You need to stay away."

"Stay away from what?" Maybe I could get more information. Wouldn't that be nice?

"I know who you are."

I raised my chin. "Joey Darling. I'm just an actress. Perhaps you're mistaking me for my alter ego."

She rolled her eyes. "Drop the airhead act, Joey. You don't want to end up like Douglas Murray, do you?"

On the positive side, she'd just admitted she knew who the dead guy was and that I was connected with him. I couldn't let this opportunity slip by. I just hoped an alien didn't burst from her chest. Based on the look on her face right now, it was entirely possible.

"That wasn't his real name."

"You figured that out, huh?" She laughed, almost as if she couldn't believe me.

"He may have died because of me."

"Don't flatter yourself."

"My picture was in his pocket. That wasn't a mistake."

Her eyes narrowed. "You really need to stay out of this."

"You keep saying that, but I have no idea why. None of this makes sense to me."

"It's not supposed to make sense to you. You're a bystander. You need to keep it that way by minding your own business. Not everyone is as nice as I am."

"Who are you?" The questions just kept escaping before I could stop them. She had information I wanted.

"Again, none of your business. You have no idea who you're dealing with. Men who have no regard for human life. Men who will kill you if you get too close."

"Who are they?"

"The less you know, the better."

"How is my father involved?"

"Who said he was involved? Think what you want, but assumptions don't prove anything."

"He's the connection between this investigation and Douglas—Max Anderson."

Military Woman shook her head. "You're crazy."

"Why were you meeting Hal?"

My question stopped her cold, but she quickly snapped out of her stupor. "We're old friends."

I shook my head, another idea coming to me. "Hal was helping those hooligans with their burglary schemes, wasn't he? Maybe even taking a cut from them. They stole that camera from Max's condo, and it has evidence on it that could incriminate you."

Her bottom lip dropped open ever so slightly. Then she went back into GI Jane mode and gnarled at me. "I'm not going to warn you again. Stay out of this. Nothing good will come from your questions. Nothing."

With that, she gave me one last dirty look and

walked away.

And I did what any good investigator would do. I followed her.

***

I lost Military Woman's car as she zoomed back to Nags Head. She must have been going one hundred miles per hour. I couldn't do that. I just couldn't. It wasn't my jam.

I'd tried in vain to find her again. She was long gone, obviously more experienced at this kind of thing than I was. Go figure.

I was getting closer to some answers. I knew I was.

Instead of going home, I headed to Oh Buoy. It was a long shot that Alexa would be there, but I desperately needed to know why she'd interviewed my dad. If she was a part of this somehow, I felt 80 percent confident I could take her down.

Sure enough, she was sitting in the corner with her notebook again. I marched right toward her and slid into the booth, sitting across from her without invitation.

Her eyes widened when she looked up and saw me. Before I could get a word out, she said, "Yes, I interviewed your father."

That had been incredibly easy. I upped my chances to 90 percent. "About what?"

"The book I'm writing has to do with dolphins. One of the characters does dolphin tours. That's it.

That's why. I didn't even know he was your father at the time. I was just doing research."

I tried to keep my expression neutral. "When did you do this interview with him?"

She looked out the window, her eyes quickly traveling from left to right in thought. "Probably four months ago."

"Four months ago is when he disappeared," I told her.

She frowned and ran her hand across her leather notebook. "I heard."

I narrowed my eyes slightly, surprised. As far as I knew, the police had never officially opened an investigation on my father. There were no signs of foul play or illegal activity. So how did she know?

"How did you hear that?" I asked.

She swallowed hard, looking pale and slightly frightened. Did I really have that effect on her? I mentally patted myself on the back.

"I went back to do follow-up questions, and the man he worked for told me he was gone. I asked when he'd be back, and his boss said he had no idea. I didn't know your father well, but he didn't seem like the type to take off like that."

She'd surmised correctly.

"Did my dad say anything interesting during the interview?"

"Oh, a lot of stuff about dolphins. It was really quite fascinating—"

I didn't have time to listen to a mini-documentary on dolphins right now. "About anything besides dolphins?"

"He did ask me if I was writing a mystery novel."

"Why is that interesting?" I was trying to follow. I really was.

"He said he could tell me some tales, if I ever wanted to change my genre. I'm writing happy ever afters—with zombies. Anyway, then he got a weird look in his eyes and got quiet."

My pulse spiked. "Did you ask him about it?"

She shook her head, almost looking sad. "No, I could read him well enough to know he was done and didn't want to talk about it."

I leveled my gaze with her. A Ravenism flashed in my mind. *Going soft at the end will get you killed.* "Is there anything else you're not telling me?"

She shook her head. "There's not. I promise."

I was going to have to take her word for that. Because I was plumb out of questions.

***

I got back to my house just as the sun sank below the horizon. I had to admit that I missed having Zane around. I missed our routines. But it was better that he wasn't home right now because I'd be tempted to spend time with him. Zane dating April changed everything.

I dropped my keys onto the foyer table, stripped my coat off, and went to take a long bath. When I finished, I dressed in my PJs and decided to go into my mystery closet. I updated the boards there and made a list of all my questions.

- Who killed Max Anderson and why? Was he connected to my father?
- Who is sending me those threats? Did they have an underground network of stalker fans?
- Who sent me the video loop? My stalkers or the killer? My bets were on the killer. Or what if they were one and the same?
- Were there links between all these crimes? There had to be.
- How had Dad gotten a picture of my mother? Did he take it himself?
- What did Jackson know that he wasn't telling me?
- Where was my father? Where, where, where?

I stared at the board and sighed. I'd gotten some answers, but not nearly enough. Did this go back to the marina? To that little beach where my mom's picture had been taken?

I turned the closet light off and closed the door behind me. I was ready to go to bed and forget everything. Maybe after I got some sleep, things would be clearer.

I stepped into the hallway and flicked the light switch on. Nothing happened.

Awesome. Had my light bulb burned out? I'd

have to wade through the darkness to make it to my room. Maybe I should have had Jackson stay the other day and request he change some light bulbs after all. But he'd probably think my most important light bulb wasn't fully screwed in—the one connected with my brilliant ideas.

I headed down the hall anyway. Just as I crossed in front of a guest bedroom, a figure lunged from the darkness.

CHAPTER 24

The man wrapped his hand over my mouth and pinned my arms to my side. I thrashed against him to no avail. He was too solid. Too strong. Too impenetrable.

Cold, hard fear shot through me. Why was this man in my house? What was he planning?

Someone had killed Max Anderson. They probably wouldn't blink an eye at doing the same thing to me.

But I couldn't die. Not yet. I had to find my dad first.

"Calm down, Joey," the man whispered in my ear. Not in a reassuring way. No, in a threatening, menacing way. Like Darth Vader—only this man was real, not a product of George Lucas's imagination.

And I was certain that when a killer said calm down, that really meant *Brace yourself while I prepare to murder you.*

I thrashed harder, but it was no use. This man easily overpowered me. I was going to have to use something other than brawn to win this battle.

Knowing that, I went still and waited. My heart pounded in my ears, the sound nearly deafening. The only other thing I could hear was the man breathing in my ear.

And he wasn't breathing hard like he was nervous. No, he seemed calm. Too calm. Like he'd done this before.

That realization didn't make me feel better.

"Good girl," he crooned, his grip loosening ever so slightly. "I tried to warn you."

His face was beside mine, close enough that I could feel the rough knit of what I assumed to be a ski mask. I could feel a hint of his warm breath. I could feel his heart beating against my back. Slowly. Steadily.

I was going to die, wasn't I? A cry caught in my throat.

"You didn't listen," he continued. "I have a feeling that's one of your bad habits. One of many."

I wanted to say something, to beg for more answers, to confirm that I did indeed have many bad habits. But my lips were clamped together, and I was unable to speak. Or scream. Or barely breathe, for that matter.

My life flashed before my eyes, and I had no idea what to do about it. So I waited. And I prayed that waiting wouldn't get me killed. Waiting didn't seem heroic or brave, but perhaps it was wise.

Please let it be wise!

"I tried to ignore your little on-camera threat, but I couldn't," he said. "So here I am. Manning up. Acting like a big boy."

Yeah, that hadn't been my best move. If I

survived this, I needed to remember never to do that again. Throw downs were a bad, bad idea.

"You're in over your head," he continued. "Do you understand that? You need to leave this alone."

I nodded, my limbs trembling uncontrollably.

"You're just like your dad, you know," he continued.

My dad? His words spurred something inside me. I struggled against his hand as I tried to speak, to ask questions, to demand answers. It only made him hold on tighter. Tight enough that my teeth ached, as well as my arms from his clamp around them.

"You want to say something?" he rasped.

I nodded, fully realizing I could be making a terrible mistake.

"Fine. I'm going to release you. If you scream, I'll shoot. Do you understand?"

I nodded again.

His hand slipped away. As soon as it did, I darted to the wall across from us, trying to keep as much space between us as possible.

Maybe I should run.

But I couldn't.

Not only did I not stand a chance of escaping, but this man had answers. Answers I desperately needed to know. Answers that felt worth dying for.

As I pressed myself into the plaster behind me, I glanced through the dark at the intruder. He wore a ski mask, and I could tell little else about him. Not even the color of his eyes. I just knew one thing: he was dangerous.

"What do you know about my dad?" My voice cracked with emotion—fear, hope, curiosity.

He leered in front of me. "Nothing I can tell you. I didn't come here to offer you solace or advice."

I raised my chin. "What *can* you tell me?"

"To be careful."

Too late for that. I was Joey the Thickheaded and Slightly Careless. "How about my dad? Is he okay? Do you know where he is?"

"You're so full of questions, aren't you? I can't give you any answers. I'm just here to give you a warning." He paused, his gaze studying me. "They told me to kill you, you know. But I won't do that. Not yet. If you're smart, you'll listen."

"Why would someone want to kill me? What did I do? Why was Max Anderson watching me?"

He let out a chuckle. Did I recognize that chuckle? I wasn't sure. I *wanted* to recognize it. Desperately.

But his laugh faded, and the atmosphere changed. In an instant, he lunged toward me. Before I could escape, he grabbed my wrist and twisted it behind me.

Then I saw something glint. A gun.

"I should kill you," he said. "It would make this easier."

"Killing is for wimps," I said. "You're not a wimp, are you?"

It was a line from Raven. I was going to roll with it. Mostly because I couldn't come up with anything better. My mind was blitzing out on me.

"Real men face their problems," I continued. "Shooting me would only prove you're scared. Are you scared? Like a little boy?"

"Shut up!" He tugged me down the hall.

Fear shot through me again. "What are you doing? I thought we were just having a conversation. We're practically BFFs at this point."

"I'm making sure you get my point." He pulled me into the spare bedroom, opened the closet door, and tossed me inside like a rag doll.

I hit the wall, and pain rippled through me. I'd deal with that later.

"Don't do this!" I yelled, desperate to get through to the man.

"Too late." He slammed the door.

"I'm going to go all backwoods crazy in here!" I yelled. "And you're going to regret this. My dad always said when I got as mad as a hornet, someone ended up in the hospital with an emotional case of anaphylactic shock."

Oh, it was the southerner in me again.

"I'll give you some time in here to think this through," the man muttered on the other side of the door. "The only person you're capable of hurting in there is yourself. Have at it."

There's no lock on the door, Dummy.

Then something scraped outside.

The dresser, I realized. The entirely way-too-heavy dresser was being shoved in front of the door.

I reached for my pocket. I didn't have a cell phone with me. I'd left it on the charger on my nightstand.

How was I going to get out of here?

At least I was alive, I decided. But being locked in a closet without food and water would be an awful way to die.

***

I wasn't sure what time it was. Or how much time had passed. I didn't have my phone, which also served as my watch. There were no windows, and the shades in the spare bedroom were closed, not allowing any sunlight in. That meant I had no way of knowing if it was still night or if morning had come.

I'd tried to figure out how long it would take for someone to figure out I was locked in here. Zane would get back from the wedding tomorrow. That was a long time not to have a bathroom, however.

Dizzy would also notice I was gone on Monday.

But . . . I was supposed to meet Jackson today. Would he think I was just being a jerk when I didn't show up? Or would he suspect something was wrong?

I curled up in a ball on the floor. I'd found a blanket on one of the shelves, but otherwise, it was empty in here. Somehow, I'd managed to get a little bit of shut-eye.

I'd tried several times to shove the door open, and now my shoulder hurt. I wasn't going to be able to move that dresser away. The carpet had locked it in place, it appeared.

I stood again and began pacing like a caged lion. Okay, I did have to go to the bathroom. Like, now. Like, *bad*.

I slumped against the wall, and tears again pressed to my eyes. How had my life turned out like this? My childhood had been relatively normal. Then my time in Hollywood felt almost like a blurry dream. And now this felt like a nightmare.

What I craved was the ordinary. Would I ever get it? Could I die in here? Alone? Without anyone who truly loved me?

Fame and recognition wouldn't keep me alive. It wouldn't help me experience true love. It definitely didn't make me feel safe and secure.

It made me feel like my whole life boiled down to this closet, which felt similar to a padded room at an insane asylum. I'd worked so hard, only to build my life on . . . nothing. Nothing that would last, at least.

I curled my arms up beneath me and lay down on the floor again, there in the corner, wishing I felt lighthearted and fun. Wishing I could compare this experience to *Panic Room* with Jodie Foster. But I couldn't.

Finally, at some point in the mindless, timeless pit I was in, I heard something downstairs.

"Joey?"

I sat up straight, suddenly forgetting about my pity party.

Who was that? It didn't matter. Someone was in my house!

I pounded on the wall. "I'm in here!"

"Joey?" The voice sounded closer.

I beat on the wall and the door and then the wall again, desperate to make as much noise as I could. "I'm in here! I can't get out."

I kept pounding, afraid whoever was here hadn't heard me. After all, shouldn't he be here by now?

"Please, help me!" I shouted.

A moment later, I heard scraping outside the door.

"I'm going to get you out," a deep voice said.

Then in a glorious moment, the door opened. It opened! I stumbled out and nearly fell right into . . . Jackson's arms.

"Joey? What . . ." He glanced behind me, as if trying to figure out what happened.

"I'm so glad you're here. And I'll tell you all about it. But I've got to run to the bathroom first!"

I scrambled past him and into the hallway bathroom, only to emerge a few minutes later. Jackson waited in the hallway, his hands on his hips and an expression of concern on his face.

I smoothed my hair back, feeling slightly self-conscious. I'd seen my reflection, and I looked hideous. Not even a high bun and some mouthwash had helped.

"Thanks for showing up, Jackson."

"What happened, Joey? What's going on?"

I told him. His expression grew more and more stormy with each detail.

"If I hadn't shown up . . ." His jaw flexed, and he

shook his head.

I swallowed hard. "Believe me—I've thought about that too. I thought about a lot of things while I was in there."

"I'm glad you're okay." He stepped closer and lowered his voice. "You are okay, aren't you?"

I nodded, but the action felt heavy and uncertain. I'd had a little too much time to examine my life while I was locked up. "Yeah, I'm okay."

He stepped back but looked unconvinced. "There's a video playing downstairs on your TV. It's looping over and over."

I froze, trying to comprehend that new fact. "What?"

"A video of your challenge to whoever killed Max Anderson."

My face paled. "I see. I actually got an email of that video a couple of days ago."

Jackson's face darkened. "You didn't report it to the police?"

"I figured you'd write it off."

He drew in a long, controlled breath before speaking. "Have I ever written off something you've said, Joey?"

I kicked my foot at nothing. "Well, no."

"Then why would I now?"

I shook my head, realizing I'd made yet another poor decision. They came naturally to me. "I don't know. The throw down was my stupid mistake, so I figured I should pay the consequences of it."

"And now the person who killed Max Anderson

has broken in and locked you in a closet. What if I hadn't come by? How long would it have taken someone else to find you?"

Tears pushed to my eyes again, and I looked away, desperately not wanting Jackson to see me like this. But it was too late. He reached for me and pulled me into a hug.

"I'm glad you're okay, Joey."

I wanted to melt in his arms, but it wasn't that kind of hug. And as deep as my thoughts were at the moment, the superficial side of me also reared its head. Because I couldn't help but wonder how I smelled.

Which was so stupid.

But I had been locked up all night.

I pulled myself together and stepped back, determined to appear stronger than I actually felt. "Speaking of which, how did you get in?"

Jackson's stern gaze had morphed into something warmer, more compassionate. "I called your Realtor and asked for the key code. I came by to get you. You didn't answer, and your car was out front. There are many things you're not, but you're usually pretty responsible."

"Thanks . . . I think."

"Listen, I'm going to send a team out to see if this man left any evidence."

"He didn't. He wore gloves." I'd tasted them. Smelled them. Felt them.

"I'd still feel better if I got a team out here."

"I understand." I smoothed my hair again, trying

to focus my thoughts. "Jackson, I think that Max Anderson was killed because he took pictures of something he wasn't supposed to see."

Jackson froze. "What do you mean?"

"I mean, I think he took photos and captured something illegal on film. Something worth killing over. Maybe not even something in connection to me. I think those punks who've been breaking in all over town stole that camera, and the bad guys wanted it back because it had evidence on it."

He shook his head, nearly looking flabbergasted. "Why would you think that?"

"Because I saw Hal from Hal's World selling it to a very suspicious woman dressed in combat gear."

"Wait. Start over, Joey."

So I did. I told him about my day and what I'd seen and what had happened and the notes my stalkers had left me.

"You're going to get yourself hurt, Joey. How many times do I have to say that?" Jackson asked.

"I just wanted to take a boat ride. And I found the place my mother's picture was taken. It just doesn't make any sense why she'd be on a beach in the middle of nowhere." I looked up at Jackson and rubbed my arms. "Can you confirm that anything I've said is accurate?"

He rubbed his jaw. "Your theory is right. We believe Max did see something he wasn't supposed to see while in the process of watching you. We believe it got him killed. What we still don't know is who killed him."

Well, at least I now knew motive and means. I just had to figure out who and what they had to do with my father.

Then I had to figure out who my stalkers were who insisted on making my life miserable.

Most of all, I needed to locate my dad. Slowly and surely, more and more clues were coming to light.

"Do you want me to call Phoebe and let her know we can't make it?"

I thought about it a moment. Part of me wanted to stay here and investigate. The other part of me knew I needed to get out. Get away from this house and this craziness. Most of all, I knew if I stayed alone too long, I'd only end up beating myself up again and replaying all of the poor choices I'd made that had led me to this point. I couldn't do that. Not now.

"I still want to go," I told Jackson.

He stared at me another moment before nodding. "Okay. Let me just let her know that we'll be running late."

***

Excitement pumped through my blood when Jackson and I took off down the road a few hours later. Not only was I excited to finally see Phoebe's place, but the weather today had turned out to be perfect. Sixty-four degrees. In February. Never mind that last week had a high of only thirty-two. Apparently, the motto around here was that if you didn't like the weather, wait a couple of days. It was proving to be true.

Plus, doing this was the perfect distraction from what had happened. If I dwelled on last night too long, I might be tempted to run. To hide. To do anything other than try to find any more answers.

Ripley hung his head from the backseat window. I gave him an affectionate rub and did some doggy talk before sliding onto the passenger seat. I noticed two cups of coffee waiting in the console.

"You didn't?" I said.

"I did. Fresh and hot from Sunset."

"Maybe you do like me, just a little bit," I teased.

He said nothing, which was just as well. Leave it to me to be awkward.

And leave it to Jackson to look fabulous wearing a deep-blue henley and ragged jeans. Simple but very effective in showing off his very defined arms and chest.

Not that I'd noticed. Except that I had. And I wanted to keep noticing. But I forced my eyes away and picked up my coffee instead.

We'd started down the road when Jackson said, "Tell me what your life was like as a famous actress in Hollywood, Joey."

His question took me by surprise, but we had at least thirty minutes to kill, so I did as he asked. I told him about celebrities I'd met, parties I'd attended, how grueling it could be to shoot a one-hour TV show with twenty-four episodes per year. By the time I finished that, we'd crossed over the Bonner Bridge, a structure that arched high above the water and gave a magnificent view of the area.

But it was what came afterward that really took my breath away. Sand dunes on either side of me and water on either side of the sand dunes.

"We're driving on a sandbar, aren't we?"

Jackson chuckled. "Well, if we want to be scientific, this whole stretch of islands is just one big sandbar."

"That's a little unnerving. Sandbars don't last forever."

"Which is precisely why some people don't want to move here. However, these sandbars have been here for centuries."

"That's comforting."

"The problem is that they naturally want to shift and move. When we build beaches and houses, we don't allow for that to happen. So all of this is really just man versus nature. We'll see who wins a hundred years from now."

"Fascinating." Ripley nuzzled me before lying down. I reached my hand back to pet him, when my hand connected with some kind of paper. Before I could stop myself, I sneaked a peek at what it was.

I let out a small gasp. It was the *Instigator*. The copy of me looking like a streetwalker.

"Joey, I can explain—"

CHAPTER 25

Before Jackson could, I glanced back and saw at least ten copies of the rag mag.

"What . . ." I couldn't even finish my question.

"It's not what it looks like. Not everything is what you assume it to be at first glance."

I swerved my gaze toward him. "Then what is this? Why would you buy all these copies? To humiliate me?"

His jaw flexed. "Do you really want to know?"

"Of course I do."

"I thought that article was disrespectful, and I knew it wouldn't make much difference—not nationally, at least—but I figured if I bought all the copies at whatever store I was in at the time, at least that many people wouldn't be seeing it."

My heart, which had felt tight, now melted in a pool of warm goo. "You did that for me?"

He shrugged. "It's no big deal. I just hate how newspapers like that twist the truth, you know? It should be illegal."

"But because I'm a celebrity, they can get away with it. Somehow that makes it okay." I glanced down at my hands. "Thanks, Jackson."

"I'm sure you'd do it for me . . . if I was a famous TV star."

I glanced behind us and saw the same car there, a black sedan following a good twenty feet back.

"There's really nowhere for cars to go. No turnoffs. This is a straight stretch from here to Rodanthe," Jackson said, as if reading my thoughts.

"I guess I'm paranoid."

"You should be. Fame makes you a target, unfortunately. It's better you're paranoid than lackadaisical."

"Living paranoid isn't a way to live."

"In your case, it might keep you alive though."

I pulled an arm across my chest, suddenly chilled. "That whole fan-club thing Adam told us about is weird."

"I have our cybercrime guy looking into it, if it makes you feel any better."

"I suppose it does. It's just . . . so creepy." I remained quiet a moment, contemplating my next words. I was going to share some information, I decided. And that was that. "I know that Douglas Murray is really a PI named Max Anderson. I'm pretty sure my father hired him."

His eyebrows shot up. "You do your homework."

"Can you confirm that my father hired him? I'm sure you've looked into Max's financial records."

Jackson didn't say anything. I waited. And waited a little bit longer.

Finally, he drew in a long breath. "I can tell you this. We found no records in his financials from your father. We were able to look on his calendar, and two weeks ago he had a meeting with someone with the initials LS."

"Lewis Schermerhorn."

"That's what we think."

"My dad is involved in this somehow. He must have hired him to follow me. But why?"

"We don't know, Joey."

I had to wonder if that was the truth.

***

Phoebe's house was located on the sound and, like most houses in the area, it stood high on stilts. I was surprised at how large it was, considering she worked at a smoothie bar and walked dogs in the summer. It turned out she rented the first story of the place and oversaw things here while the owner left for the winter.

Jackson kissed her cheeks as we walked in. "Good to see you, Phoebs."

"You too, Jax." She smiled and gave me a quick hug. "I'm so glad you made it here. You're going to love Hatteras Island and want to move here. I promise you."

"I thought I was already living in paradise."

"It's really like the next step after paradise, especially in the summer when it gets super busy up on the northern beaches. It's quieter down here."

"And more likely to be wiped off the face of the earth if a major hurricane ever hits the area," Jackson said.

"Minor details." Phoebe slapped his arm. "Okay, enough of that talk. You're going to mommick her."

"Mommick?"

"Ignore her. She likes to talk like a High Tider." He paused. "Or as it's so often said, Hoi Toider."

"A High Tider? I'm so confused."

"Some of the natives here on the island talk with a slight, almost British accent. Some people call it Old English. It's especially noticeable down in Ocracoke, but you can hear it here too. Don't be deceived though. Phoebe is not a High Tider."

"But I think it would be fun to be one and have that cool accent."

"I love cool accents," I added. "I used to always want to be British, just so I could sound sophisticated."

"You should talk Spielberg into doing a movie down here."

As if Spielberg listened to me. "You obviously didn't hear about Tweet Gate."

"Tweet Gate?" she questioned.

"I'll tell you later."

She threw her shoulders back. "Anyway . . . welcome to my home! I'm so glad you're here. But before I try and be overly hospitable, Jackson, could you help me put a picture up? It's a two-person job."

"No problem."

"Joey, make yourself at home. There are drinks in the fridge. We'll be right back."

As they disappeared down the hallway, I

lingered by the bookshelf in the living area. I stared at the pictures there. I knew I was being nosy, but I just couldn't stop myself.

Because there were pictures of Claire here. I stared at them.

Claire looked exactly as I'd imagined. She was slender, blond, and beautiful, but not in an overblown way. In a very natural way. Her face and hair both looked sun kissed, and her smile was bright and easy.

And there were pictures of her and Jackson here. A different Jackson though. A happy Jackson who had warmth radiating from his eyes. Who smiled. Who kissed his wife's forehead as they sat on the beach, looking cozy and happy.

Claire's death had changed him, I realized. Death usually did that. I wasn't surprised by that fact. I just hadn't expected the difference to be so dramatic.

When people like Claire suffered an untimely death, they tended to be immortalized as perfect. I'd seen it before. No one could ever live up to them.

Not that Jackson was taking applications or that I was tempted to apply. But this was just one more reason why I had to keep my growing feelings for Jackson under control.

I would never measure up.

"All done! Okay, lunch is ready, and then we're going paddle boarding," Phoebe announced.

I jumped away from the bookcase, afraid for a second that she'd been able to read my thoughts. I cleared my throat, keeping my gaze away from Jackson's. "In February?"

"Just don't fall in the water, and you'll be okay!"
Comforting. Or not.

***

Paddle boarding had been fun. Phoebe had even been
brave enough to let Ripley sit on the edge of her
board, and the two had formed quite a picture
together. The sun had just begun to sink on the
horizon as we wrapped up our time on the water. We
returned to the house, where Phoebe had left some
eastern North Carolina–style barbecue in the
crockpot. Normally I wouldn't eat pork, but this time
I'd make an exception.

In truthfulness, I made a lot of exceptions.
Unfortunately.

We ate and talked about life on the island and
problems with beach erosion. Phoebe talked about
some sea turtles that had been rescued from the
sound recently. It was all nice. Casual. Normal.

I didn't realize how much I'd craved normal until
now. Normal was good. Normal kept you grounded.

After we finished eating, Jackson's phone rang,
and he excused himself. I picked up my own phone to
check my text messages. I'd missed a call from
Rutherford. No surprise. My best friend, Starla, had
also texted me. Then there was one from a number I
didn't recognize.

**It's Shawn. I've been doing
some research. Call me.**

**You'll want to know what I
learned.**

Interesting. I'd given him my phone number
before I left Sunset that day we met and asked him to
let me know if he heard anything else. Apparently, he
had.

I texted him back, anxious to hear what he'd
learned. Just as I finished, parts of Jackson's
conversation drifted over to me.

"I understand," he said. "I'll send you the
pictures from his condo. I took some of my own, just
for reference. Okay, got it. Thanks."

He punched in a few things and then set his
phone down as Ripley jumped in circles. Jackson
grabbed his leash and spoke in soothing tones to the
canine.

"I'm going to take Ripley on a quick walk before
we head back," Jackson said. "You want to come?"

I did want to. But I didn't. "I'm going to help
Phoebe clean up some."

"Got it. I'll be back."

As he stepped out the door, I saw that he'd left
his phone. I remembered the conversation. *I'll send
you the pictures from his condo. I took some of my own,
just for reference.*

My heart pounded erratically in my ears. I
shouldn't. I shouldn't.

But he had photos from Douglas Murray's/Max
Anderson's place. What if there was some kind of clue
in those pictures? Something that would give me the

answers I so desperately craved? Answers about my father.

Phoebe was distracted with a phone call in the other room. Jackson was gone. And his phone was here on the TV stand, beckoning me.

My hands shook as I picked it up. I glanced around one more time before hitting the button. The screen flashed on.

I needed a code.

My throat went dry. I'd seen him punch in some numbers earlier today. I hadn't meant to watch so carefully. Not really. But I had. And I knew it.

So I used it.

A picture came up on the phone.

It was a picture of a gold cross with a rose twisted around it. A chain was stretched through a loop on the top. A necklace. A broken necklace.

My heart nearly stopped.

I'd seen that cross before. I knew exactly where.

Anastasia had been wearing it in one of her pictures.

This connected Douglas Murray/Max Anderson/Mark Hamill to Anastasia's murder.

"What do you think you're doing?" a deep voice asked behind me.

I'd been caught.

CHAPTER 26

"Jackson, I'm sorry. I can explain—"

He snatched the phone from my hands. "Save it."

"No, really, I—"

"I realized I'd forgotten my phone and came back to get it. It's a good thing I did." He scowled at me again, but this was a different kind of scowl. This was an honest one, one full of hurt and anger. And I deserved it. I more than deserved it.

But even knowing that didn't make the icky, awful feeling in my gut go away.

"I'm sorry. I don't know why I—"

"I don't want to hear your excuses, Joey." He shook his head like a disappointed father. "I've got to take Ripley out."

He stormed out the door, and I felt like roadkill. Worse than roadkill. I felt like the flies that ate on roadkill. Worse than the flies. I felt like the maggots left behind by the flies that fed on the roadkill.

"Everything okay?" Phoebe asked, coming back into the living room. "I thought I heard something heated out here."

I swallowed hard, unsure what to even say. "I

think I messed up, Phoebe. Again. I mess up. A lot."

She squeezed my arm. "We all do."

"I appreciate you asking me here, and I really hope I didn't ruin all of this. But I may have, and for that, I'm really sorry."

"What happened?"

"Jackson left his phone, and I saw a picture from a crime scene." I shook my head. "I know it was wrong. I shouldn't have done it. But, Phoebe, it connects the murder of Mark Hamill—"

"Mark Hamill died?"

I shook my head. "I mean Douglas Murray—no, Max Anderson!—to the disappearance of my father."

"You looked on his phone?" It was like she didn't hear the second part of what I'd said. Which made sense. Because to her, the first part would be way more important. It showed my lack of integrity.

"I shouldn't have done it," I repeated.

I waited for a lecture. For her to scold me. I deserved every moment of it.

"He'll get over it."

I blinked, certain I hadn't heard her correctly. "What?"

She shrugged. "Jackson. He'll get over it. Give him time."

"I betrayed his trust."

She leaned closer. "Joey, I haven't seen his eyes light up around someone like they do around you since Claire."

Her words almost knocked the wind out of me until I remembered the truth. "He doesn't like me like that, Phoebe. He barely likes me at all. Especially not now."

"You might be surprised."

***

Silence.

Sometimes I could appreciate it, and sometimes I hated it.

Right now was one of those times that I hated it because it was awkward and heavy and filled with tension. Not even Ripley panting at my neck could make anything better.

"I am sorry," I finally muttered somewhere on the middle of the sandbar with a road running over it.

Jackson didn't say anything for a moment and then, "I'm just not sure I can trust you."

Heat warmed my cheeks. Yes, I deserved that comment. But the fact was that Jackson hadn't proven himself to be all trustworthy either. He was keeping secrets from me. Sure, maybe there were professional boundaries in place. I got that. But he wasn't totally innocent.

It was so hard to keep that to myself. To not blurt it out, to point out the hypocrisy of it all.

Don't show your hand.

It was what I kept telling myself. I hoped it was the right move.

Jackson glanced in his rearview mirror again. He'd done that several times.

I looked behind us.

The black sedan. It was back.

"It *was* following us earlier," I muttered. I hadn't been losing my mind.

"It's definitely been behind us for a while." Jackson's words were controlled, but his grip on the steering wheel tightened.

"Coincidence?" I asked, knowing my words were absurd.

"Doubtful." His gaze flickered to the rearview mirror again. "They're gaining on us."

"Why would they do that?" I grabbed the armrest, my blood pressure skyrocketing. I knew the answer, and it wasn't that the driver was going to pass us.

"Your seat belt is on, right?" Jackson asked.

I nodded, feeling tension stretch throughout my entire body. "It is."

"Hold on."

"What are you doing?"

"I'm just trying to keep us alive." He accelerated.

I glanced in the side-view mirror. The car behind us accelerated also.

Then it moved into the other lane. The lane with oncoming traffic—only no one was there right now. Were they going to pass us? That had to be it. This was all a mistake. They'd get in front and be on their merry way.

When they were beside us, Jackson tapped the brakes, slowing down. The other car seemed to anticipate his move. Instead of charging forward and becoming leader of the pack, it rammed into us from the side.

Jackson righted the steering wheel. But before we could fully get back on track, the car rammed us again.

I looked up and realized we were careening right toward the enormous sand dune.

CHAPTER 27

As the sand dune got closer, I could only think of one thing: Ripley. I had a seat belt. That poor dog didn't.

So I did what any decent human being would have done. I threw myself in front of him. I used myself as a seat belt, the best I could.

The truck collided with the sand, which might as well have been a ten-foot-thick brick wall.

The air bags expanded, sending white powder into the air.

Ripley lunged forward. Into my arms. Fur covered my face. Claws dug into my legs.

The wretched sound of metal mangling and scraping and crushing filled the air. Momentum lunged us forward. Glass broke. Jackson yelled something.

At once, everything stopped. The silence was resounding and mighty. A buzz filled my ears, and I reminded myself to breathe.

Then came a pop and a sizzle from the hood.

I glanced over and untangled myself from dog fur and limbs. I drew back until I could see the canine's face. "Are you okay, Ripley?"

Ripley licked me, and I released my breath. Then

my gaze fell on Jackson. A small trickle of blood crept down his forehead, but he appeared to be otherwise okay.

The car had passed us and zoomed over the bridge, but there was no way we would be catching up.

"You okay?" Jackson muttered.

"I think." I did a quick self-evaluation and couldn't figure out anything specifically that was wrong. Except that I hurt all over. And my right arm throbbed. Despite my seat belt and the air bag, I'd somehow rammed into something hard. The dashboard? The door? I didn't know. Broken glass littered my hair like a twisted confetti of sorts.

Jackson grabbed his phone and called in the incident. The Dare County Sherriff's Office promised to have someone out within five minutes.

I drew in a deep breath, my heart racing. That had been close. Too close.

A strange smell filled the air. Was that . . . gas?

As soon as the thought crossed my mind, alarm washed over Jackson's features. He grabbed my hand. "We need to get out of here, Joey. Now."

I didn't argue. I tugged on the door. It wouldn't budge.

I tugged harder. Nothing happened.

Panic tried to seize me.

"I can't get out, Jackson." My pitch climbed higher than a kite in a windstorm.

He threw his door open and grabbed my hand. "Come on."

I pressed my seat belt release. Nothing happened again. No clicks. No give. Nothing.

The lifesaving strap continued to hold me in this truck that could burst into flames at any minute.

Fear—real fear—flashed through me. Again and again. My head spun as I grabbed at the strap around my waist. Why wasn't the seat belt coming off?

In three seconds flat, Jackson reached into his pocket, pulled out a knife, and cut the seat belt off. He grabbed my arm and hauled me out of his truck. I wasn't sure if he was carrying me or if everything was happening as if in an alternate reality, but somehow we flew across the sand. Ripley stayed on our heels.

Just as we got twenty feet away, fire exploded from the truck. Jackson shielded me, pulling me to his chest to keep away any flying shrapnel. Ripley barked at our feet, staring at the wreckage as if he knew something bad had just happened.

"Are you okay?" Jackson asked.

I felt too dazed to answer. My ears were ringing. I could feel the heat from the flames.

What had just happened? Was this real? Or was I on the set of *Relentless*? Or was this a dream? A dream about *Relentless*?

"Joey?"

I looked up and saw Jackson staring at me. I finally nodded, even though I had no idea if I was okay. I knew he just needed a response, that he needed to know I heard him.

"You're bleeding."

I glanced down at my right arm. Sure enough, a huge gash cut through my sleeve and into my flesh. Blood rushed out at an alarming rate.

My head spun at the sight.

At once Jackson stripped off his shirt, revealing a white undershirt beneath. I tried not to stare, thankful that the blood gushing from my arm could distract me. He stepped closer and wrapped his shirt around my arm to stop the bleeding.

"Help should be here anytime now," he said, his voice suddenly gentle and calming. Gone was the bitterness from earlier.

But when I looked at his bicep—because I couldn't help but look—I saw a tattoo. Of a skull and crossbones with words in a different language beneath them.

My heart nearly stopped.

That was the same tattoo a waitress had told me a man had. A man who'd met with my father before he disappeared.

That man had been Jackson.

***

"You met with my father," I muttered.

Jackson squinted. "What?"

I pointed to his tattoo, outrage rushing through my blood. "You met with my father before he disappeared. It was you. In Fatty's. Erma told me he met with someone. I didn't realize it was you until now."

"Joey—" He reached for me.

I jerked back, throwing myself off balance and nearly tumbling into the sand in the process. "Don't try to tell me that I'm wrong. I know more than you think about your involvement with my dad."

He raised a hand, as if to say *slow down.* "Joey—"

"Save your cockeyed excuses! You have a police file on my dad. You met with him at Fatty's. And you even met with him at some dark warehouse one night," I rushed. "Yet whenever I talk about him, you act like you don't know a thing. Now who's the one who's untrustworthy?"

He stopped trying to reach for me, to placate me, and locked his jaw in place. I saw regret in his eyes. I didn't care. It was too late for me to care.

"Are you a part of this? Did you have something to do with my dad's disappearance? You and the chief?" All the things that I'd bottled up inside for so long escaped from me like the eruption created from mixing Coke and Mentos.

Ripley whined beside me and nuzzled my hand. But not even my furry friend could calm me down.

Jackson opened his mouth, and I knew what he was going to say. Deny, deny, deny. I was over it.

"Don't even tell me that I've got it all wrong," I said. "I have evidence. Pictures. Witnesses. I saw your file with my own eyes at the police station."

Before he could say anything—not that he would and not that there was any good excuse—a sheriff's cruiser pulled up, followed by an ambulance. Nine one one had arrived.

Medics began checking me out, and I threw one last scowl toward Jackson. I'd gotten it wrong before. I'd believed Zane when I shouldn't have. But there was no way I had it wrong now. Jackson had betrayed me, just like every other man I knew.

As the medics led me toward the ambulance, the only thing I regretted was not saying goodbye to Ripley.

***

I lay in a curtained-off room in the ER, listening to beeps and unseen footsteps and murmured conversations taking place just out of sight. I felt alone and mad, and my head hurt. I had too many bad memories of the hospital. Memories of my car accident. Of Eric showing up and acting like the perfect spouse while everyone watched. Of the lies and insults he'd whispered when no one was listening. When would I ever forget them?

At that moment, a shadow appeared on the other side of the curtain, and a deep voice said, "Knock, knock."

I supposed that was what you did when there wasn't a door.

Metal scraped against metal as the hooks attached to the partition slid to the side. Jackson appeared.

The one person I didn't want to talk to. Not by a long shot. But I couldn't go anywhere, thanks to the IV hooked to my arm. Stupid IV.

"How are you feeling?" Jackson paused beside my bed. Tension radiated between us, like the eerie calm in a nuclear aftermath.

"I've been better. Six stitches and a concussion. Yay for me." I rubbed my arm where a bandage had been placed over my stitches. "Where's Ripley?"

It seemed like a safe enough topic.

"Phoebe came and got him."

I finally pulled my gaze up to him. "And how are you?"

I almost didn't want to ask, but I did anyway out of common decency.

"I'm okay."

He glanced at my uninjured arm, his eyes zeroing in on an old scar there. It was deep, running from the underside of my arm, above my elbow, halfway down my forearm.

"What's that from?" he asked.

My throat went dry, so dry that I could hardly swallow. Did I tell him the truth? That I'd cut myself on a broken vase when Eric had pushed me down the stairs? That the police never noticed because I'd been in a car accident while driving myself to the hospital?

"Car accident," I croaked. I couldn't tell him the truth. Wouldn't. He already thought I was incompetent. Hearing about Eric would only make me seem weaker. I'd already felt like less of a person since our marriage and divorce. There was no need to add to the feeling.

Jackson's eyes narrowed, as if he doubted my words.

How did he know? Did he have an internal lie detector?

But this wasn't a discussion that we needed to have now. Not when there were so many other things hanging between us.

Jackson cleared his throat, his features still tight. "I did meet with your father a couple of days before he disappeared."

My heart pounded in my ears. Nothing else mattered except this conversation. "Did you know him from church?"

"Not really. I'm unable to do a lot with the church because of my schedule. I do participate in a Bible study, but he wasn't a part of it. We met at Fatty's because of my police work."

"Why hadn't you been able to tell me about this before?"

"It's complicated, Joey." He shifted, his face still pinched. "I know that explanation isn't going to satisfy you. If I could answer your questions, I would."

"It's not an explanation. Why can't you say more?" My voice climbed higher, and I leaned toward Jackson, desperate to reach through his double-talk and hear the truth. "You'd rather see me suffer through not knowing what happened to my dad?"

His features squeezed at my words. "It's not like that. It goes deeper than you think, and it would put an entire operation at risk."

"An entire operation? What does that mean?" I didn't know, but I didn't like the sound of it. Fear shot through me as worst-case scenarios bombarded my thoughts.

Jackson opened his eyes, and I saw the pain there, the agony of desire versus obligation. "I can't tell you. Can you understand that? Can you try to understand that?"

Compassion tried to win, but anger took first place instead. "This is what I understand. You know information that you refuse to share. Meanwhile, I'm going through sleepless nights wondering about my father. Not knowing is like a curse."

His jaw flexed, and he remained quiet for a moment. Finally, he said, "I'm sorry, Joey."

He was trying to end this conversation, but I wasn't ready for that. "Somehow my father was involved in a police investigation—I'm sorry. You called it an *operation*. That must mean he was in trouble. You have to tell me more."

"I've already said too much, Joey."

"Hardly." My voice sounded surprisingly hard. "What about that necklace you found at Max's place? It belonged to Anastasia. Is she connected with all of this . . . this . . . madness?"

Jackson remained quiet a moment before nodding. "We believe she is. Somehow. Whatever Max caught on camera, we think is connected with whatever got Anastasia killed. In fact, we believe he may have unwittingly stumbled upon her killer."

Silence more awkward than someone asking for your autograph under a bathroom stall stretched between us. If he wasn't going to give me answers, then I had nothing to say to him.

"Do you want me to drive you home?" Jackson finally broke the silence.

I shook my head. "No, I'll find another way."

"Joey . . ." His voice sounded pleading.

It made something snap inside me. "Look, I know you're doing your job. I realize you have limitations. But this is my father's life we're talking about, and to me, his life is more important than any *operation* you have going on."

His throat visibly tightened, and he stepped back. "I understand. Are you sure you can get another ride home?"

I nodded. I wouldn't accept a ride from him. Even if it meant somehow signaling my stalkers to do it instead.

CHAPTER 28

I knew I should have gone to church the next morning—my weary soul needed some back-to-my-roots refreshing—but my pain medication and the long day yesterday kept me in bed. When I did wake up, my thoughts played over and over in my head.

Jackson admitting he knew more than he would tell me. Anastasia's necklace. Max Anderson's involvement in this.

As I drank my coffee, I checked my phone. Shawn still hadn't texted me back. I was anxious to know what he'd learned. And the fact that he hadn't responded gave me a moment of worry. I hoped he hadn't gotten himself in trouble

I texted him again.

> **It's Joey. Haven't heard from you. Hope all is well. Would love to talk.**

I lowered my phone, fingers crossed that I'd hear from him soon.

Then I moved on to the next item on my to-do list. I had to talk to Bert Philpot again. He was the one who'd started that nonprofit, and that nonprofit tied my father with those international workers, including Anastasia. I had to figure out what he knew.

I pulled my aching body out of bed, made myself another crappy cup of coffee, and sat down at my kitchen table. I found the man's number online and dialed.

A woman answered on the first ring. "Bert's Storage."

"I'm trying to reach Bert." I looked out the bay window at the serene beach outside and rolled my shoulders, wishing my body didn't ache so much.

"I'm sorry. He's not available."

"Do you know when he will be available?" I needed to speak with him as soon as possible. And I needed different—better—coffee. Preferably from Sunrise.

"No, ma'am. I sure don't."

I needed something more detailed than that. "If you don't mind me asking, is he out for lunch and returning later today, or is he out of town?"

The woman, who sounded fresh out of high school with her thin, high-pitched voice and uncertain tone, sighed. "Honestly, I don't know where he is. I haven't been able to get in touch with him in two days. I'm getting a little worried. This isn't like him."

I closed my eyes, reality hitting me. This was somehow connected with that nonprofit he started. And that nonprofit was somehow connected with international workers and that seafood-processing plant in Wanchese.

"Thanks for your help," I rushed. "I hope you're able to reach him soon. Have you let the police know?"

"Should I? I've been on the fence."

I frowned. "Call Detective Sullivan with the Nags Head PD. At least let him know."

I mentally patted myself on the back. At least no one could fault me for keeping sensitive information to myself. And I wouldn't have to talk to Jackson myself. Win-win!

When I hung up, I grabbed my keys. I couldn't stay here. I had to head to Wanchese. I didn't know what I would do when I got there, but I had to do something.

***

I ended up at the warehouse where I'd been taken by a killer several weeks before. The same warehouse I'd also gone to with Maria Salvatore. And the warehouse where I'd met Adam. Adam, who was one of my fans. Who was someone who worked in this area. And who was someone who seemed very observant.

I wasn't sure how to track him down here. So I did the only thing I could think of: I walked into Shipwreck Bay Seafood and asked for him. To my surprise, he appeared a few minutes later.

"Joey Darling?" He blinked, as if in disbelief. "What . . . I wasn't . . . how can I help you?"

"I have a few questions for you. Do you have time?"

"Sure, I just signed out for my lunch break."

I nodded outside. "You want to take a walk?"

"Uh . . . yeah."

I was pretty sure I made him nervous, and I needed to put him at ease. We stepped outside into the temperate, sunny day. The fishy sea scent around us was becoming comforting—something I never thought I'd think. We strolled near the docks.

"I wasn't expecting to see you again," Adam said. "What can I do for you?"

"Adam, did you ever meet a man named Bert Philpot?"

"Who?" His face scrunched in thought.

"He was a man who started an outreach to some of the international workers in the area."

He pulled his head back in recognition. "Oh, him. Yeah, I do remember him. He was handing out flyers after work one day, mostly to the internationals. I almost look Middle Eastern, so he handed one to me."

Good. This was a start. "Who did he work with here?"

He sighed. "I don't know. We don't have a ton of international workers here. Only a few. He offered them financial counseling, food, and even clothes. It all seemed legit."

"Anything strange about it?" We stepped over a thick rope strung across the ground.

Adam thought a moment and shook his head. "No, I can't say there was. What's going on?"

I decided to level with him. "The truth is that my father disappeared four months ago. I believe something happened, something connected with the operations here in Wanchese and the nonprofit Bert started. I also wonder if all this is somehow connected with Anastasia."

"Anastasia worked here."

I paused. "At Shipwreck Bay?"

Why didn't I know this?

"Yeah, she worked in the café. The international student workers have to be placed in a job where they interact with the public. She actually started at the drugstore but got moved over here in September. Some of the students head home then, but she wasn't leaving until a little later."

That fact may have led to her untimely death.

"We were all shocked when she died," Adam continued. "For the longest time we thought she must have slipped and fell. Then we heard it was murder. I don't know why someone would want to kill her."

I lowered my voice and glanced around, making sure no one else was close enough to hear my next question. "Do you believe her death could have something to do with her work here?"

He pressed his lips together. "I don't know. There were a couple of men at the seafood company who liked to give her a hard time. I'm not saying they hurt her or anything. There was one other time she seemed pretty upset when she was leaving work."

"Did she say why?"

"No, but I thought she'd been crying. And her

hands were shaking."

"How about the men? What do you know about them?"

He shrugged. "I just know they work the night shift. We don't usually take deliveries in the evening, but every once in a while a catch from down farther south will be ready in the evening. We have to have someone here to receive it. One of the guys is the night manager."

"When was that?"

Adam frowned. "Two days before she died."

I sucked in a deep breath. "One more question: When is the next time one of these night deliveries is supposed to take place?"

"Actually . . . tonight."

CHAPTER 29

That did it. Whatever had happened went back to this marina. All of it. And I was going to figure out what.

After leaving Adam, I'd talked to Charlie, and he gave me permission to hang out in his dolphin-tour ticket shack. He left at six, and that was when I moved into the small space.

What did I hope to discover? I wasn't sure. But I was going to discover *something*.

I would stay on the sidelines. I wasn't going to interject myself into a dangerous situation. But I'd watch and observe and record. Then I'd report and walk away.

That had been easier than flubbing an audition.

I'd brought Sunset coffee with me. My warmest black sweater. My black knit hat.

I could do this.

I *would* do this.

I opened the ticket sales window ever so slightly—just enough so I could peer outside. What was I expecting to see? I had no idea.

I knew that most of the operations in this area closed down in the evening. The seafood-processing-plant workers went home. There could be a few stray fishermen coming in with their catches of the day.

I didn't see anything for the first three hours. Yes, three hours. So I played on my phone. Took selfies. Caught up on all the online gossip concerning myself. I had no idea that my breakup with Eric was a publicity stunt or that I was secretly pregnant. It was that picture of me in the bathing suit, wasn't it? I knew it!

I had a new cell phone, one that was cheaper than my last, which had died when it fell into the ocean while I was tossing a Frisbee with Zane. I was still learning to use my new phone, which was a step down from my bells-and-whistles old phone. That kind of phone wasn't in my budget right now.

Technology wasn't my friend, but I had to make sure I knew how to take pictures. Unfortunately, nighttime pictures on a cell phone were usually grainy.

At nine, my phone vibrated—yes, I'd remembered to put it on vibrate this time. Yay, me! Though I didn't recognize the number, I answered.

"Joey? It's me. Shawn."

Shawn from Seaside Condos. The war vet. "I tried texting you back, but you didn't respond. Is everything okay?"

"I started out just trying to see what I could find out, but I've gotten into some pretty deep stuff. We need to talk."

I straightened. "Okay, let's talk."

"In person. You've got to see it for yourself."

I bit down on my lip. I couldn't ruin this

operation. I had to stay and see if this was all for nothing or not. "I really want to hear what you have to say, but it's not a good night."

"It's about the man who died."

I glanced at my watch. I wanted to know what he'd learned. Desperately. But I couldn't leave right now.

"I can try to meet you at eleven at Willie's." It was the only place open at that hour. "Would that work? I'm tied up with something right now."

"Sure, that will work. And, Joey . . . be careful whom you trust in the meantime." His words had an ominous ring that I didn't particularly like.

Of course, I was now wondering what he'd discovered and why he had to tell me in person. At least I'd been smart enough to suggest meeting in a public place. Not that I thought Shawn was dangerous. In fact, he seemed harmless and kind.

But a girl could never be too certain.

I used my binoculars to watch the harbor in the distance. Finally, just after 10:00 p.m., I saw movement on the water.

A boat pulled up to the docks at Shipwreck Bay. As it did, three people stepped from the factory.

I zoomed in on one. Military Woman! She *was* involved with this.

They talked to the men on the boat, who then began to unload some boxes from the hull.

Why would they be making a delivery at this hour? And in boxes, at that?

I pulled out my camera and took a few pictures.

Unfortunately, I couldn't see anything in them. Anything at all.

I was going to have to leave this shack.

I didn't want to, but I didn't have any other choice.

I crept from the safety of my hideout, careful not to make any sounds. I dodged behind cars and any other obstacles I could find as I tried to get close. Finally, I reached the building, stood at the corner, and prayed no one came this way.

I raised my phone. Yes, I could make out details here. I snapped photos of everything. From here I could clearly read that the boxes were marked *shrimp*. Shrimp? What was so secretive about that?

Somehow, I just knew this was all connected. There was more to this than just a nighttime seafood delivery.

Strains of the conversation drifted up to me. They said something about barracudas and fish scales. What in the world were they talking about? It must be barracuda season. It was the second time I'd heard it mentioned.

One of the men said something to the other . . . in a different language. I tried to place what it might be. I closed my eyes. I'd had to learn bits of certain languages for the show.

Was that . . . Russian? It was my best guess.

Just then, one of the men dropped a box. He muttered curses as the items inside tumbled to the ground.

I sucked in a breath. Were those . . . guns?

I let that sink in for a moment.

Illegal arms trafficking. Was that what all of this had been about?

I quickly took more pictures.

That was what had been going on. Someone was packaging these weapons at the bottom of their seafood shipments, somehow using the product to conceal the weapons. They'd then loaded them into the delivery trucks, which were hijacked. I vaguely remembered hearing that news story at Dizzy's house. The weapons were then taken to a kingpin of some sort who'd sold them and made a killing . . . literally.

At that moment, the crab pod beside me crashed to the ground. I hadn't even touched it!

One of the men glanced my way, and I quickly ducked behind the building. I couldn't risk being caught. Or was it too late for that?

"Did you hear something over there?" one of them asked.

Run!

I slid my phone back into my pocket. I had to get out of here. Now. Before my good luck turned bad.

***

When I was on the causeway back to Nags Head, I reached for my phone to call Jackson and tell him what had happened. My problem was that my phone wasn't in my pocket.

I closed my eyes.

I knew I'd put it in the pocket of my black leather coat when I'd taken off.

So where was it?

I felt on the floor of my Miata and everywhere else I could think of. It wasn't in here.

And that would mean I'd dropped it at some point as I ran back to my car.

Dread filled me. I knew what that meant. I had to go back and look for it. It had all the evidence I needed, not to mention my personal information.

So I did. I went back. And my phone was nowhere to be found.

The men were gone. The docks were quiet. It was almost like nothing had happened.

Except I had proof that it had.

Or, I'd *had* proof that it had.

This wasn't good. It wasn't good at all.

I turned around and rushed back to my house. I had to use the phone there and call Jackson, even if it was almost midnight. He had to know.

He answered on the first ring, and I began one majorly long run-on sentence about what had happened.

"You did what?" he screeched.

I didn't know he was capable of screeching.

"I didn't want to be the girl who cried wolf," I said, pacing my living room like a frenzied wind-up doll. "I decided to get proof first."

He let out a long, heavy sigh. "That wasn't a smart move, Joey."

"I know, but I was trying to be safe. And now I've

left my phone."

"Even if someone found it, they're not going to link it back to you and know that you were taking pictures . . . right?"

"Well, that would be true, except the picture on my home screen is of me at the People's Choice Awards. Don't judge." I stopped pacing long enough to rest my forehead against the wall. If I wasn't on the phone, I might have banged it there.

He sighed. "Okay, but you were there earlier today, you said. It doesn't mean anything. They could think you left it earlier."

"Except I turned the lock off my phone so I could take pictures tonight. It kept getting in my way and freezing it up."

"So anyone can get on your phone and look at the pictures there?" Disbelief lilted Jackson's voice.

"Yes, that's right." I did bang my head this time. But softly. Just enough to make myself feel better. "And, Jackson, they were talking about barracudas and fish scales. Does that mean anything?"

"Joey . . ." He sighed. "You have no idea what you've gotten yourself into. Do me a favor. Stay at your place. Don't go anywhere. I'm coming over to get you. Okay?"

"What are you going to do with me? Lock me up? Turn me over to the mayor? Parade me around town as an example of what not to do?" I deserved it. I would deserve every minute of it.

"Your first suggestion isn't bad. At least I would know you'd be out of trouble behind bars."

"Jack—"

"But of course, I can't do that. I'm not sure where I'll take you. But I know you shouldn't be at your place alone, especially if one of those guys has found your phone. You have no idea what you've gotten yourself into. No idea."

As I hung up, uneasiness filled me. No, I had no reason to feel uneasy. Jackson would arrive, he'd protect me, and that was that.

Except my life was never that easy.

Someone pounded on my door a couple of minutes later. Jackson had gotten here fast. I rushed toward it, so ready not to be alone.

Except when I looked out the peephole, it wasn't Jackson. It was another familiar face instead.

CHAPTER 30

Shawn. I'd forgotten I was supposed to meet him!

"I'm sorry I stood you up," I started. "It's been one of those nights. And right now really isn't a good time."

"I have to tell you something. Now." He leaned on his arm crutch as he stood outside on my stoop and sounded genuinely concerned.

"It has to do with the man who died at the Polar Plunge?"

He nodded. "It does. I'm sorry to come here. I really am. But I knew I had to get through to you somehow."

With a touch of hesitation, I pulled the door open. Shawn wasn't involved in this, I reminded myself. I'd already ruled him out as a possible suspect. He would have a hard time going in the water with his disability. Plus, what would his motive be?

"Come on in," I said.

Jackson would be here soon enough. Maybe Jackson needed to hear whatever Shawn had to say also, so it would all work out.

I didn't move from the entryway. Instead, I

rubbed my hands together and looked up at Shawn, anxious to hear what he'd learned. "So what's going on?"

"You'll never believe who's involved in Max Anderson's murder."

My eyebrows flickered up. "You discovered Mark Hamill's real name?"

"You thought he looked like Luke Skywalker too? Anyway, I've been busy doing the armchair detective thing. It beats doing my job in upper management."

"Okay . . ." I rubbed my arms, feeling chilled and impatient.

"I discovered that—"

Before he could finish, someone pounded on the door. Jackson! I reached over and threw it open. Sure enough, Jackson stood there with . . . Military Woman.

My heart pounded in my ears, and I backed away from the door.

Jackson hurried inside, gave a fleeting glance toward Shawn, and grasped my uninjured arm. "Are you okay?"

I froze before whispering, "Jackson, she was there." I dramatically angled my eyes toward Military Woman.

His face didn't even register surprise. "She's on our side, Joey."

"What do you mean, *our* side?"

"Joey," Shawn said. "We should really talk."

I glanced at Military Woman, my throat thick and tight with fear. She stood near the door, an icy look on her face, as if she just dared me to defy her.

"Joey . . ." Shawn continued.

I glanced around the room at everyone there, trying to figure out whom I could trust.

"Joey, they're both involved," Shawn said. "They're dirty. I've got proof."

"Dirty cops?" My mind raced.

"That's right," Shawn said. "That's what I was so desperate to tell you."

I glanced over at Jackson and Military Woman. Jackson shook his head, moving like there was a wired explosive in the room.

"Don't listen to him, Joey," he said.

"Who is she?" I pointed to the woman.

Military Woman stepped forward. "I'm Charlotte Neville, an undercover agent with the DEA. Don't listen to him, Joey."

"But I saw you. Down at the docks tonight."

"I was undercover," Charlotte said. "Please, we need to get you out of here."

"Joey, they're not telling you the truth," Shawn said. "They're both getting a cut in order to look away."

My spine straightened. "To look away from what?"

"Everything that the Barracudas have been doing in this area and how they've exploited this coastline for their own gain," Shawn said.

"That's why they said Barracudas?" I shook my head. "What are they? A gang?"

Shawn squinted. "You've never heard of the Barracudas?"

I shrugged. "Should I have?"

"They're a notorious international crime ring known for trafficking weapons and drugs," Jackson said. His gaze darted to Shawn, while his hand hovered over his gun.

"And they're using Shipwreck Bay Seafood as a front?" I muttered.

"You're better at this detective thing than I gave you credit for," Charlotte said. "But you're not safe right now."

"Because the Barracudas are on their way?" I asked. "You're right. We should get out of here. Shawn, you should come with—"

Something clicked behind me. A gun.

They were already here, I realized.

Jackson and Charlotte drew their weapons and pointed them at me.

No, at Shawn.

Who was obviously holding a gun behind my head.

My skin felt like it was trying to peel itself away from my body.

"Put them down or I'll kill her," Shawn said, almost sounding amused. "You two were never supposed to be here."

"Don't hurt her," Jackson said.

"Shawn . . . you were in on this?" I muttered.

"Come on, Joey. You had to see it," Shawn said. "We're practically BFFs."

I sucked in a breath. That was what I'd said to the man who attacked me in my house. Shawn had been that man. And . . . I'd never told him where I lived.

I should have put this together sooner.

The mood in the room became electrified.

Shawn pressed the gun into my temple, all signs of his disability now gone. He'd been faking it this whole time? What a loser.

"This is the last time I'm going to say it," he growled. "Put your guns down. Now."

Jackson and Charlotte both did as they were told.

I sucked in a deep breath. This was why my superfans had told me to watch Episode 210. It wasn't the bank robbery. No, in that episode, the bad guy had actually been at the crime scene acting like an observer. In truth, he was hunting for information.

"You were never staying at Seaside, were you?" I asked, feeling like a fool.

He shook his head. "No, I wasn't."

"You were just there to watch and see what the police discovered because you were the one who really killed Max Anderson. I walked right into it by asking you questions. Everything you've said to me has only served as a distraction." How could I have been so dumb?

"Anyone could have fallen for it, Joey," Jackson said, still looking edgy.

I shook my head. "No, *you* wouldn't have."

"We've been trying to nail these guys for months," Charlotte said. "That's why I worked at Shipwreck Bay. So I could get an inside track."

"We didn't, however, know that Shawn was a

part of this," Jackson continued.

"Why not just plan an entire operation around tonight?" I asked. "You could have caught everyone in the act at the docks this evening, and this whole thing would be done."

"It's not that easy," she said. "We're trying to figure out who their leader is. We want to cut off the head of the snake. That's why I was undercover."

"Why risk everything to come here?" I asked.

"They found your phone," Charlotte said. "They're going to come and kill you. That's why we need to get you out of here."

"No one is going anywhere." Shawn pressed the gun deeper into my head. "I've been tasked with taking care of this . . . taking care of her. It wasn't supposed to be this complicated."

This was all my fault.

"I looked through all the Polar Plunge pictures. I didn't see you," I continued, desperate to keep him talking.

"Half of the people aren't recognizable. I wore a wig, a tutu, and sunglasses."

"And what are fish scales?" I said.

"It's what some people call high-quality heroine," Jackson said.

"Now, enough of this chitchat. Let's take a walk outside," Shawn ordered. "One wrong move, and she dies. Understand?"

Jackson nodded slowly. "We'll do what you say. Just don't hurt her."

"Good. Then walk."

"What are you going to do?" I asked.

He smiled, a soulless kind of smile that made my insides shrivel. "You'll find out soon enough."

CHAPTER 31

Water splashed at my ankles. At my calves. Up to my hips.

Every time a wave crashed, the water climbed higher and higher. My body lost more and more feeling. I couldn't breathe. The cold was so biting. Consuming. Pervasive.

At Shawn's order, Jackson tied a rope around my midsection. He'd already tied up Charlotte to another pier piling—the one behind me. Occasionally, Charlotte would voice an idle threat. I knew all about those. I was the queen.

Jackson leaned closer as he tightened the ropes. "I'll get you out of here, Joey," he whispered above the roar of the water.

I didn't see how that was possible. My body would only last fifteen or twenty minutes in this water. Then it would begin to shut down.

I'd acted in an entire episode about this, so I should know. Hollywood would never make things up.

Another wave crested right near the piling, and a mist of ocean water hit my face. My entire body tensed, and my lungs tightened even more.

"Make it snug!" Shawn ordered, standing close enough to act if anyone tried anything. Plus, there was his gun. Aimed at us. His finger on the trigger. "Make any moves, and I'll just shoot her."

Rain started to fall, so there was no one on the beach, not even any of the crazy fishermen who practically lived on these shores. No one in their right mind would be out tonight.

My legs were already numb. The tide was coming in fast, yet this would be a slow, painful way to die. My vessels would constrict. Blood flow to my heart would be compromised.

This was going to be a Shonda Rhimes way to end the season. With drama. Lots and lots of drama.

I was going to become part of the Graveyard of the Atlantic.

What would Rutherford think when I wasn't available anymore to do the press junket with Jessica for *Family Secrets*? He'd probably be okay because at least this would draw publicity to me and, therefore, the movie. Meanwhile, Eric would go on camera and talk about how he'd tried to get me help.

And why was I thinking about these things now? I should be devising an escape plan. Or praying for mercy. Anything but thinking about Rutherford and *Family Secrets*.

Think, Joey. Think. How do you get out of this?

I couldn't use my baloney move since I couldn't feel my legs—and I was tied up.

However, I could arch my back. That would mean when Jackson stepped away, there could be some give within the ropes. If I could slide them off, then maybe I would stand a fighting chance.

The rain continued to come down on my face in rivulets as I tried to make myself bigger than I was. I glanced around me. The moon was covered by the clouds, and the only light came from a few random houses on the other side of the dunes.

Jackson tightened the rope with an apologetic frown and stepped back.

Another wave crested on me, and saltwater filled my mouth. Something tangled around my legs— seaweed or other marine life. I was going to stick with seaweed.

I glanced at Shawn. A sheen covered his face. Probably left by the rain, because he didn't seem nervous. No, he almost seemed like a professional. I mean, who else carried rope with them just in case they needed to tie people up to a pier? And why not just shoot us? Why end it this way?

I had a feeling the Barracudas liked to make a statement. And killing someone this way definitely had style.

What would he do now? Would he tie Jackson up? If so, was that my opportunity to strike? I supposed it didn't matter since my back-arching move didn't work. I wasn't going anywhere.

"I'm going to make you watch," Shawn said, a sinister tone to his voice. "I think that will be worse for you than letting you die too. Don't you think?"

"I don't know why you're involving Joey in this. She has nothing to do with the investigation."

"That's where you're wrong. She's becoming the face of the Nags Head PD. Or haven't you heard? Any case done in relation to Joey will become national news. We can't have that happening. We have too much at stake."

"What did you do to my dad?" I asked, my voice barely audible over the roar of the ocean.

Shawn shook his head. "I'm sorry. I don't handle those sides of the operation."

Fire ignited in me. I would fight this.

Just then I glanced behind Jackson. It was rainy and hard to see, but was that a figure moving out there?

Was that . . . Zane? I'd recognize his crazy curls anywhere.

What was he doing back from the wedding already? And what was he thinking? Out here there was nowhere to hide. Everything was exposed and open.

He dove to the ground, army-crawling on the sand, and blending in perfectly with the darkness.

I thought he did, at least.

I looked away, determined not to give away his whereabouts.

Just like that, he darted toward the water and dove in.

Zane and his dolphin-like ways. How could he stand it? The water was so cold that it hurt. Really hurt.

"It doesn't have to end this way," Jackson said. He remained near me, hands raised, probably to put

Shawn at ease.

Shawn still pointed his gun at him.

I looked over and saw . . . a fin in the water?

No, it was Zane's suit. That ugly suit he wore as part of his endorsement deal.

I had to use this to my advantage.

"Shark!" I screeched. "There's a shark in the water!"

Shawn's gaze darted toward the waves.

As soon as he looked away, Jackson swooped in like a seagull on a bread crumb, a description that in retrospect didn't seem very flattering to Jackson.

The two fell into the water. It was all blurry. And I was so cold. And my teeth wouldn't stop chattering.

But the best I could tell, the two of them wrestled right there where the waves receded and broke.

Finally, Jackson was on top of Shawn. He jerked his arm back and punched him in the face.

Shawn went still.

Jackson pulled out his handcuffs and jerked Shawn's arms behind him.

As he did, Zane emerged from the water. He slopped toward me and began struggling with the rope holding me in place.

"I'll get you out of here," he said.

My teeth chattered so badly that I could hardly say thank you.

Just then more officers arrived, pounding across the sand toward us. They could help Charlotte get free, I hoped. And help Jackson apprehend Shawn.

And . . .

Nothing else mattered right now.
This was all over, I realized.
It was truly all over.

***

"So there was an international crime ring operating out of Wanchese?" I pulled the blanket more closely around me, still shivering at my core. I sat on my couch, sipping on some coffee as I tried to warm up.

Jackson tried to take me to the hospital, but I refused. No more hospitals. Not if I could help it.

Charlotte seemed to have bounced back quickly. She'd changed clothes—though I had no idea where they came from—drank some coffee, and was now in full GI Jane mode as she recounted what happened to her colleagues. She and Raven had way more in common than Raven and I did.

Meanwhile, Zane gave his statement to another officer in my kitchen. He also seemed fine after simply changing and getting a warm drink. In fact, he almost seemed invigorated.

Maybe I was just a wimp.

Jackson shifted on the couch beside me. He had hardly left my side, and I could see the concern in his crinkled eyes.

"That's correct," he said. "It's more complicated than that. The people who were apprehended tonight are just one arm of the Barracudas. But they were bringing guns in at night, packing them in the seafood containers, and then the trucks were hijacked."

"Why didn't you watch the trucks then?"

"We did, but the shipments were irregular, and Shipwreck sends out multiple shipments per day. It was a big task."

"Anastasia must have discovered what was going on," I surmised. "Maybe she came back to the dock one night and overheard the men speaking in Russian. Most people couldn't understand it, but she could. That fact ended up getting her killed."

"That's correct. We still don't know why her necklace was found in Max's place. Probably only Max can tell us that. His camera had been wiped clean and offered no clues."

"There were drag marks on the shoreline where my mom's picture was taken," I blurted. "I know it might be nothing, but it could be something, right?"

"We've been working with the Coast Guard. We believe there are some illegal operations taking place right here in these waters. Those guns you saw? We believe there's a tradeoff going on before they arrive at the warehouse. That could very well be what those marks were. Or it could have simply been a fisherman who stopped there."

My throat tightened. "But my mom . . . and my dad. I'm still having trouble piecing this together."

"Anastasia came to your father for help because there were very few people here she could trust. When he realized what was going on, he came to me."

Blood drained from my face. "He did?"

Jackson nodded. "You have to understand, Joey,

at that point, none of this was my call. The DEA stepped in."

"I stepped in," Charlotte said, coming into the room. "You could have ruined our whole operation."

I didn't like her tone. "Well, what were you waiting for? It was all happening right there on the docks, and I'm sure that wasn't the first time."

She scowled. "I'm trying to get the name of the person who's in charge of the entire operation," she said. "We wanted to shut down the entire operation instead of just taking down the henchmen."

Well, that made sense, I supposed. I pulled my blanket more tightly around me. "Oh. So I did ruin it?"

She crossed her arms. "We'll have to reevaluate now."

My gaze shot to Jackson's. "What about my father? I'm still not sure how he fits with this. Yes, Anastasia talked to him. Yes, he talked to you. But now he's gone . . ." My voice cracked.

Jackson and Charlotte exchanged a glance, and another round of worry shot through me.

"Apparently, you and your father are a lot alike. He suspected something was going on down on the waterfront, and he started to stay late to figure out what," Charlotte said. "He unofficially became one of our informants. I mean, let's face it—he had an inside track with the fishermen there that we won't ever be able to achieve."

"My dad?" That didn't even sound right.

She nodded. "He had clear boundaries he was supposed to keep. He was instructed to watch but not get involved. Everything was fine for the first week."

"And then . . ." I held my breath, not sure I wanted to know.

"Something happened to spook him," Jackson said, softening his voice. "He came to me for advice, and I told him he should back off and that law enforcement would take over."

"What happened?" I held my breath.

Jackson shifted closer to me. "He wouldn't tell me the details. He just said he saw someone from his past. He wondered if this person could be involved, but he was having trouble believing it. I had no idea whom it might be. He refused to tell me."

"My mom . . ." I remembered her picture. That had to be it. My temples began throbbing.

"That's my guess, though I didn't realize that until I saw her picture when I was with you," Jackson said. "I think we can safely assume he saw your mother while he was looking for the bad guys."

"So my mom is somehow involved in this?" It made no sense. She'd left to pursue modeling. She couldn't be involved in an international crime ring.

Jackson leaned with his elbows on his knees. "It's all assumptions. We don't really know at this point."

My gaze locked with his. "You really don't know where my dad is?"

"We don't, Joey. We told him to a take a step back and clear his head. The last thing we wanted was someone who was emotionally involved. Then he disappeared, and no one has been able to find him since. We have people looking into it."

I turned to Charlotte. "Including your DEA peeps?"

"Even my DEA peeps. Sorry." She frowned.

"Do you believe something happened to him? That these guys got hold of him? Is his body going to wash ashore like Anastasia's did?" The words left a bitter, acidic taste in my mouth. I couldn't even go there . . . yet I had no choice but to face that thought.

"We don't believe that, based on the chatter we heard," Charlotte said.

"And we believe that Max Anderson was hired by your father to keep an eye on you," Jackson added.

That was right. Max. Where all this had started.

"Then why did he die?" I took a sip of my coffee, trying to appear normal even though I felt anything but.

"We believe that this crime ring heard you were in town. We believe they perceived you as a threat and, therefore, were keeping an eye on you. Max Anderson picked up on this as he was watching you. He must have seen something that got him killed."

I wrapped my arms across my chest. "I don't like where any of this is going."

"I can assure you that we're working on it," Charlotte said. "Detective Sullivan was legally sworn to not repeat any of this information. It's all been highly classified, and the whole operation could have been ruined. You may not understand that now, but you will eventually. We're going to keep trying to find the head of the organization. We believe they're based out of this area."

I nodded. "What about Bert? Have you heard from him?"

"They were holding him hostage," Jackson said. "Our guys found him a couple of hours ago, and he's doing okay."

"Why would they hold him hostage?"

"From what I understand, after he talked to you that day in Fatty's, he started to get suspicious and wondered if your dad's disappearance had something to do with one of the international students. Specifically Anastasia. He went to Shipwreck Bay Seafood a couple of nights ago and asked too many questions. I suppose they would have killed him, but they decided to blackmail him instead. They wanted to use his storage sheds to help them remain undetected."

"I'm glad he's okay. He seems like a genuinely nice man." I tugged the blanket more tightly around me. "And by the way, I have a fan I need to give you."

"A fan?" Jackson asked.

I nodded. "I found it in my father's things. It's an oriental folding fan, and it has some blood on it."

"And this is the first time you're mentioning it?"

"I thought it might be because Dizzy had something to do with this. She uses those things all the time. But it turns out she got it at the drugstore where Anastasia used to work. I'm sorry I kept it from you, but I had no idea it might be connected with someone else's murder. I thought . . ." I shook my head. "I don't know what I thought."

When Charlotte excused herself, Jackson turned

to me, dropping some of his professionalism. "Are you really okay, Joey?"

I nodded, though barely. I'd really thought I was going to die out there tonight. "I guess. I don't know what to think."

"I just got word from the chief that you're going to be starting your 'research' with the department next week. I'm not sure if you heard, but the ABC News story ran during prime time today. The story about how you and I *worked together* to solve the murder of Simon Philips."

I tugged at my collar self-consciously "Those weren't my words."

He nodded. "I know. The mayor loved it. I think you'll like it too. The story made you sound somewhat legendary."

"I'll . . . have to check it out online." I paused, hating the tension stretching between me and Jackson. "That's great to hear. For me, at least."

He lowered his gaze before slowly drawing his head up. "Listen, Joey, maybe we should start over."

Start over? Starting over sounded like a great idea. A smile feathered my lips. "You know what? That sounds wonderful. Let's try to put the past behind us."

He extended his hand. "Deal."

Another jolt of electricity shot through me, and I quickly pulled my hand away.

Jackson opened his mouth to say something, when a shadow came over us. I looked up and saw Zane there.

"Sorry to interrupt, but, Joey, can we talk a minute?" he asked.

Jackson nodded and rose. Was it my imagination, or did he almost look hesitant? It was probably my imagination.

"Of course." Jackson joined the others in the kitchen.

Zane sat beside me. It was the first real chance I'd had to talk to him since this whole fiasco began. Before I could say anything, he pulled me into a long, warm hug.

A hug that I needed. That I craved. That made me believe that someone actually cared about me as a person and not a means to an end.

"Thank you," I said. "How'd you know?"

"I got home and went out to my balcony. I saw what was happening, and I knew I had to do something. I did what I do best: I hopped in the water."

"Well, you may have very well saved my life." I rubbed a hand along his arm. "I didn't think you were going to be back yet from the wedding."

He shrugged. "I came back early."

"Did you have fun?"

He twisted his lips. "April and I . . . we broke up."

I squeezed his arm. "Zane, I'm so sorry."

He shook his head. "Don't be sorry. I'm the one who called things off."

"Why? I thought you really liked her."

His gaze locked with mine. "There was one small problem."

"What's that?"

"You were all I could think about when I was with her."

My heart pounded in my ears. "Really?"

"Yeah, really. I know you said you're not ready to date, but . . . when you are, I'll be there."

"I . . . I appreciate you telling me that."

He glanced at Jackson in the distance. "And one more thing. I guess I always have felt a little competitive with Jackson. But I want to put that behind me. I'm sorry I said what I did about him. He . . . he was good for Claire. He was there for her when she passed, and that says a lot."

I smiled. "Thanks for telling me that."

He squeezed my hand. "When all of this is over and you've recovered from today, I have some new adventures I want to tell you about. Hashtag: bucketlistsrock."

"Oh, do you?" I could only imagine what he was planning.

"Yeah, you're going to love them . . . especially the one involving the Goat Man."

"The goat man?"

He nodded. "Yeah, he lives in the woods and only comes out at night when—"

Before he could finish, another officer stepped inside the house. He had something white in his hands. A square piece of paper.

My heart lurched. I knew exactly what that was. Everything else became silent around me as I listened to him read it to Jackson.

"We've been way too easy on you. It's time to get serious about your investigations. We'll be watching. Signed, your biggest fans."

My blood went cold. What did they have planned next? And why couldn't I ever catch a break?

###

Coming March 2017:
Safety in Blunders

Reign of Error

My name is Joey Darling, and I'm a disgrace to imaginary detectives everywhere.

When actress Joey Darling discovers a mermaid tail with drops of fresh blood on it while hiking in a remote nature preserve, she knows something suspicious is going on.

As details surface, Joey realizes she's dealing with a problem she has encountered one too many times: someone desperate for fame who falls victim to a predator. With the help of her neighbor Zane Oakley and the opposition of local detective Jackson Sullivan, Joey hunts for answers, unaware of the deadly net in which she's about to entangle herself.

Joey knows she's a fish out of water when it comes to cracking cases, but can she use her talent—acting—to help find the missing woman? Or will Joey end up swimming with sharks?

Preview: CHAPTER 1

Zane Oakley hooked his arm through mine as we walked down the path, and for a moment I felt like Dorothy in *The Wizard of Oz*. I wondered who that would make Zane? The Cowardly Lion? No, Zane was fearless. The brainless Scarecrow? The heartless Tin Man? None of them seemed to fit my thrill-seeking neighbor.

We walked down a mix of gravel road and walking path through a nature preserve in Nags Head on one of his adventures. He was calling it *The Goat Man Project* and had chosen to record it using filmography similar to *The Blaire Witch Project*. He wore a Go Pro on his forehead, recording everything that happened on our daylong excursion.

"We're here with the GMRO—also known as the Goat Man Researchers Organization. Now, the Goat Man is known to only come out at night," Zane said, whispering conspiracy-like. "So we probably won't find him. We're just looking for evidence of his existence."

"Hoofprints?" I suggested.

"Yes, like hoofprints. Stray hair. A strange *baaaing* sound."

"Or maybe a cashmere sweater or some tasty cheese." Zane cut me a confused look, and I shrugged. "What? That's what I think about when I think of goats."

"You sound glib now, my friend, but that will all change soon. The Goat Man is no laughing, cashmere sweater–wearing matter. He likes to chase people through these woods."

"As long as he doesn't kill them."

"He reserves that right for small woodland creatures." Zane lowered his voice and swung his head my way. "Or so they say."

I shivered and moved a little closer to Zane as the path narrowed. "Okay, that is a little creepy . . . especially when you say it in that voice. And how long has the Goat Man been said to haunt these woods?"

"Decades basically. Teens come out here all the time to search for him."

"Well, it really is pretty here." I glanced around. With the exception of sand dunes, the Outer Banks was mostly flat. This nature preserve, however, must have been built on top of some centuries-old dunes. I nearly felt like I was in the mountains instead of a little stretch of islands off North Carolina's coast.

There were eight-foot drops on one side of the road and high hills on the other. In the distance, I could see where the foliage cleared and the Albemarle Sound began. I would have never imagined this area would be out here.

The good news was that it was nice outside today. Unseasonably warm for March. Warm enough that I'd worn a tank top for our hike, and I could feel the promise of summer on its way.

Zane crouched down as he walked, reminding me of a character from *Scooby Doo*, as he tried a little too hard to look sneaky. There was nothing to be sneaky about out here. We were the only ones hiking these lonely trails.

"What was that?" Zane froze and grabbed my arm. "Did you hear that?"

I halted, wishing I could say I wasn't scared. But part of me was. Because it was kind of creepy out here. And something shuffled in the woods not terribly far away.

My shoulders tightened. "A squirrel?"

"Too big to be a squirrel."

"A deer?"

"Sounded like a human to me. Maybe two of them."

The noise stopped. Instead of feeling better, the skin on my neck crawled even more. Was that a . . . moan?

No. It was just the breeze. Or a bird.

That was not the Goat Man. It wasn't. Because he wasn't real. Just like Bigfoot and the Loch Ness Monster weren't real.

Zane glanced over at me, his expression ultraserious, which didn't make me feel better. Then a smile cracked his face, and he elbowed me. "Just kidding. It was probably a deer."

I slapped his well-defined arm. "Not funny."

He snapped out of melodrama and pointed to a

road in the distance. "My granddad used to have a cabin over there. Hashtag: ohhowtheyearsgoby."

"People used to live out there?"

He sauntered at a normal pace now, dropping his act for a minute. "There used to be a village here, complete with schools, churches, and a store. Everyone headed out in the forties—probably because of the Goat Man. *Then* developers tried to turn this into another neighborhood during the boom of the 1970s. *Then* some local conservatory groups purchased it. The people who already had homes here were grandfathered in, however."

The forest seemed to close in even tighter, branches reaching for my arms. Algae-filled water crept closer, and roots felt like they were rising up. I'd always had a great imagination, which sometimes worked in my favor (e.g., acting) and sometimes didn't (e.g., right now).

"I don't know how I would like living back here," I said, glancing around for verification that something dangerous lurked close by. "I mean, I realize that we're not that far away from civilization. Still, it feels so isolated, like I've been dropped into the middle of nowhere."

"That's what some people like."

"I guess."

"The Goat Man likes it." Zane made a ghastly expression, and he raised his hands like a supernatural being.

"You said your granddad lived out here?"

Zane dropped his act. For now. "Yep. He built a

canal from his house all the way out to the sound. We'd take the boat out and go fishing."

I smiled as the image filled my mind. "That sounds really nice."

"When we weren't doing that, we sat on the porch and just looked out over the water. I'd drink lemonade and listen to his tales about life as a fisherman in this area. That would last all of fifteen minutes, and then I'd get restless and try to figure out a way to rig a zipline from the house to the water."

"That sounds like you. Adventurous and out of the box, even as a young boy."

"After we got tired of fishing and ziplining, my granddad made up stories about buried treasure here. My brother and I would search everywhere hoping to find it."

"What little kid wouldn't?"

"That is, until I ran into the Goat Man." His voice turned serious. "Then I never came out here to visit my granddad again."

I turned toward him sharply. "Really?"

A grin cracked his face. "No, of course not."

I elbowed him. "Zane Oakley, you should be ashamed of yourself."

In response, he hooked his arm around my neck and pulled me toward him. He planted a friendly kiss on my forehead.

That was right. *Friendly.* We were friends, even though he'd confessed that he liked me. I wasn't quite ready to return the sentiment, although at times I was very tempted. When it came to Zane, what was there not to like? He had a lean beach body, curly hair that was neatly trimmed at the sides, a contagious smile, and he was up for anything.

"Oh, Joey," he muttered. "What did I ever do without you?"

"I'm sure there are plenty of people who'd line up to go on one of these adventures with you." *Plenty of women.* I kept that silent. He had a steady stream of admirers.

"But there's no one like you."

"Flattery, my dear. I'm not supposed to like it . . . but I do. I really do."

"I know." Zane picked me up over his shoulder and twirled me around.

I chuckled, feeling nearly giddy. The familiar scent of surfboard wax, salt water, and coconut oil filled my senses. It was a pleasant combination that always made me want to drink in more.

I hadn't had this much fun since . . . well, since Zane took me go-carting. Or when he'd made me climb a lighthouse at sunset. Wherever Zane was, there was fun, and lots of it.

He set me down, and our gazes caught. I saw the longing in his eyes. He wanted to kiss me.

I'd seen the look plenty of times before.

And it would be so easy to get lost in Zane. To forget about my problems. To pretend my ex-husband hadn't crushed my self-worth. To imagine my father hadn't disappeared, possibly at the hands of an international crime ring. To stop trying to figure out if my future was in Hollywood or somewhere else.

But I couldn't forget those things. I needed to deal with my issues instead of falling back into my normal MO of covering my pain with the highs of stardom or romance.

To break the moment, I poked Zane in the stomach and made a funny face. "You're a troublemaker. You know that, right?"

He shrugged and turned away, acting like our exchange hadn't affected him. And maybe it hadn't. I still couldn't read him at times. Part of me thought he was a womanizer. The other part thought maybe I could be the one to change him.

And that was never a healthy thought.

We began walking again. Searching for the Goat Man was one more thing on Zane's bucket list. And he was paid to document all his adventures as part of an endorsement deal with Slick Ocean, a surfboard company. He lived their motto of "Life is an adventure."

He was living what he called "the good life." He did a little realty work, a little licensed massage-therapy work, and a little of this and that also. Mostly he grabbed whatever opportunities he could to surf and have fun while still making enough money to live.

"So when does the Castle and Beckett thing start?" he asked.

It could have been my imagination, but tension seemed to stretch in his voice as he asked the question. Which was weird, since the whole Castle/Beckett thing was Zane's idea. Maybe he'd never thought I'd see it through to fruition or that the mayor would approve it.

I needed an "in" at the police station, and Zane had recommended that I ask the mayor to let me be an unofficial consultant as a part of my acting research. The mayor loved getting publicity for this area, and he used my fame to help him do that as often as possible. This was the one time I'd tried to use this to my advantage.

"Tomorrow," I said. "Everything had been done. Background check. Drug check. The mayor may have even looked into my history of fashion faux pas. I'm not sure."

He chuckled, but it faded quickly. "How often will this consulting be happening?"

"Once a week. I just have to figure out how to balance that and still pay my bills."

"After your movie comes out, you won't have to work quite so hard, will you?"

I shrugged. "I think you're underestimating the amount of debt I have. My life is representative of the house in *The Money Pit*."

"Bummer. I loved that scene where the bathtub fell through the floor."

I kicked a rock off the path and listened as it tumbled down a cliff. "That was a great scene. But speaking of money, I would have to say that it just made me miserable. It started to control my life and make me into someone I didn't want to be. All I want right now is to find my father."

I felt Zane's eyes as he glanced over at me. "No

new leads?"

I shook my head, remembering all the events of the past couple months. I'd discovered some answers, but those answers had only led to more questions. "No. Nothing."

We continued down the wooded path, past little signs identifying wildlife, such as mosquito ferns and a devil's walking stick.

"What about your stalker fan club?" Zane asked. "Anything else from them?"

"Thank goodness, no." I'd thought I only had one stalker. Then I realized I had two. Then it came to light that I had a whole fan club of twisted little people who watched my every move.

So far they hadn't tried to harm me. But they did enjoy manipulating me in their efforts to keep my alter ego, Raven Remington, alive. They couldn't seem to handle both the fact that my show, *Relentless*, had been canceled and that I wasn't actually Raven Remington.

"Check out that cemetery over there." Zane pointed to some tombstones in the distance.

"Let's go closer," I told him, thankful to have something new to occupy my thoughts.

We trotted up to the edge of the property, and I looked around, remembering for a moment those who had lived here decades and decades earlier. They'd been the true pioneers, living on this weathered sandbar without the ease of the technology we had today. Ease that gave plenty of advance notice for hurricanes that could put this whole place under water or winds that could send houses tumbling into the sea.

I paced around the perimeter, giving my respects. Then I stepped beyond the cemetery toward the stretch of water in the distance. It was like a treasure that we'd stumbled upon—a mostly untouched beach.

Serenity washed over me. Until I saw something I shouldn't.

"You've got to be kidding me," I muttered.

"What is it?" Zane asked.

I pointed at something sticking out from beneath some underbrush. "Is that a . . . mermaid tail?"

I felt silly even asking. I mean, mermaids were just as real as the Goat Man or Bigfoot, right?

We crept closer. It had to be my eyes. I was seeing things.

That couldn't possibly be a mermaid tail because . . . mermaids weren't real, I reminded myself again.

But from a distance, it definitely looked like shimmery scales and a luminescent tail hiding beneath the brush. But it also looked empty . . . deflated . . . lifeless. Almost like a snake skin that had been shed.

By a mermaid.

"Zane, you didn't do this, did you? For ratings." My voice shook.

"No way. I would have coordinated this better and called it the Mermaid Researchers Organization."

He had a point.

We stopped beside it, and I held my breath as I

took a closer look.

"Whoa . . ." Zane muttered.

It was definitely a mermaid tail . . . and fresh blood was splattered across it.

If you enjoyed this book, you may also enjoy:

Squeaky Clean Mysteries:

Hazardous Duty (Book 1)

On her way to completing a degree in forensic science, Gabby St. Claire drops out of school and starts her own crime-scene cleaning business. When a routine cleaning job uncovers a murder weapon the police overlooked, she realizes that the wrong person is in jail. But the owner of the weapon is a powerful foe . . . and willing to do anything to keep Gabby quiet. With the help of her new neighbor, Riley Thomas, a man whose life and faith fascinate her, Gabby seeks to find the killer before another murder occurs.

Suspicious Minds (Book 2)

In this smart and suspenseful sequel to *Hazardous Duty*, crime-scene cleaner Gabby St. Claire finds herself stuck doing mold remediation to pay the bills. Her first day on the job, she uncovers a surprise in the crawlspace of a dilapidated home: Elvis, dead as a doornail and still wearing his blue-suede shoes. How could she possibly keep her nose out of a case like this?

It Came Upon a Midnight Crime (Book 2.5, a Novella)

Someone is intent on destroying the true meaning of Christmas—at least, destroying anything that hints of it. All around crime-scene cleaner Gabby St. Claire's hometown, anything pointing to Jesus as "the reason for the season" is being sabotaged. The crimes become more twisted as dismembered body parts are found at the vandalisms. Someone is determined to destroy Christmas . . . but Gabby is just as determined to find the Grinch and let peace on earth and goodwill prevail.

Organized Grime (Book 3)

Gabby St. Claire knows her best friend, Sierra, isn't guilty of killing three people in what appears to be an eco-terrorist attack. But Sierra has disappeared, her only contact a frantic phone call to Gabby proclaiming she's being hunted. Gabby is determined to prove her friend is innocent and to keep Sierra alive. While trying to track down the real perpetrator, Gabby notices a disturbing trend at the crime scenes she's cleaning, one that ties random crimes together—and points to Sierra as the guilty party. Just what has her friend gotten herself involved in?

Dirty Deeds (Book 4)

"Promise me one thing. No snooping. Just for one week." Gabby St. Claire knows that her fiancé's request is a simple one she should be able to honor. After all, Riley's law school reunion and attorneys' conference at a posh resort is a chance for them to get away from the mysteries Gabby often finds herself involved in as a crime-scene cleaner. Then an old friend of Riley's goes missing. Gabby suspects one of Riley's buddies might be behind the disappearance. When the missing woman's mom asks Gabby for help, how can she say no?

The Scum of All Fears (Book 5)

Gabby St. Claire is back to crime-scene cleaning and needs help after a weekend killing spree fills her work docket. A serial killer her fiancé put behind bars has escaped. His last words to Riley were: *I'll get out, and I'll get even*. Pictures of Gabby are found in the man's prison cell, messages are left for Gabby at crime scenes, someone keeps slipping in and out of her apartment, and her temporary assistant disappears. The search for answers becomes darker when Gabby realizes she's dealing with a criminal who is truly the scum of the earth. He will do anything to make Gabby's and Riley's lives a living nightmare.

To Love, Honor, and Perish (Book 6)

Just when Gabby St. Claire's life is on the right track, the unthinkable happens. Her fiancé, Riley Thomas, is shot and in life-threatening condition only a week before their wedding. Gabby is determined to figure out who pulled the trigger, even if investigating puts her own life at risk. As she digs deeper into the case, she discovers secrets better left alone. Doubts arise in her mind, and the one man with answers lies on death's doorstep. Then an old foe returns and tests everything Gabby is made of—physically, mentally, and spiritually. Will all she's worked for be destroyed?

Mucky Streak (Book 7)

Gabby St. Claire feels her life is smeared with the stain of tragedy. She takes a short-term gig as a private investigator—a cold case that's eluded detectives for ten years. The mass murder of a wealthy family seems impossible to solve, but Gabby brings more clues to light. Add to the mix a flirtatious client, travels to an exciting new city, and some quirky—albeit temporary—new sidekicks, and things get complicated. With every new development, Gabby prays that her "mucky streak" will end and the future will become clear. Yet every answer she uncovers leads her closer to danger—both for her life and for her heart.

Foul Play (Book 8)

Gabby St. Claire is crying "foul play" in every sense of the phrase. When the crime-scene cleaner agrees to go undercover at a local community theater, she discovers more than backstage bickering, atrocious acting, and rotten writing. The female lead is dead, and an old classmate who has staked everything on the musical production's success is about to go under. In her dual role of investigator and star of the show, Gabby finds the stakes rising faster than the opening-night curtain. She must face her past and make monumental decisions, not just about the play but also concerning her future relationships and career. Will Gabby find the killer before the curtain goes down—not only on the play, but also on life as she knows it?

Broom and Gloom (Book 9)

Gabby St. Claire is determined to get back in the saddle again. While in Oklahoma for a forensic conference, she meets her soon-to-be stepbrother, Trace Ryan, an up-and-coming country singer. A woman he was dating has disappeared, and he suspects a crazy fan may be behind it. Gabby agrees to investigate, as she tries to juggle her conference, navigate being alone in a new place, and locate a woman who may not want to be found. She discovers that sometimes taking life by the horns means staring danger in the face, no matter the consequences.

Dust and Obey (Book 10)

When Gabby St. Claire's ex-fiancé, Riley Thomas, asks for her help in investigating a possible murder at a couples retreat, she knows she should say no. She knows she should run far, far away from the danger of both being around Riley and the crime. But her nosy instincts and determination take precedence over her logic. Gabby and Riley must work together to find the killer. In the process, they have to confront demons from their past and deal with their present relationship.

Thrill Squeaker (Book 11)

An abandoned theme park. An unsolved murder. A decision that will change Gabby's life forever. Restoring an old amusement park and turning it into a destination resort seems like a fun idea for former crime-scene cleaner Gabby St. Claire. The side job gives her the chance to spend time with her friends, something she's missed since beginning a new career. The job turns out to be more than Gabby bargained for when she finds a dead body on her first day. Add to the mix legends of Bigfoot, creepy clowns, and ghostlike remnants of happier times at the park, and her stay begins to feel like a rollercoaster ride. Someone doesn't want the decrepit Mythical Falls to open again, but just how far is this person willing to go to ensure this venture fails? As the stakes rise and danger creeps closer, will Gabby be able to restore things in her own life that time has destroyed—including broken relationships? Or is her future closer to the fate of the doomed Mythical Falls?

Swept Away, a Honeymoon Novella (Book 11.5)
Finding the perfect place for a honeymoon, away from any potential danger or mystery, is challenging. But Gabby's longtime love and newly minted husband, Riley Thomas, has done it. He has found a location with a nonexistent crime rate, a mostly retired population, and plenty of opportunities for relaxation in the warm sun. Within minutes of the newlyweds' arrival, a convoy of vehicles pulls up to a nearby house, and their honeymoon oasis is destroyed like a sandcastle in a storm. Despite Gabby's and Riley's determination to keep to themselves, trouble comes knocking at their door—literally—when a neighbor is abducted from the beach directly outside their rental. Will Gabby and Riley be swept away with each other during their honeymoon

. . . or will a tide of danger and mayhem pull them under?

Cunning Attractions (Book 12)

Politics. Love. Murder. Radio talk show host Bill McCormick is in his prime. He's dating a supermodel, his book is a bestseller, and his ratings have skyrocketed during the heated election season. But when Bill's ex-wife, Emma Jean, turns up dead, the media and his detractors assume the opinionated loudmouth is guilty of her murder. Bill's on-air rants about his demon-possessed ex don't help his case. Did someone realize that Bill was the perfect scapegoat? Or could Bill have silenced his Ice Queen ex once and for all? Gabby Thomas takes on the case, but she soon realizes that Emma Jean had too many enemies to count. From election conspiracy theories to scorned affections and hidden secrets, Emma Jean left a trail of trouble as her legacy. Gabby is determined to follow the twisted path until she finds answers.

While You Were Sweeping, a Riley Thomas Novella

Riley Thomas is trying to come to terms with life after a traumatic brain injury turned his world upside down. Away from everything familiar—including his crime-scene-cleaning former fiancée and his career as a social-rights attorney—he's determined to prove himself and regain his old life. But when he claims he witnessed his neighbor shoot and kill someone, everyone thinks he's crazy. When all evidence of the crime disappears, even

Riley has to wonder if he's losing his mind.

Note: *While You Were Sweeping* is a spin-off mystery written in conjunction with the Squeaky Clean series featuring crime-scene cleaner Gabby St. Claire.

The Sierra Files:

Pounced (Book 1)

Animal-rights activist Sierra Nakamura never expected to stumble upon the dead body of a coworker while filming a project nor get involved in the investigation. But when someone threatens to kill her cats unless she hands over the "information," she becomes more bristly than an angry feline. Making matters worse is the fact that her cats—and the investigation—are driving a wedge between her and her boyfriend, Chad. With every answer she uncovers, old hurts rise to the surface and test her beliefs. Saving her cats might mean ruining everything else in her life. In the fight for survival, one thing is certain: either pounce or be pounced.

Hunted (Book 2)

Who knew a stray dog could cause so much trouble? Newlywed animal-rights activist Sierra Nakamura Davis must face her worst nightmare: breaking the news she eloped with Chad to her ultra-opinionated tiger mom. Her perfectionist parents have planned a vow-renewal ceremony at Sierra's lush childhood home, but a neighborhood dog ruins the rehearsal dinner when it shows up toting what appears to be a fresh human bone. While dealing with the dog, a nosy neighbor, and an old flame turning up at the wrong times, Sierra hunts for answers. Her journey of discovery leads to more than just who committed the crime.

Pranced (Book 2.5, a Christmas novella)

Sierra Nakamura Davis thinks spending Christmas with her husband's relatives will be a real Yuletide treat. But when the animal-rights activist learns his family has a reindeer farm, she begins to feel more like the Grinch. Even worse, when Sierra arrives, she discovers the reindeer are missing. Sierra fears the animals might be suffering a worse fate than being used for entertainment purposes. Can Sierra set aside her dogmatic opinions to help get the reindeer home in time for the holidays? Or will secrets tear the family apart and ruin Sierra's dream of the perfect Christmas?

Rattled (Book 3)

"What do you mean a thirteen-foot lavender albino ball python is missing?" Tough-as-nails Sierra Nakamura Davis isn't one to get flustered. But trying to balance being a wife and a new mom with her crusade to help animals is proving harder than she imagined. Add a missing python, a high maintenance intern, and a dead body to the mix, and Sierra becomes the definition of rattled. Can she balance it all—and solve a possible murder—without losing her mind?

Holly Anna Paladin Mysteries:

Random Acts of Murder (Book 1)

When Holly Anna Paladin is given a year to live, she embraces her final days doing what she loves most—random acts of kindness. But one of her extreme good deeds goes horribly wrong, implicating her in a string of murders. Holly is suddenly thrust into a different kind of fight for her life. Could it also be random that the detective assigned to the case is her old high school crush and present-day nemesis? Will Holly find the killer before he ruins what is left of her life? Or will she spend her final days alone and behind bars?

Random Acts of Deceit (Book 2)

"Break up with Chase Dexter, or I'll kill him." Holly Anna Paladin never expected such a gut-wrenching ultimatum. With home invasions, hidden cameras, and bomb threats, Holly must make some serious choices. Whatever she decides, the consequences will either break her heart or break her soul. She tries to match wits with the Shadow Man, but the more she fights, the deeper she's drawn into the perilous situation. With her sister's wedding problems and the riots in the city, Holly has nearly reached her breaking point. She must stop this mystery man before someone she loves dies. But the deceit is threatening to pull her under . . . six feet under.

Random Acts of Malice (Book 3)

When Holly Anna Paladin's boyfriend, police detective Chase Dexter, says he's leaving for two weeks and can't give any details, she wants to trust him. But when she discovers Chase may be involved in some unwise and dangerous pursuits, she's compelled to intervene. Holly gets a run for her money as she's swept into the world of horseracing. The stakes turn deadly when a dead body surfaces and suspicion is cast on Chase. At every turn, more trouble emerges, making Holly question what she holds true about her relationship and her future. Just when she thinks she's on the homestretch, a dark horse arises. Holly might lose everything in a nail-biting fight to the finish.

Random Acts of Scrooge (Book 3.5)

Christmas is supposed to be the most wonderful time of the year, but a real-life Scrooge is threatening to ruin the season's good will. Holly Anna Paladin can't wait to celebrate Christmas with family and friends. She loves everything about the season—celebrating the birth of Jesus, singing carols, and baking Christmas treats, just to name a few. But when a local family needs help, how can she say no? Holly's community has come together to help raise funds to save the home of Greg and Babette Sullivan, but a Bah-Humburgler has snatched the canisters of cash. Holly and her boyfriend, police detective Chase Dexter, team up to catch the Christmas crook. Will they succeed in collecting enough cash to cover the Sullivans' overdue bills? Or will someone succeed in ruining Christmas for all those involved?

Random Acts of Greed (Book 4)

Help me. Don't trust anyone. Do-gooder Holly Anna Paladin can't believe her eyes when a healthy baby boy is left on her doorstep. What seems like good fortune quickly turns into concern when blood spatter is found on the bottom of the baby carrier. Something tragic—maybe deadly—happened in connection with the infant. The note left only adds to the confusion. What does it mean by "Don't trust anyone"? Holly is determined to figure out the identity of the baby. Is his mom someone from the inner-city youth center where she volunteers? Or maybe the connection is through Holly's former job as a social worker? Even worse—what if the blood belongs to the baby's mom? Every answer Holly uncovers only leads to more questions. A sticky web of intrigue captures her imagination until she's sure of only one thing: she must protect the baby at all cost.

The Worst Detective Ever:

Ready to Fumble

I'm not really a private detective. I just play one on TV.
Joey Darling, better known to the world as Raven Remington, detective extraordinaire, is trying to separate herself from her invincible alter ego. She played the spunky character for five years on the hit TV show Relentless, which catapulted her to fame and into the role of Hollywood's sweetheart. When her marriage falls apart, her finances dwindle to nothing, and her father disappears, Joey finds herself on the Outer Banks of North Carolina, trying to piece her life back together away from the limelight. A woman finds Raven—er, Joey—and insists on hiring her fictional counterpart to find a missing boyfriend. When someone begins staging crime scenes to match an episode of Relentless, Joey has no choice but to get involved.

Reign of Error

Sometimes in life, you just want to yell "Take two!"
When a Polar Plunge goes terribly wrong and someone dies in the icy water, former TV detective Joey Darling wants nothing to do with subsequent investigation. But when her picture is found in the dead man's wallet and witnesses place her as the last person seen with the man, she realizes she's been cast in a role she never wanted: suspect. Joey makes the dramatic mistake of

challenging the killer on camera, and now it's a race to find the bad guy before he finds her. Danger abounds and suspects are harder to find than the Lost Colony of Roanoke Island. But when Joey finds a connection with this case and the disappearance of her father, she knows there's no backing out. As hard as Joey tries to be like her super detective alter ego, the more things go wrong. Will Joey figure this one out? Or will her reign of error continue?

Safety in Blunders

My name is Joey Darling, and I'm a disgrace to imaginary detectives everywhere. When actress Joey Darling discovers a mermaid tail with drops of fresh blood on it while hiking in a remote nature preserve, she knows something suspicious is going on. As details surface, Joey realizes she's dealing with a problem she has encountered one too many times: someone desperate for fame who falls victim to a predator. With the help of her neighbor Zane Oakley and the opposition of local detective Jackson Sullivan, Joey hunts for answers, unaware of the deadly net in which she's about to entangle herself. Joey knows she's a fish out of water when it comes to cracking cases, but can she use her talent—acting—to help find the missing woman? Or will Joey end up swimming with sharks?

Christy Barritt

Carolina Moon Series:

Home Before Dark (Book 1)

Nothing good ever happens after dark. Country singer
Daleigh McDermott's father often repeated those
words. Now, her father is dead. As she's about to flee
back to Nashville, she finds his hidden journal with hints
that his death was no accident. Mechanic Ryan Shields
is the only one who seems to believe Daleigh. Her
father trusted the man, but her attraction to Ryan
scares her. She knows her life and career are back in
Nashville and her time in the sleepy North Carolina
town is only temporary. As Daleigh and Ryan work to
unravel the mystery, it becomes obvious that someone
wants them dead. They must rely on each other—and
on God—if they hope to make it home before the
darkness swallows them.

Gone By Dark (Book 2)

Ten years ago, Charity White's best friend, Andrea, was
abducted as they walked home from school. A decade
later, when Charity receives a mysterious letter that
promises answers, she returns to North Carolina in
search of closure. With the help of her new neighbor,
Police Officer Joshua Haven, Charity begins to track
down mysterious clues concerning her friend's
abduction. They soon discover that they must work
together or both of them will be swallowed by the
looming darkness.

Wait Until Dark (Book 3)

A woman grieving broken dreams. A man struggling to regain memories. A secret entrenched in folklore dating back two centuries. Antiquarian Felicity French has no clue the trouble she's inviting in when she rescues a man outside her grandma's old plantation house during a treacherous snowstorm. All she wants is to nurse her battered heart and wounded ego, as well as come to terms with her past. Now she's stuck inside with a stranger sporting an old bullet wound and forgotten hours. Coast Guardsman Brody Joyner can't remember why he was out in such perilous weather, how he injured his head, or how a strange key got into his pocket. He also has no idea why his pint-sized savior has such a huge chip on her shoulder. He has no choice but to make the best of things until the storm passes. Brody and Felicity's rocky start goes from tense to worse when danger closes in. Who else wants the mysterious key that somehow ended up in Brody's pocket? Why? The unlikely duo quickly becomes entrenched in an adventure of a lifetime, one that could have ties to local folklore and Felicity's ancestors. But sometimes the past leads to darkness . . . darkness that doesn't wait for anyone.

Light the Dark (a Christmas novella)

Nine months pregnant, Hope Solomon is on the run and fearing for her life. Desperate for warmth, food, and shelter, she finds what looks like an abandoned house. Inside, she discovers a Christmas that's been left behind—complete with faded decorations on a brittle Christmas tree and dusty stockings filled with loss. Someone spies smoke coming from the chimney of the empty house and alerts Dr. Luke Griffin, the owner. He rarely visits the home that harbors so many bittersweet memories for him. But no one is going to violate the space so near and dear to his heart. Then Luke meets Hope, and he knows this mother-to-be desperately needs help. With no room at any local inn, Luke invites Hope to stay, unaware of the danger following her. While running from the darkness, the embers of Christmas present are stirred with an unexpected birth and a holiday romance. But will Hope and Luke live to see a Christmas future?

Cape Thomas Series:

Dubiosity (Book 1)

Savannah Harris vowed to leave behind her old life as an investigative reporter. But when two migrant workers go missing, her curiosity spikes. As more eerie incidents begin afflicting the area, each works to draw Savannah out of her seclusion and raise the stakes—for her and the surrounding community. Even as Savannah's new boarder, Clive Miller, makes her feel things she thought long forgotten, she suspects he's hiding something too, and he's not the only one. As secrets emerge and danger closes in, Savannah must choose between faith and uncertainty. One wrong decision might spell the end . . . not just for her but for everyone around her. Will she unravel the mystery in time, or will doubt get the best of her?

Disillusioned (Book 2)

Nikki Wright is desperate to help her brother, Bobby, who hasn't been the same since escaping from a detainment camp run by terrorists in Colombia. Rumor has it that he betrayed his navy brothers and conspired with those who held him hostage, and both the press and the military are hounding him for answers. All Nikki wants is to shield her brother so he has time to recover and heal. But soon they realize the paparazzi are the least of their worries. When a group of men try to abduct Nikki and her brother, Bobby insists that Kade

Wheaton, another former SEAL, can keep them out of harm's way. But can Nikki trust Kade? After all, the man who broke her heart eight years ago is anything but safe...Hiding out in a farmhouse on the Chesapeake Bay, Nikki finds her loyalties—and the remnants of her long-held faith—tested as she and Kade put aside their differences to keep Bobby's increasingly erratic behavior under wraps. But when Bobby disappears, Nikki will have to trust Kade completely if she wants to uncover the truth about a rumored conspiracy. Nikki's life—and the fate of the nation—depends on it.

Distorted (Book 3)

Mallory Baldwin is a survivor. A former victim of human trafficking, she's been given a second chance, yet not a night goes by that she doesn't remember being a slave to weapons dealer Dante Torres. Despite being afraid of the dark and wary of strangers, Mallory is trying to rebuild her life by turning her tragedy into redemption. To former Navy SEAL Tennyson Walker, Mallory seems nothing like the shattered woman he rescued two years ago, and he can't help but be inspired by her strength and resilience. So when a stalker suddenly makes Mallory vulnerable once again, Tennyson steps up as her bodyguard to keep her safe. Mallory and Tennyson's mutual attraction can't be ignored, but neither can Mallory's suspicion that Tennyson is keeping a terrible secret about her past.

Standalones:

The Good Girl

Tara Lancaster can sing "Amazing Grace" in three harmonies, two languages, and interpret it for the hearing impaired. She can list the Bible canon backward, forward, and alphabetized. The only time she ever missed church was when she had pneumonia and her mom made her stay home. Then her life shatters and her reputation is left in ruins. She flees halfway across the country to dog-sit, but the quiet anonymity she needs isn't waiting at her sister's house. Instead, she finds a knife with a threatening message, a fame-hungry friend, a too-hunky neighbor, and evidence of . . . a ghost? Following all the rules has gotten her nowhere. And nothing she learned in Sunday School can tell her where to go from there.

Death of the Couch Potato's Wife (Suburban Sleuth Mysteries)

You haven't seen desperate until you've met Laura Berry, a career-oriented city slicker turned suburbanite housewife. Well-trained in the big-city commandment, "mind your own business," Laura is persuaded by her spunky seventy-year-old neighbor, Babe, to check on another neighbor who hasn't been seen in days. She finds Candace Flynn, wife of the infamous "Couch King," dead, and at last has a reason to get up in the morning. Someone is determined to stop her from digging deeper into the death of her neighbor, but Laura is just as determined to figure out who is behind the death-by-poisoned-pork-rinds.

Imperfect

Since the death of her fiancé two years ago, novelist Morgan Blake's life has been in a holding pattern. She has a major case of writer's block, and a book signing in the mountain town of Perfect sounds as perfect as its name. Her trip takes a wrong turn when she's involved in a hit-and-run: She hit a man, and he ran from the scene. Before fleeing, he mouthed the word "Help." First she must find him. In Perfect, she finds a small town that offers all she ever wanted. But is something sinister going on behind its cheery exterior? Was she invited as a guest of honor simply to do a book signing? Or was she lured to town for another purpose—a deadly purpose?

The Gabby St. Claire Diaries: a tween mystery series

The Curtain Call Caper (Book 1)

Is a ghost haunting the Oceanside Middle School auditorium? What else could explain the disasters surrounding the play—everything from missing scripts to a falling spotlight and damaged props? Seventh-grader Gabby St. Claire has dreamed about being part of her school's musical, but a series of unfortunate events threatens to shut down the production. While trying to uncover the culprit and save her fifteen minutes of fame, she also has to manage impossible teachers, cliques, her dysfunctional family, and a secret she can't tell even her best friend. Will Gabby figure out who or what is sabotaging the show . . . or will it be curtains for her and the rest of the cast?

The Disappearing Dog Dilemma (Book 2)

Why are dogs disappearing around town? When two friends ask seventh-grader Gabby St. Claire for her help in finding their missing canines, Gabby decides to unleash her sleuthing skills to sniff out whoever is behind the act. But time management and relationships get tricky as worrisome weather, a part-time job, and a new crush interfere with Gabby's investigation. Will her determination crack the case? Or will shadowy villains, a penchant for overcommitting, and even her own heart put her in the doghouse?

The Bungled Bike Burglaries (Book 3)

Stolen bikes and a long-forgotten time capsule leave one amateur sleuth baffled and busy. Seventh-grader Gabby St. Claire is determined to bring a bike burglar to justice—and not just because mean girl Donabell Bullock is strong-arming her. But each new clue brings its own set of trouble. As if that's not enough, Gabby finds evidence of a decades-old murder within the contents of the time capsule, but no one seems to take her seriously. As her investigation heats up, will Gabby's knack for being in the wrong place at the wrong time with the wrong people crack the case? Or will it prove hazardous to her health?

Complete Book List:

Squeaky Clean Mysteries:
#1 Hazardous Duty
#2 Suspicious Minds
#2.5 It Came Upon a Midnight Crime (a novella)
#3 Organized Grime
#4 Dirty Deeds
#5 The Scum of All Fears
#6 To Love, Honor, and Perish
#7 Mucky Streak
#8 Foul Play
#9 Broom and Gloom
#10 Dust and Obey
#11 Thrill Squeaker
#11.5 Swept Away (a novella)
#12 Cunning Attractions
#13 Clean Getaway (coming soon)

Squeaky Clean Companion Novella:
While You Were Sweeping

The Sierra Files:
#1 Pounced
#2 Hunted
#2.5 Pranced (a Christmas novella)
#3 Rattled
#4 Caged (coming soon)

The Gabby St. Claire Diaries (a Tween Mystery series):
#1 The Curtain Call Caper
#2 The Disappearing Dog Dilemma
#3 The Bungled Bike Burglaries

Holly Anna Paladin Mysteries:
#1 Random Acts of Murder
#2 Random Acts of Deceit
#3 Random Acts of Malice
#3.5 Random Acts of Scrooge
#4 Random Acts of Greed
#5 Random Acts of Fraud (coming soon)

The Worst Detective Ever:
#1 Ready to Fumble
#2 Reign of Error
#3 Safety in Blunders
#4 Join the Flub (coming soon)
#5 Blooper Freak (coming soon)
#6 Flaw Abiding Citizen (coming soon)

Carolina Moon Series:
Home Before Dark
Gone By Dark
Wait Until Dark
Light the Dark (a Christmas novella)

Suburban Sleuth Mysteries:
#1 Death of the Couch Potato's Wife

Stand-alone Romantic-Suspense:
Keeping Guard
The Last Target
Race Against Time
Ricochet
Key Witness
Lifeline
High-Stakes Holiday Reunion
Desperate Measures
Hidden Agenda
Mountain Hideaway
Dark Harbor
Shadow of Suspicion

Cape Thomas Series:
Dubiosity
Disillusioned
Distorted (coming in 2017)

Standalone Romantic Mystery:
The Good Girl

Suspense:
Imperfect

About the Author:

USA Today has called Christy Barritt's books "scary, funny, passionate, and quirky."

Christy writes both mystery and romantic suspense novels that are clean with underlying messages of faith. Her books have won the Daphne du Maurier Award for Excellence in Suspense and Mystery, have been twice nominated for the Romantic Times Reviewers' Choice Award, and have finaled for both a Carol Award and Foreword Magazine's Book of the Year.

She is married to her Prince Charming, a man who thinks she's hilarious—but only when she's not trying to be. Christy is a self-proclaimed klutz, an avid music lover who's known for spontaneously bursting into song, and a road trip aficionado.
When she's not working or spending time with her family, she enjoys singing, playing the guitar, and exploring small, unsuspecting towns where people have no idea how accident-prone she is.

Find Christy online at:
www.christybarritt.com
www.facebook.com/christybarritt
www.twitter.com/cbarritt

Sign up for Christy's newsletter to get information on all

of her latest releases here:
www.christybarritt.com/newsletter-sign-up/

If you enjoyed this book, please consider leaving a review.

81157301R00198

Made in the USA
Columbia, SC
16 November 2017